MURDER in Season

Also by Rosie Sandler

The Gardener Mysteries Series

1. *Seeds of Murder*
2. *Murder Takes Root*
3. *Murder in Bloom*
4. *Murder Bears Fruit*
5. *Murder in Season*

MURDER in Season

ROSIE SANDLER

embla books

First published in the UK in 2026 by

embla books

An imprint of Bonnier Books UK
5th Floor, HYLO, 105 Bunhill Row,
London, EC1Y 8LZ

A CIP catalogue record for this book is available from the British Library.

ISBN: 9781471421099

Also available as an ebook and an audiobook

1

Typeset by IDSUK (Data Connection) Ltd
Printed and bound in Great Britain by CPI (UK) Ltd, Croydon CR0 4YY

FSC www.fsc.org MIX Paper | Supporting responsible forestry FSC® C013604

At Bonnier Books UK, we are committed to publishing sustainably. Find out more here: bonnierbooks.co.uk/sustainability

The authorised representative in the EEA is Bonnier Books UK (Ireland) Limited.
Registered office address:
Block B, The Crescent Building, Northwood, Santry
Dublin 9, D09 C6X8, Ireland
compliance@bonnierbooks.ie

www.bonnierbooks.co.uk

To the village of Silver End in Essex and its wonderful residents on its centenary. Here's to the next 100 years!

1

Avery Sinclair is a greyhound in human form – all long, sinewy limbs and sculpted face. She stands framed in her doorway to welcome me to the village of Greenhaven in Essex, her hair scraped back from her pale, angular face. Her detached house is a fine flat-roofed example of the stunning white modernist buildings that fill the village's neat streets, and I'm keen to see inside. It's the first Monday in November, and I have been summoned to Greenhaven to build a centenary garden, to mark one hundred years since the first of these houses were built.

My dog – and loyal companion – Mouse stands beside me on the doorstep, his unruly dark coat, thickset trunk and enthusiastic tail forming a stark contrast to the sighthound elegance of our host.

'Hello there!' says Avery. 'You must be Steph.' She holds out a hand, which I shake.

Looking past me, she shivers. 'Come in, out of the cold.'

I'm happy to oblige: it's one of those bitter days, when the dark clouds sit low, seeming to turn the air itself grey.

Our host shuts the door behind us, then bends towards my canine companion, 'And I take it this fine fellow is Mouse?'

This is all the encouragement he needs to tug on the lead in order to lick her hand.

'Sorry!' I say.

'Nonsense,' she says, patting his head before straightening up. 'He's only being friendly. I wasn't sure how your journey would go, but I'm just making a pot of coffee, if that suits?'

'Music to my ears,' I say, as we follow her through the hall. Despite the dullness of the day, this space is filled with light and warmth. I stop short at the entrance to Avery's living room. I've read up on Greenhaven in advance and, like all of the houses I've seen on my drive through Greenhaven, Herons has the original metal-framed windows made by the Crittall company.

French windows with floor to ceiling fixed panes or 'side-lights' on either side offer an expansive view out to a large, elegant garden, filled with foliage in different shades of green. There are plain white walls and two enormous portraits in a vibrant, expressionistic style.

She glances up from a glass topped circular wood coffee table and catches me looking around, a rather bemused Mouse still on the lead at my side.

'What do you think of the place?' she asks. 'Oh! Do take him off the lead. I've put a cushion down near the fireplace.'

I release Mouse and point to the large cushion, watching as he pads obediently over to it and settles himself in a rather formal, upright position, his beloved soft toy, Mr Rabbit, between his feet.

'I love it,' I say, responding to Avery's query as I turn back towards her. 'Is the furniture original?'

She gestures for me to take a seat in a cream leather armchair with dark wood arms and a curved back, and hands me a cup and saucer. Noting the art deco design of orange flowers on the white china, I say, 'I'm guessing this is the same period?'

Instead of answering straight away, she holds up a dog biscuit with a tilt of the head. When I nod, she places it at Mouse's feet before taking the chair opposite me, her own cup and saucer on her lap. Mouse glances at me for approval, and I say, 'Go on, boy: you can eat it.'

He takes up the biscuit and begins to crunch it loudly.

'I have another in my pocket,' Avery confides to me with a wink.

I smile. 'Thank you.' I've decided I like this woman.

'In answer to your questions about the furniture and china, yes to both. The sofa and chairs have been re-covered, but they're the ones my grandparents bought from the Co-operative department store in the village, when they moved here from Glasgow back in the early nineteen-thirties. And the coffee set is Crown Devon. It was my grandmother's.'

'I don't know much about china, but I do have a Susie Cooper set in my brother's loft, awaiting its permanent home,' I say, referring to a famous twentieth-century ceramic designer. 'I couldn't resist it when I saw it in a charity shop.'

'Oh, which one?'

'White with red spots.'

'Oh, that's great fun!'

Inhaling the aroma of rich coffee from the floral cup, I don't realise I've closed my eyes until I hear my host laughing. I open them abruptly.

'You're a coffee lover, I take it?' she says.

I pull a face. 'You've caught me. This smells amazing.'

'I buy it directly from a specialist importer in Colchester. It's all Fairtrade, etc. etc.' She waves an expressive hand.

I take a sip. 'It's delicious.' Glancing around the room, I say, 'The windows are Crittall, aren't they?'

'That's right. The factory is still going strong in nearby Witham. I've heard they're especially popular in Africa. There used to be a factory out there. It's because the metal frames don't get eaten by termites.'

I stare at her and she laughs. 'I know. I sometimes surprise myself with my rather . . . esoteric knowledge.'

'Do you have similar knowledge about horticulture?'

She smiles and shakes her head. 'I just about know a dahlia when I see one, and I know my bay tree from my cherry laurel, but that's about my lot, I'm afraid.'

I laugh. 'I promise not to come to you if I'm stuck on plant identification. Will we be visiting the site today?'

'That's the plan.' She checks her watch. 'Let's have our coffee, and then we'll walk over. You won't meet your volunteer helpers till Wednesday, I'm afraid, but you can get an idea of the terrain in the meantime.'

As we sip our drinks, she fills me in on a little of the village's history, some of which I know already from material she emailed to me, along with my own research. Greenhaven is a 'model village' or 'garden village': a housing estate built to high specifications by a factory owner for his workers. Built between 1926 and the early 1930s by the furniture manufacturer, Ernest Patterson, it is considered a fine example of a purpose-built, self-contained community in the modern movement style.

Avery goes on to tell me that the current Mr Patterson is called Martin, and is the grandson of Ernest, the industrialist who founded the factory in 1899, with the aim of mass producing affordable furniture. Patterson & Sons swiftly became one of the most profitable manufacturing plants in the UK, with a reputation for style and durability, and its goods were exported all over the world.

Avery sighs. 'Ernest's son John inherited the business, which was meant to go to his older boy, Charles, when he retired. In fact, Charles – supposedly the reliable son – surprised everyone by running off with one of the factory girls, leaving his hapless younger brother, Martin, to pick up the pieces.' I stare at Avery wide-eyed, and she nods grimly.

'The factory isn't still in use, is it?' I ask.

She shakes her head. 'Like I said, Martin is hapless. In fact, feckless might be a better word – the man is a waste of space, and a blight on the Patterson family name.' Her tone is bitter. 'He wanted to make money from the factory, but wasn't prepared to do a day's work to that end. He hired a manager, and absented himself almost entirely. The manager turned out to be a useless man, who ran the business into the ground. Martin had to declare bankruptcy for the company ten years ago. He still lives in Greenhaven – you'll see him around – and his personal wealth appears undiminished. He's certainly managing to keep Eagles going.'

'Eagles?'

'That's the big house, originally built for Ernest. It's on The Avenue, to the right of the village hall and the row of shops.'

'I'm guessing grandson Martin isn't too popular in Greenhaven?'

She sighs. 'I'm afraid you're right about that. A lot of people lost their jobs when the factory closed, and understandably they blamed Martin for not being proactive in running the business. Greenhaven is a shadow of the place it used to be.'

'How long have you been here?'

She looks surprised. 'I grew up here. My parents both worked in the factory, my mother as a floor manager and my father in the accounts department.'

'What about you? Did you work there?'

She shakes her head. 'I've always worked in the arts. I'm one of the lucky ones: I didn't rely on the Pattersons for my livelihood.'

We finish our coffee, and Avery gives Mouse his second biscuit, then we head back to the hall.

There's a pile of thin newspapers on a small table, and Avery says, 'Oh, take a *Maven*, won't you?'

I take the top one from the pile and read its title, *The Green Maven*. 'Is this the local newsletter?' I ask Avery.

'Well, we prefer to call it a newspaper. You know what a maven is?'

I think for a moment. 'An expert?'

She smiles. 'Precisely. Stella, who set up the paper, is from New York originally. I believe the term is more common over there.'

I thank Avery, then roll up the paper and push it into one of the deep pockets of my jacket. I put Mouse on his lead and we set out into the cold, to visit the site of my new project.

* * *

Greenhaven is bigger than I'd realised. Avery points out that there are a number of side roads leading off Hogs Green Road – the main road into the village – and The Avenue, where the village hall and shops are sited. All are lined with the preserved, largely flat-roofed white houses.

Avery says, 'Ernest didn't want the whole village to comprise identical buildings, so he hired a number of prominent architects, meaning every set of houses is a little different from the others.' She points out a row of terraces in which each house boasts a V-shape window, protruding like a small triangular tower; another row features a miniature metal-railed balcony.

'It's beautiful,' I say, and she nods and smiles.

She points a few metres ahead. 'We're coming to the site now.'

I know from my initial communication with Avery that the rectangular plot covers one hundred metres by sixty-five – a bit smaller than a football pitch, according to my dad, who knows more about such matters than I do – but that, for reasons not fully clear, I have not been allocated the entire plot for the project.

I see the metal Heras fencing before we reach it – freestanding, interlocking panels, such as you often see around building sites and festival grounds. The site is opposite the village hall and the Co-op and, from the way it lies, it forms a large island in the middle of the roads. I can already see how it could become a central hub for the village.

Avery takes a key from her pocket and unlocks a padlock, releasing one section of the fencing, which she lifts to the side with my help, and we step inside.

It's pretty overgrown, but that's to be expected from a long-neglected plot. As it's November, many of the common thugs have died back. But the long thorny stems of brambles, now brown and woody, fill whole areas.

One small wildflower that is still in green leaf is the dead-nettle – a plant that resembles the stinging nettle but, unlike the latter, is from the mint family, with square stems instead of round ones, and no sting – lacking the tiny hairs that carry the toxin. Where the stinging nettle bears groups of drooping greenish-white flowers, the dead-nettle has far prettier, to my mind, white or purply-pink blooms.

I'm a big fan of the 'right plant, right place' mantra, first popularised by renowned Essex-based gardener Beth Chatto in the 1960s. So, as wild dead-nettle does well here, I'll make sure I acquire some of the cultivated forms, such as *Lamium orvala*, known as the balm-leaved red dead-nettle, which is taller and more upright and stocky, or *Lamium maculatum*, the spotted dead-nettle, which has pretty silver-green leaves.

Turning to Avery, I say, 'Could I use the entire site?'

She frowns. 'I'm not sure the budget will stretch . . . There's also some rubble over in that area.' She points to the right.

'Rubble, we can clear,' I tell her. 'I really think, given the multi-functional garden you want here, I'll need all of the available space.'

'Let me talk to the committee.'

'That would be great – thank you.'

Returning my attention to my surroundings, I lift my gaze from the undergrowth and see that there are some beautiful trees, including one with giant brown seed pods hanging from it like streamers.

Turning to Avery, I say, 'Oh my goodness – that's *Catalpa bignonioides* – the Indian bean tree!'

She nods. 'There's another one outside the village hall. They were even more spectacular earlier, when the pods were still green.'

'Fantastic,' I say, starting to plough through ivy and woody brambles to investigate further. I'm glad of my thick gardening trousers as the bramble thorns snatch at my legs. I can already see that there's a mass of scrawny hazels, willows and elders, most of which will have to come out.

Glancing behind me, I notice that Avery is staying beside the gate. She catches my expression and says, 'I know it's rather a mess, but we have a small team of volunteers lined up to help you clear the area.'

Mouse tugs on his lead, but I tie him to the nearest tree. I don't want him vanishing into the undergrowth.

I look back at Avery. 'I'm going to do a recce. Don't feel you have to stay.'

'Oh no, I have to remain with you.' I regard her quizzically, until she adds, 'It was a condition of the Heritage Society that you have a chaperone.'

'In case I . . . what? Steal the weeds?'

She smiles, but it doesn't reach her eyes. 'I know: it's ridiculous. But it was the only way to get them to agree to your appointment.' I'm examining an oak sapling, trying to decide if we could dig it up and move it to another spot, but I stop and look at her again.

'The Heritage Society is happy for me to be carrying out this project?' I check.

'Oh, yes.' There's a pause, then she adds, 'But some of the other villagers were less keen.'

My heart sinks. 'You'd better tell me who my enemies are.'

'It's not that bad. Some felt that the money would be better spent . . . elsewhere.'

'And what do you think?'

'Oh, the garden was my idea. Greenhaven needs an outdoor space. It will be a precious place, where people can sit and reflect.'

I can only hope the village dissenters will come around to Avery's way of thinking.

2

I don't spend long on my first perusal of the garden site. A cold drizzle has started, and I'm aware of both Mouse and Avery waiting for me. I turn back reluctantly and untie Mouse on my way to join Avery at the gate.

After we've stepped out to the street, Avery locks the panel behind us, and hands me a key on a fob bearing the name Magpies.

'I did mention you'll be sharing the house?' she checks.

'Yes. Who am I sharing with again?'

'Nellie Dawn. She's a fabulous sculptor and painter, who we're lucky enough to have secured as our artist in residence, thanks to an arts fund the Patterson family set up decades back, which Martin has been unable to redirect for his own benefit. Nellie's been here for several months already, and we've commissioned a sculpture from her for the garden.' She must catch my look of concern, because she says, 'I'm sure the two of you can land on something that will be sympathetic to your overall design. She has various ideas, but hasn't started on the design process. Where was I? Oh yes, Nellie has the front bedroom at Magpies – which is the largest, I'm afraid. But you have your pick of the remaining two rooms.'

'I'm sure that will be fine.'

'There should be some food in the fridge and cupboards – I made sure Nellie stocked up. She doesn't always remember to shop for herself, but she seemed thrilled by the idea of having someone to cook for.'

'Lucky me,' I say with a smile. 'I can't say cooking's my thing.'

'Oh well, we can't all be good at everything, can we?' She seems ready to leave, but then something occurs to her. Fixing me with a look that I can't read, she says, 'I should probably mention that there is also Timmy.'

'Who's Timmy?'

'He's Nellie's little dog.'

'Oh – a friend for you, Mouse!' I say, and he makes a rumble of approval in his throat.

'Yes, well, let's hope so,' says our host, patting his head.

She raises a hand in farewell and strides away, turning up her hood, before I can follow up on her enigmatic statement. Is Timmy vicious, or perhaps territorial?

I decide to leave the van outside Avery's for now. It's only a short walk along Argent Street, past some of the lovely white terrace houses, to Hogs Green Road. Here, we turn right and a moment later reach the metal gate of a rather grand detached house with a privet hedge for privacy and the name Magpies on a sign beside the front door.

I glance across the road, and find my attention drawn to an even grander edifice. Woodpeckers is a beautifully maintained cream building with a green front door, a flat roof, and one of the V-shape towers formed of Crittall windows, opening on to a green metal balcony. While I admire the house, a stunning vintage car draws into its driveway. The MG M-type open-top sports car is in the same racing green shade as the trims on the building. With a low whistle of appreciation for the immaculate vehicle, I give in to Mouse's tugs on the lead. He's never been a fan of standing in the rain. As I let him lead me to the front door of our new place of residence, I look back to see a couple climb out of the car, both dressed in vintage clothing, he in a trench coat and she a fur-trimmed camel coat with a matching hat. I don't know much about fashion, but I recognise the styles as dating from the 1920s or thereabouts.

'I might have to befriend the neighbours, so I can get a closer look at that car,' I tell Mouse, as I turn the key to our lodgings.

'Another new home, boy,' I say. As we step over the threshold, I think about my bank account, where my previously depleted funds are now swelling nicely, like a tray of dried peas soaking in water. My ex-husband Ben lost all of our money, along with our house, in some risky business deals. Now, Mouse and I move from one project to another, each placement providing free accommodation and a generous pay packet thankfully protected from Ben's reckless optimism.

I close the front door behind us and we stand in our new hallway. It's quiet inside and smells of furniture polish. The banisters and floor are made from a pitch pine which gleams from years of care. As in Avery's house, the Crittall windows allow plenty of light through. I trace a rainbow light effect on the floor to a pair of stained-glass windows high up – a touch of art deco frivolity which has been allowed to slip into the otherwise minimalist architecture.

'This is lovely,' I say softly, and Mouse rumbles his agreement.

Raising my voice, I call, 'Hello! Is anyone home?' There's no response, but I had already figured that Nellie and Timmy must be out – Mouse has neither growled nor barked, and the house has that stillness that only comes from a lack of inhabitants.

'Let's explore,' I say to Mouse, taking him off the lead. He sniffs his way to the right while I step through the nearest door to my left. It's the living room, and runs from the front to the back of the house. The wood flooring runs throughout here as well, and there's a sideboard and nest of tables that I recognise from the Patterson furniture archives, which I've looked up online, while doing my initial research. I suspect the sofa and three armchairs – all with wooden frames and padded seats and backs – were also sourced from the village factory. The ceiling and alcoves boast black and silver light fittings made from metal and glass which are like miniature modernist sculptures or tiny UFOs.

I continue my exploration of the house. The kitchen is small but functional, with free-standing units that are no doubt also originals. There's a metal framed table with a Formica top in a faded yellow and black geometric design, that I reckon dates from just after WWII. The table is pushed against the wall; around its three accessible sides are metal stools with yellow cushioned seats.

A final room on the ground floor is filled with canvases, sketchbooks, and some form of wire framing that could be the base for a sculpture, but I will have to wait and ask Nellie when she returns.

I make my way upstairs, where I find Mouse sniffing around a good-sized bedroom at the back of the house. A large bay window is framed by red curtains in a print that reminds me of kinetic sculptures by the artist Alexander Calder, whose work I've seen in an art gallery and loved. The bed has a walnut frame and is already made up, with a bedspread in the same fabric as the curtains. The wooden floorboards bear a large rug in similar colours.

'Isn't this lovely?' I say to Mouse. 'Do you like it?'

He looks up at me and I stroke his head and soft ears.

'Let's just take a quick look at the other room,' I say, striding out and pushing open the remaining door on this side of the house. But this is a box room, a single bed and tiny wardrobe taking up all of the space.

'OK: that makes the decision easy,' I say to Mouse. 'Will you come with me to fetch the van?' He follows me downstairs and, once he's established that the rain has stopped, we jog back to Avery's, where we climb inside our beloved van, I strap us both in, and we drive the two minutes to Magpies. In case Nellie owns a vehicle and is used to parking in the drive, I pull up on the road outside. Mouse grabs Mr Rabbit, and I bring in his bed and blanket. Up in our new bedroom, I place his bed on the floor near the radiator for warmth, and he leaps on to a sofa by the window, to gaze out at the garden.

'Shall we take a look out there?' I suggest.

Leading him back downstairs, I open the French windows from the living room and we step outside. The garden is mature and – although unimaginative – well-tended and attractive, with many evergreen shrubs. There's an ancient apple tree in the middle of the lawn, and a selection of laurels, privet and cotoneaster along the perimeter fences. A blackbird is pecking around in the dead leaves, while a robin sings from a holly tree. There are clearly not too many cats in the vicinity.

I leave Mouse to continue his explorations outside while I head back into the house and through to the cosy kitchen, where I make coffee in a cafetière and sit at the table with a mug bearing an illustration of Eagles, the Patterson house. There are several similar mugs in the cupboard, each displaying a different Greenhaven building. I've never visited a village with its own mugs before. The residents are clearly very proud of their heritage.

Removing my jacket, I discover my forgotten copy of *The Green Maven*. Clearing space on the cluttered tabletop, I lay it down and begin to read. There are the expected articles about sports teams and fixtures, plus listings for events in the village hall and its incorporated library.

And then, inside the back cover, I find a gossip column. There's no other word for it. Written by someone who goes by the name 'the Green Raven' – and whose profile picture is a photograph of a green feather – the column is an observation of a number of villagers.

Although those mentioned are not referenced by name, I'm pretty sure the other residents will recognise them by description alone.

What the Little Bird Saw *with the Green Raven*

Caw, Caw! Green Raven here, bringing you up to date with all the juicy worms this bird has discovered during flights about the village.

First of all, Ms Burberry Trench has been spotted a number of times, climbing out of a car in Argent Street. And who was sighted behind the wheel of the vehicle in question? None other than Mr On-the-Board himself. This Raven cannot help but wonder what Mrs On-the-Board makes of all this. Or is she too busy furnishing her new £100k extension to get her feathers in a ruffle about her husband's flightiness?

Meanwhile, Sulky Teenager has got himself into another spot of bother with our local law enforcement. Constable Dodo gave Sulky a 'slap on the wrist'. As far as this bird can see, Dodo's gentle slaps don't seem to have made a mark. Maybe it's time to rethink law and order in the village, Dodo?

In other news, your resident Raven spotted Acne Boy creeping out of the House of Many Daughters via a side door at gone midnight on Tuesday! Rumour has it, the Many Daughters' parents were at the *Totally Legal Lock-in* at the Greenhaven Arms. It's clearly time to lock up your daughters – or at least not leave them unchaperoned of a night-time.

That's all for now from your green feathered friend. And remember: I have my beady eye on you . . .

Green Raven

Mouse has finished his exploration of the garden, and appears at my side. I tip back the rest of my coffee and say, 'Right, boy, time for a proper walk.'

I shut the French windows in the living room and then head back to join Mouse in the hall but, when I open the front door, it transpires that the rain has restarted. He gazes out at the drizzle and whines quietly.

'It's no good. We've been cooped up all day. We both need the exercise.'

The first minute or two of our walk is a tug of war which I come close to losing, until Mouse thankfully becomes distracted by the new sights and scents, and we begin to enjoy ourselves.

After a couple of minutes, and without directly aiming for it, we arrive back at the garden site.

A figure is standing there, beneath a red and white golf umbrella, gazing through the fencing into the wilderness. The person turns as I approach, and I see it's a thin white man of medium height, with greying hair and beard, big brown eyes, and a pervading air of sadness.

'I don't think we've met,' he says, stepping towards me. 'Kieran Galloway. Are you the person they've brought in to make the garden?' Despite his Scottish name, his accent is local. He holds out a hand, which I shake. His handshake is cold and wet, and I wonder how long he's been standing here.

'That's right – Steph Williams.'

'And who's this?' he asks, looking down at Mouse.

'This is Mouse.'

The dog makes a rumble in his throat and licks Kieran's hand. The man pats his head and says, 'Hello, boy. You're rather nice, aren't you?' Mouse barks once and Kieran nods approvingly. 'Clever, too.'

'He is pretty bright,' I agree. 'But I am his biased human companion.'

He smiles, but it's weak, as if diluted by the watery atmosphere.

'Are you involved in the garden project?' I ask him. 'I've been promised volunteers.'

He shakes his head. 'It's just all a bit too . . . painful for me.'

I frown. 'What is?'

'Do you know about the site – what was here before?'

'Was it not just a piece of wasteland?'

'It was not. There was a bungalow with a garden on part of this land.'

I look again at the overgrown plot. 'Really? What happened to it?'

'It was burned down with my grandparents inside. They both died in the fire. They were buried together in the village cemetery.'

I put a hand to my mouth. 'Oh my god! I'm so sorry, Kieran! That's awful.' He nods, and I see his eyes are wet with held-back tears. 'When did this happen?' I ask.

'Oh . . . it was back in the 1980s.' He swipes the tears away from his eyes with the heel of his hand. 'Stupid of me to still get so upset.'

'Not at all. It must have been traumatic. Did they find the cause of the fire?'

'It was arson,' he says dully.

My eyes grow wide. 'Arson? What . . . ? Who . . . ?'

'Oh,' he says darkly, 'Everyone knows who. But, strangely enough, the police never managed to pin it on anyone.' When I say nothing, he says, 'Money and power rule.'

I had thought I was coming to a quiet little village for a bit of peace after my previous eventful postings. Instead, I'm reading scurrilous gossip in the local paper, finding out about arguments over funding and, worst of all, learning about a double murder, if what Kieran claims is true. I can't help wondering if it suits him to believe there was someone to blame for his grandparents' death, instead of it being a horrible accident. I've seen people fuelled by anger after the death of a loved one.

Meeting Kieran's eye, I say gently, 'Can I ask . . . Why wasn't your grandparents' bungalow rebuilt after the fire?'

He shrugs. 'There was enough housing in the village. And then, more recently, the site became a destination for the local teens to hang out and smoke and drink, so all this Heras fencing was brought in.'

I take a deep breath. 'How do you feel about the centenary garden?'

'I like the idea. I've been promised a tree in my grandparents' memory, which they would have loved.'

'Have you decided on a species?'

He laughs again. 'It's obvious you're a gardener: straight to the plants.'

I pull a face. 'Sorry! We can talk about that down the line.' I hesitate, then ask, 'Do you know if the rubble is still on site?'

'Most of it was cleared, after the local kids started hanging out here. But I think you'll find the foundations are still in place, over there.' He points to a large section, just visible from our viewpoint, where the ivy has gone rampant.

Weirdly, hearing this has the effect of inspiring me. I am wondering if I might be able to incorporate the foundations of the house into my design.

3

When we get back from our walk, there's a red Citroën Berlingo parked in the driveway. Mouse and I hear Timmy yapping before we've even reached the doorstep. The door is opened and a small ball of golden fur hurls itself out and begins running around us in circles. Mouse stands very still, as if afraid he might accidentally stand on the little dog. Timmy's tail is wagging even as he carries on barking.

'Well, you're an enthusiastic little thing, aren't you?' I say, laughing.

Mouse bends down to lick Timmy's nose, which sends him into even more of a frenzy.

Nellie stands on the doorstep, also laughing. 'Sorry! I thought I'd shut him in the studio, but he managed to get out!' Her voice is pure Geordie and she has a mass of copper curls which bounce as she moves, like living creatures. Everything about her seems animated.

'No worries,' I say with a smile. 'Mouse doesn't seem too bothered.'

I take the opportunity to study our new human housemate. She's in her late twenties, I'd guess, and dressed in dungarees in a vibrant splash print. She's small, so she's had to turn up the dungarees several times at the bottom. She has freckles and bright green eyes to go with her red hair.

She catches me sizing her up, and smiles. 'Yep: I am a complete mess.'

'Not what I was thinking at all!' I assure her.

But before I can say more, she's distracted by her dog and says, 'Oh, Timmy, no!' I turn to take in Timmy, who's attempting to run underneath Mouse's stomach, while Mouse backs away. 'Leave him alone now,' says Nellie. But Timmy is nothing if not persistent.

Nellie steps outside in her bare feet and picks up her dog, who licks her chin. 'Yuck!' she says. She turns to look at me. 'Shall we go in?'

'Sounds good.' I've started to notice that the rain is now poking its way down the back of my neck like cold fingers. I inch my way out of my wet jacket and hang it on the coat stand in the hall.

'There's a pot of coffee on the side,' she says, leading the way into the kitchen.

'I already love it here,' I say. 'Oh – do you bother taking off shoes in the house?' I ask, glancing down at her bare feet.

She shakes her head. 'The floors are all hardwood, apart from the rugs, which I steam clean every blue moon.'

'Sounds like my kind of cleaning regimen.'

She looks back and winks. 'I can tell we're going to get along just fine.'

She puts Timmy down in a basket I hadn't noticed in a corner of the kitchen, whereupon he jumps straight back out. Mouse retreats behind my legs.

Nellie looks apologetically at Mouse. 'Timmy's a bit full on, isn't he?' she says. She addresses me: 'Should I put him in another room?'

I glance down at Mouse. 'What do you think, boy? Can you cope with Timmy's enthusiasm?'

Mouse looks dubiously at his little tormentor. I crouch down, physically holding back the small dog with one hand, to prevent him from getting to Mouse.

'OK: that's enough, Timmy,' says Nellie. She scoops him up and takes him out of the room. We hear a door shut, and then the sound of Timmy barking and whining piteously.

'I'm sorry,' I say to Nellie, as she strides back in.

'Don't be: he has to learn, especially if we're going to all get along. Now, are you ready for that coffee?'

'I really am.'

I take a seat on a stool at the Formica kitchen table. The scent of coffee fills the air as Nellie brings the cafetière to the table, along with two mugs. 'Do you take milk?'

I shake my head and she pours the steaming liquid into the mugs, handing one to me. It bears an image of a house similar to the one opposite.

'Thanks. It smells great.' Holding up the mug, I turn the photo towards her. 'Is this Woodpeckers?'

'That's it.'

'I saw a couple pulling up outside there, in a beautiful MG.'

She frowns before saying, 'Is that a car?'

I laugh. 'Sorry, I'm a bit of a petrolhead.'

When she still looks bemused, I explain, 'I love cars.'

'Oh, right!'

'They were driving a gorgeous vintage green car, basically. And, as far as I could tell, they were dressed in era-appropriate clothing.'

'That'll be Stella and Jeremy,' she says. 'Stella's the editor of the paper you've got there. You're lucky – I don't always remember who's who. On the other hand . . .' She gets up and collects a large sketchbook from the worktop near the cooker. Bringing the book to the table and sitting back down, she opens it to show me pages filled with sketches and watercolours. I must show my surprise at the subject matter, because it's her turn to laugh. 'Yeah – I'm not sure what the equivalent of "petrolhead" is for someone who's into doors and gates.'

'Portalhead?' I suggest, and she laughs again.

She pushes the book towards me and I turn the pages, stopping every now and then to admire a beautiful entry way.

'That one's Wrens,' she says, when my eye is caught by a stunning double door inset with vertical panels featuring a stack of diamond shapes in stained glass. 'I've been commissioned to do a series of paintings of it. It's a gorgeous building.'

'I thought the village was all modernist architecture,' I say, 'but I would have said the pattern in this glass was more art deco?'

'Yeah. I think the idea behind the village was to focus on utility over design – the typical modernist ideal of function over form.' When I look blank, she explains, 'The idea that use is more important than ornament. So, everything needs to be functional above all. But I get the impression some of the architects – there were a bunch of them involved in designing Greenhaven – let the odd bit of art deco frippery creep in.'

'Like the stained glass in our hall,' I say.

'Exactly.' She smiles. 'Oh – I wasn't sure what you eat, by the way. I thought I'd do a veggie chilli tonight, if you fancy?'

'That sounds perfect, thank you. I am vegetarian, so that was a good call. Avery told me you got some shopping in. You'll have to tell me what I owe you.'

She shakes her head. 'You can get it next time.'

'Is there just the Co-op on The Avenue?'

'Yeah, but it's pretty well stocked. And did you see there's a fish and chip shop – though that might be less appealing for you – and a Boots? Oh, and the library, of course, in the village hall. It's not open every day but, if you get an Essex Libraries' card, you can use it, and they'll even order books in for you.'

'This place seems to have everything,' I say. 'But then, I suppose it was built as a model village.'

She grins. 'D'you know, when I first heard the term "model village", I pictured one of those miniature villages with tiny houses – you know, everything doll-size?'

I laugh. 'That would make my job a lot easier! I reckon I could create one of those fairy gardens out of a few foil containers, some plastic trees, and an upturned lid for a pond.'

'Yeah – and my sculpture could be made out of a few pins and some papier mâché.'

We're silent for a moment, enjoying the miniaturised visions of our artistic endeavours.

Then Nellie says, 'I suspect the first Mr Patterson was a control freak.'

Taken by surprise, I laugh before saying, 'How do you mean?'

'Well, if you give your workers everything on their doorstep, they never need to leave, do they? So he gives them a school, a village hall, a dentist's, a doctor's, a police officer, a library, a department store . . .'

'I hadn't thought of it like that.'

She meets my gaze and raises her eyebrows. 'Creepy, really.'

I laugh. 'That might be a bit strong?'

'No, the family were really strict. Did Avery tell you about the housekeeper they accused of stealing from them?' When I shake my head, she continues, 'Nancy O'Donoghue, she was called. She worked for the family for years. And then, one day, out of the blue they accuse her of stealing this statue off the mantelpiece.'

'I take it she hadn't stolen it?'

'Well, her house was searched and it was never found. But they fired her anyway.'

'Really?'

'Yeah. And she'd never put a foot wrong before then. All the older folk I've talked to here say she was really hard-working and discreet – didn't discuss the family outside the Eagles and all that.'

'Did she get another job?' I ask.

'Nope. No one would employ her without a reference,' says Nellie. Without warning, she pushes back her chair and leaps to her feet, shouting, 'Biscuits!'

I'm reeling from what Nellie's just told me, but I'm distracted by Mouse, who barks on hearing one of his favourite words. I stroke his head. 'OK, boy. They're in the van. I'll get you one in a bit.'

Nellie is rummaging in a wall cupboard; she looks over at us and says, 'Oh, I have some for Timmy in a jar on the side. Mouse can have one.'

'That would be great, thanks. I haven't unpacked the van yet.'

She stops rummaging and stares at me. 'You have a van? Oh, my god! That's brilliant! Sometimes it's hard to fit everything in my Berlingo.'

'I'll be happy to help if you need to move larger pieces. You said you're working on a series of paintings? I'd love to see some of your work.'

'Sure. And I need to see your designs for the garden – Avery told you I'm making the sculpture?'

'She did. I've only got roughs so far, but I should be able to crystallise things in the next few weeks.'

We finish our drinks and head off – I to unload the van, and Nellie to the dining room, to work on a painting.

I don't have a lot of belongings and, as towels have been provided along with bedding, it doesn't take me long to bring in my holdall filled with clothes, and a couple of bags containing Mouse's food and toys.

I spend some time in the bedroom, messaging my mum and dad to let them know all is well, and sending further messages to my boyfriend Mike and brother Danny before putting my clothes away in the wardrobe and chest of drawers.

Nellie calls me about an hour later and I go down for dinner. Mouse accompanies me, and I fill his and Timmy's bowls with food and water while Nellie dishes out our dinner.

'This chilli is amazing,' I say as we sit at right angles at the tiny table, trying not to bump knees.

'The secret's in the chocolate,' she says.

'Oh, I've heard that. I've never tried it, though.'

'It has to be dark chocolate, and not too much.' Timmy is sitting at her feet, staring up at her as if he's starving. 'You've got your dinner there,' she tells him, pointing to his bowl. 'Anyway, this one's not safe for you.' Looking at me, she says, 'He once got into a box of chocolates at my parents' at Christmas. We had to drive about twenty miles to find an open vet's. He was so ill.'

'Did he learn from it?' I ask.

She raises an eyebrow. 'You've met Timmy. What do you think?'

'How old is he?' I ask, expecting her to say two or younger.

When she answers, 'Seven,' I stare.

'I know. He's yet to come out of the puppy stage. I have tried puppy training, believe it or not. But he's so enthusiastic about everything, it's hard to be strict.' She reaches down to stroke his head.

She insists on clearing the plates after we've finished. I'm delighted to discover there's a small dishwasher in the little kitchen, which she loads before opening the fridge and bringing a plate to the table.

'Ta-da!'

'Wow!' I say, which is the only possible response to the beautiful pavlova, covered in cream and topped with blackberries, raspberries and mandarin segments.

'Yeah. You will put on weight if you live with me,' she says, setting the plate on the worktop as there isn't room on the cluttered table, and cutting two slices. She brings them over on two mismatched china side plates and hands one to me with a teaspoon.

'Thanks so much. I'll take my chances,' I tell her.

'That's good. I haven't had anyone to cook for in a while.'

She sounds sad, so I ask, 'Were you in a relationship?'

'Yeah. It ended, after four years. That's part of why I took this residency,' she says.

'I'm sorry to hear that.'

After playing with her teaspoon for a moment, she looks at me, lifts her chin and says, 'Hey, if they didn't appreciate what they had, why should I want to be with them?'

'Absolutely.'

But a tear trickles down her cheek, and I reach across to squeeze her arm.

We sit in silence as we eat our dessert. Despite her proximity, she feels a long way away.

4

A habitual early riser, I'm awake the next morning by six, ready to continue our exploration of Greenhaven and its environs. As I pull on my running clothes, Mouse stirs from his bed near the radiator where he has slept with Mr Rabbit and his favourite lead between his paws. The heating hasn't come on yet, and the room is chilly. Despite the curtains, I can feel a draught coming through the large bay windows. At least we got a good night's sleep: Nellie took Timmy up to bed with her last night and shut the door, so we wouldn't be disturbed by the little dog.

'Hey boy,' I say, 'fancy a run?' He stirs and opens one eye. The second time I say the word 'run', he practically leaps out of bed, making me laugh.

While Mouse settles Mr Rabbit in the bed before picking up his lead, I pull on my running trainers. Then we head down to the hall where I clip on his lead. Opening the door, I see dark clouds are still lurking, stretching above our heads like the wings of giant crows. I suppress a shiver, and we set off.

We start by heading towards the garden site, not because I especially want to view it again this morning, but because I know it's on the way to the village shops, which I'm keen to check out.

I slow at the tall fencing that borders the site. Peering through at the mass of overgrowth beyond, I say, 'What do you think, boy? I reckon we can make something pretty good.'

He tilts his head enquiringly and I turn to continue our run. But, at that moment, he barks once to alert me to the approach of a tall, broad-shouldered white man in a dark wool overcoat and scarf.

'Ms Williams?' the man calls.

It occurs to me that the site seems to be attracting people, even before I've built the garden.

'That's right.' The newcomer has the flushed cheeks and protruding belly of a heavy drinker.

'Martin Patterson. I own Eagles, the big house.' He nods towards the imposing white building on the far side of the site, just visible above the fencing.

'Good to meet you,' I say, proffering a hand. But his own hands remain firmly in the pockets of his expensive-looking coat.

I feel suddenly vulnerable, and find myself wishing I was dressed in more than my jogging shorts and vest.

'I'm glad I caught you,' he says brusquely. 'You've probably heard that I'm opposed to this renovation project.' Mouse starts grumbling at Martin's terse manner, so I shorten his lead to keep him close as the man continues: 'I'm off to Scotland shortly for a couple of days, and I didn't want to come back and find the whole plot had been dug up without my consent.'

I frown. 'I'm sorry – does the site belong to you?'

He puffs himself out like a cockerel. 'Well, my family used to own the whole village, of course.'

I don't point out that the emphasis is clearly on the past tense, *used to*. Instead, I tilt my head and say, 'But I believe the Heritage Society is in charge of the centenary garden project?'

He sighs. 'Look, I don't know what Avery and her gang have been saying, but there are building remains on this site, along with god knows what detritus.' He gestures to the area beyond the metal fencing as he continues, 'I simply don't believe the site is safe. As I'm sure you're aware, final veto rests with me, as the sole surviving member of the Patterson family.'

'Really?' I say, holding his gaze. 'That's not the impression I was given, when I took the job.' I'm getting cold standing still in my running clothes, but I manage to keep my teeth from chattering. I've already recognised that Martin is a bully, and I need to hide any hint of weakness.

The staring contest goes on a little too long. At last, he says, 'Just make sure you don't start work without my sign off on your plans.'

As I have no intention of complying with this order, I change the subject. 'I've been reviewing the village's picture archives on Facebook. Does your house still have the original Japanese garden? If so, I'd love to see it in real life, for my research.'

He's clearly wrong-footed by my sudden change of tone, and I look down to pat Mouse's head as I conceal a smile.

Clearing his throat, he says, 'Oh, yes, the . . . er . . . Japanese garden is still pretty much in its original state. I'm sure John, my gardener, will show you around.'

'That would be great, thanks.'

He nods. 'Knock on the door of John's bungalow to the left of Eagles. I'll let him know to expect you.'

I'm about to repeat my thanks when he turns and strides away, relieving me of the need.

Mouse makes another grumble as we watch the man's back recede, and I look down and say softly, 'My sentiments entirely.'

Then he and I set off jogging again, soon passing the row of shops and the large village hall, with the library boasting its own entrance on the far left-hand side.

The pavements are wide, and we run side by side. Mouse matches my pace, his tongue lolling, and I feel a surge of happiness. It's always exciting to be at the start of a new project, with all the possibilities that that entails.

Before we reach the countryside, we pass some newer houses: a series of 1950s council semis with cream facades, plus some red-brick, boxy, 1980s designs. I know that Greenhaven originally consisted of around five hundred houses, but I'd estimate that there are at least another two hundred on the outskirts. I remember Avery's reference to the conflicting views in the village on how the funds should be spent. With so many residents, it's no wonder it's hard to reach a consensus. And now it seems Martin Patterson will be adding his own special brand of obstructiveness to the mix. I wonder, not for the first time, if my job is going to be a tough one.

5

After my run with Mouse, there's no sign of Nellie and Timmy, so we grab breakfast and head over to pay a visit to Avery, as I want to run a couple of things by her, in her role as chair of the Heritage Society committee – and my employer.

She welcomes us with a big smile, and invites us inside. As she and I sip coffee from her pretty china, I mention meeting Martin Patterson.

'And how did you find him?' she asks.

I shrug. 'He made it pretty clear that he doesn't want the money spent on my services, and he believes he should have the power of ultimate veto.'

She sighs. 'I'm so sorry. The man is an obstinate you-know-what.'

I can think of a number of words and phrases that would fit, but I hold my tongue. Instead, I say, 'So long as he doesn't really have the authority to prevent the garden being built, then I don't really care, to be honest. He can throw his weight around, but I'm not easily intimidated.'

She eyes me for a moment before saying in a thoughtful tone, 'No, I don't suppose you are.' She puts down her cup and sits back. 'Well, I can certainly reassure you on that score.

Martin Patterson has no more claim to that land than to this house.'

Glancing around, I say, 'I take it . . .'

'Oh, the house is mine. I have the deeds to prove it.' She sighs. 'I'm afraid Martin has always been spoilt. He grew up with money, and inherited the factory and Eagles. He had no real drive or motivation to work. Unfortunately, that led to the failing and ultimate buyout of Patterson and Sons.'

'So what happened? Didn't the buyer want to keep it going?'

She shakes her head. 'Sadly, Martin didn't adequately vet the buyer. I think he was so keen to get out of the burden of inherited duty that he didn't think to ensure the workers and the village would be looked after. The buyer turned out to be an asset stripper, a vulture. He sold what he could from the factory, then lost interest. Employees found themselves unemployed. Young people had to move away to find work. That steady whirring of machinery had been the heart of the village. Without it, the village began to die. It's only in the past couple of years that we've seen an influx of funds from heritage groups and the like, and have been able to begin the restoration of what was a near-perfect example of the modernist movement.'

She laughs unexpectedly. 'Christy on the committee has been saying I should record a documentary about Greenhaven. I certainly seem to have plenty to say.'

'Perhaps you could time it for the centenary celebrations,' I suggest. 'If you don't try for anything too ambitious.'

'Maybe so.' She sets down her coffee cup. 'Now, was there something you wanted?'

'Yes: I'd like to poll the villagers, and it occurred to me that *The Green Maven* would be a good place to do it.'

'Poll them?' she looks concerned. 'What about?'

'Only about how they'll be using the new garden. It would help to inform the design.'

'Ah! Like the intention behind the design of the houses: let the people's ultimate use determine the design,' she says, echoing Nellie's words. 'I like that idea.'

'So, who do I need to contact about the newspaper?'

'The editor is based at Woodpeckers – do you know it?'

'Yes, opposite Magpies.'

'That's right. Just knock and ask for Stella. She'll love your suggestion. She's always looking for content.'

'Great. Thanks.'

'Was there anything else?'

I nod. 'Initially, you told me I could only use the site up to what I now know to be the remains of the destroyed bungalow. As I said yesterday, I don't think that's enough space for the sort of multi-functional garden the village needs.'

'Yes. I said I'd mention it to the committee. I'll email them later today.'

'That's great – thanks.'

I drain my coffee and get up to leave, calling to Mouse. As Avery opens the door to show us out, she says, 'Oh, and Steph, if you do get any interference with the garden build, refer them to me.'

She closes the door before I can respond, leaving me hoping I'm not going to find protesters when I turn up to the garden site the next day to meet my volunteers.

6

As I push the doorbell beside the green front door of Woodpeckers, I'm still a little unsettled at the idea that I might be going up against some of the village by using the Heritage Society's precious funds to make a garden. But I'm here, and I've been tasked to do a job, so I determine to make sure the ultimate product is something that will benefit as many of the villagers as possible.

A loud barking sets up inside the house, and I hear a man's voice calling a command before the door is opened by a tall white man with thick brown hair pushed back from his forehead, and hazel eyes. 'Dashing' is the rather dated word that springs to mind – although this might be the product of the aviator jacket he's wearing.

'Yes, hello?' he says in a confident, deep voice. 'How can I help?' He has a smile that forms wrinkles at the corners of his eyes and immediately puts me at ease.

'Hi. I'm Steph Williams, the . . .'

'. . . the garden designer!' he says, holding out a hand. 'Jeremy Pargeter. How can I help?'

'Actually, I was hoping to talk to Stella,' I tell him.

'Ah, my better half. Stella!' he calls over his shoulder. 'You have a visitor.' Turning back to me, he says, 'Please come in.'

I gesture to Mouse. 'Is it OK to bring Mouse in or should I take him home first?'

Jeremy pats Mouse on the head and Mouse licks his hand. 'What a fine chap. Is he OK with other dogs?'

'He loves them.'

'Then please bring him in to meet our two.'

As we enter the hall, I move to take off my boots but he says, 'We don't bother with that. The dogs don't take theirs off.' He strides towards a door with glass panels. As he opens it, two Old English sheepdogs come trotting out. They are so well trained that they stop, standing quietly, one on either side of Jeremy. 'Good girls,' he says, placing a hand on each head. 'Greta, Marlene, meet Steph and Mouse.'

He pronounces his second dog's name 'Marlena', so I ask, 'After Garbo and Dietrich?' and he nods. I hold on to Mouse's lead until it's clear that all three dogs are delighted with the encounter, and then I unclip it. There is much sniffing and tail wagging. Marlene and Greta have long plume-like tails. 'They're gorgeous,' I say.

'Yes, we're rather lucky.'

A woman appears in the doorway behind Jeremy. She's black and petite, with a paisley silk headscarf and a matching shirt dress with a pleated skirt. The outfit makes me think of films from the 1940s, though I'm not great on fashion history. 'Hello,' she says with a warm smile.

'Darling, this is Steph, who's going to make a beautiful garden for the village.'

'Great to meet you,' she says. 'And I see we have another visitor.' She may have lived in the UK for a long time, but she's retained more than a hint of her New York accent.

'This is Mouse,' I say.

'What a sweet boy,' she says. 'He's obviously good with strange dogs.'

Remembering Timmy, I say, 'Although he is finding Nellie's dog a bit full on.'

She and Jeremy laugh. 'That's Timmy!' she says. 'Do come in. Tea? Coffee?'

'Coffee would be great,' I say, following her into the room.

'I'll sort the drinks and keep the dogs out of your hair,' says Jeremy.

'Thanks, love,' says Stella, leading me into a large rectangular sitting room that runs from the front to the back of the house. 'Take a seat,' she says, gesturing to a sofa with a wooden frame and cream leather upholstery. I can't help wondering about the practicality of the colour choice with two large, hairy dogs on the premises.

As I sit in the middle of the comfortable sofa, she takes the matching armchair to my right and sits forward. 'So, what can I do for you?'

'It's about *The Green Maven*,' I tell her. 'I'm hoping you'll include an article for me.'

'Ah, great! Let me grab a notebook in that case.'

She gets up to open a drawer in a curved walnut bureau, and I take the opportunity to glance around the room. Wooden display cabinets placed in the room's corners are filled with colourful china; a large fireplace provides a focal point at the centre of the long wall, and floor to ceiling shelves on either side of the front window are lined with books.

The French windows with side lights are identical to those in Avery's house, Herons, as well as at Magpies. Through them, I can see some beautiful shrubs and trees in the back garden. A further two windows along the side of the room, and another at the front of the house, mean the space is, again, filled with light. When I have enough saved for my and Mouse's home, I shall have to consider a modernist house, if it's not outside my budget.

'Right,' says Stella, sitting back down with a spiral notebook and pen in hand, 'shoot.' I explain my ideas for the questionnaire while she nods and makes notes. Part way through, Jeremy comes in with a tray of drinks and hands us each a mug.

'Milk and sugar?' he asks.

'No, thanks. This is great.'

'Right,' he says, when we're both settled with drinks and a slice of Bakewell tart with a pastry fork on the side, 'I'll leave you to it.'

After he's left, Stella takes a sip of her tea before saying, 'I love the idea of canvassing the village. But I'm afraid you should be prepared for a backlash.'

I frown. 'Avery did hint that not everyone wants the money to be spent on a garden.'

'That's right. I don't know if you've explored the whole village yet, but some of the residents are keen to see the money go on replanting some of the gappy hedges, taking out a number of diseased and dead trees, that kind of thing.'

'I can understand that,' I say. 'If there are funds left over after the garden, perhaps I can take a look at some of those maintenance projects. Is there anything else that people feel the money would be better spent on?'

'A number of the younger families have children, so there's a lot of call for a playground,' she says. 'You may have seen that we do have a set of swings and a slide near the old church, but it's right next to the graveyard, and it's not the most welcoming spot.'

I smile. 'Well, that's sorted.'

'It is? The Heritage committee haven't mentioned plans for a playground.'

'I did list it, but perhaps it was missed when the information was shared.'

She makes more notes. 'That's great. I can make sure we mention that in the paper, so everyone's aware.'

'Thanks, I'd appreciate that.'

'So, what's going into the questionnaire?'

'It's mainly going to be about usage. I want to know how often people envisage visiting the garden and playground, and how long they think they'll spend there. There's other things, too: will they be alone or accompanied by friends or family? Will they use it as a meeting place? Should there be picnic tables or just benches? If it's OK with you, I'll type it all out and email it over.'

She gets up and fetches a business card from the top of the bureau, handing it to me. 'My email's on there. I know it's a bit rushed, but is there any chance you could get it to me by eight this evening?'

I check my watch. 'I'd better get on!'

'If you can, I'll include it in the issue I'm sending to press on Thursday.'

'Thanks so much.'

'It's a pleasure. I'm excited to see what you create.'

Despite my best intentions, however, I find myself caught up in our conversation, and we've moved from my previous employment to her former role as a freelance journalist on national newspapers before I finally get up to leave.

It's only then that I remember the Green Raven. 'Oh, one more thing: who writes the gossip column?' I ask her.

'I honestly have no idea.' With her being in charge of the paper, this seems unlikely – but her expression is inscrutable. 'All I can tell you is that the first column was emailed to me around nine months ago. It had a gently mocking tone, which I found endearing. It reminded me of Elizabeth Gaskell's novel, *Cranford*.'

I smile at this reference to the nineteenth-century comedy of manners, which examines the foibles of a group of villagers.

Stella sighs. 'It has become more . . . biting since then, though. I should probably kill the column, but it is very popular in the village.'

'To be honest, I'm surprised you haven't been sued for libel.'

'I think the targets of the column all know that, in order to defend the column, I would only have to prove there was truth in the Raven's allegations, and that wouldn't be hard to do.'

'Fair enough. Does the email address not give a clue to the writer's identity?'

She raises her eyebrows. 'Green raven at gmail dot com.'

'I guess you would have thought of that,' I say with a laugh.

'If you fancied contributing an ongoing column while you were here,' she says, walking me to the glass-panelled living-room door and opening it to allow me through, 'that could be interesting. Perhaps something charting your progress with the garden?'

I hesitate, not wanting to commit to more work. 'Hmm,' I say at last. 'Can I think about it?'

'Of course,' she says, before calling over my shoulder, 'Jeremy, our guest is leaving.'

After a moment, another glass-panelled door opens at the end of the hall, and her husband re-emerges, with all three dogs. 'Good to meet you, Steph,' he says.

'You, too. Thanks for the coffee and delicious cake.'

'Any time. I'll look forward to seeing what you make for us.'

Calling Mouse to heel and glancing at the Old English sheepdogs, I say, 'Before I go, I was wondering if Marlene and Greta might like a walk with Mouse?'

'I'm sure they'd love that, wouldn't they, darling?' he says to Stella, who nods.

'I always think they must get a bit bored, just hanging out with each other and the two of us,' she says. 'And they've obviously taken to your lovely boy.'

'When I email you, I'll suggest a time.'

'We can take them out in the countryside,' she says. 'There are lots of good walks from the village.'

'Perfect. Mouse loves to explore.'

We smile and I take my leave, having to persuade a reluctant Mouse to step out with me into a drizzle so cold and thin, it's like frozen needles. By the time we've made the short trip across the road and stepped in at the door of Magpies, my hair is soaked and plastered to my head, and I'm shivering. At least Mouse's thick fur has insulated him.

But I sigh with pleasure as I close the front door behind us and remove my wet jacket: the central heating is on, and the house is warm and welcoming.

7

Nellie insists on treating me to another delicious evening meal, this time a pie filled with roasted squash and tomatoes, seasoned with sprigs of rosemary. She even serves it early and insists on clearing up afterwards, to give me time to work on my questionnaire for Stella.

After we've eaten, I settle myself with my laptop at a table beside the living room window, while Nellie watches *Bridgerton* on the TV. Timmy seems finally to have worn himself out, and I notice that Mouse becomes far more confident while the little dog sleeps, placing himself at Nellie's feet to observe the human goings-on on the box. The yellow curtains are closed, revealing an abstract print of dandelions, and the room feels cosy.

I create a new Word document on my laptop, then reflect for a moment on what I want to ask the residents of Greenhaven.

Deciding to make my questionnaire a call to action, I type:

Have your say: the Greenhaven centenary garden is for you!

I set out a series of questions, focusing around usage, including whether the residents are looking for a place just to sit in contemplation, or whether they'd like a corner for exercise equipment, and what they'd ideally want in the children's play area.

After giving the questionnaire a quick read through, I attach it to an email and send it to Stella, asking her to improve anything that doesn't read well, and to check she's OK with printing the results. I add a suggestion that we walk the dogs on Sunday morning.

My inbox pings just before I shut down my laptop, and I see it's an email from Avery. It simply reads:

> Committee all onboard with use of whole plot for garden, provided you can keep it within budget.

With a smile, I send a quick acknowledgement before shutting down and joining Nellie on the sofa, in front of *Bridgerton*.

'Have you seen it before?' she asks, after hitting the pause button.

Mouse, who is apparently engrossed in the period drama, turns from his position near the TV set to see why the people on the screen have stopped moving.

'Sorry, boy,' says Nellie, pressing play.

'No,' I whisper. 'But it's fine.'

My phone rings with a video call about ten minutes into my viewing, while a woman with red hair who looks vaguely familiar is admitting to . . . I guess I'll never find out her secret.

'Oh, it's my boyfriend,' I say, looking at my screen. Grimacing, I confess, 'I hate that word.'

Nellie laughs. 'What would you prefer?'

I shrug. 'There is no better option.'

'Shouldn't you answer the poor guy?'

'Oops! Good point!' I press the green button and Mike's face appears.

'Hiya,' I say. 'Meet my new housemate, Nellie. Nellie, meet Mike.'

I turn the screen towards her, and they wave and smile at one another.

'I'll take this upstairs,' I tell Nellie, and leave the room. Mouse, I note, remains to watch the drama. It's a shame he won't be able to fill me in on the big reveal.

8

'Where's my favourite canine?' Mike asks, when I continue the call from the sofa in my bedroom.

'Watching *Bridgerton* with Nellie.'

'What – no sharks or wolves?'

'No sharks or wolves. Apparently, humans in period costume are just as entertaining. How about Edward?'

'He's never watched *Bridgerton*, as far as I'm aware.' He considers for a moment, '. . . unless he takes control of the remote when I'm at Coleton Fishacre.' This is the stunning National Trust property where Michael works as under gardener.

We both laugh at the image of his cat settling in with the remote control.

'I'm going to have my work cut out here,' I say after a moment.

'Is the site in that bad a state?'

'Well, it's pretty overgrown, but it's not just that . . .' I fill him in on the lack of consensus in the village. 'But I'm having the village newspaper print a questionnaire, asking what everyone wants from the new garden. Hopefully, that will help get most people on side.'

'Great idea. Sometimes, I envy you. I love it here, of course, but you get to create entirely new worlds in each place you visit.'

I smile. '"Entirely new worlds": I like that.'

'You can't tell me the spiral garden you made for the flower show wasn't at the very least a kingdom in miniature.'

'There was something fairy-tale-ish about it, wasn't there?' I say. 'And hopefully I'll be able to do something equally magical here, if I can get all the villagers behind me.'

'I'm sure you will. I have faith in your ability to charm anyone and everyone.'

I shoot him a sceptical look. 'It's in your interest to say that. You want to get in my pants.'

He lifts his hands in surrender. 'Fair, I may be a bit biased . . .'

'How's your work?' I ask him, and he fills me in on November jobs in the huge grounds at Coleton Fishacre, from the raking of leaves to the deadheading of late-flowering perennials and the mulching of perennial borders, which apparently goes on for months.

By the time we finish our call, Mouse has appeared in the bedroom with his blue lead and Mr Rabbit between his jaws. As he carefully places the treasured items in his bed and settles down for the night, I wander back downstairs to say goodnight to Nellie. But the living room's in darkness. Spotting a light emanating from beneath the dining room door, I open it, expecting to find her sketching or painting. Instead, she's on the phone.

'Oh!' she says. 'Hold on a minute.'

'Sorry to disturb you; I just came to say goodnight,' I say.

She raises a hand and nods, then waits until I've exited and closed the door behind me before recommencing her conversation. As I head back to the stairs, I'm sure I don't imagine the words, 'No, it's all right – she didn't hear anything.'

As I clean my face and teeth and pull on my fleecy pyjamas, I try to dismiss the sense that I was being discussed, reminding myself that I've only just met Nellie, and she was almost certainly having a private conversation about herself or the other person on the call.

Nonetheless, I lie awake in bed for some time, feeling a sense of discomfort that's hard to shake.

9

The next morning is Wednesday – the day I'm set to meet my volunteers. I feel like a fool for my unease the night before. Nellie was probably talking to someone who was concerned for their own privacy, and the conversation had nothing to do with me.

'Stop believing the world revolves around you,' I reprimand myself, as I pull on my trainers.

Mouse, who is waiting by the door, glances back at me in bemusement.

'It's all right, boy,' I tell him. 'Just talking to myself.'

He makes a rumble in his throat and returns to staring at the door, clearly impatient for me to open it.

'Come on, then,' I say, pulling my lime-green woolly hat over my thick curls before opening the door and letting him exit first.

Timmy starts barking from inside Nellie's room as we pass her door. 'Shhh,' I say quietly. 'Try not to wake Nellie.'

'Already awake,' comes her voice from inside, still husky from sleep.

'Sorry,' I call.

'No, you're all right. This one needs to go out for a wee.'

'I'd offer to let him out, but . . .'

'You get Mouse out to safety before I release the Tiny Terror,' she says.

With a laugh, I do as she suggests.

Outside, there's a wind so cold that I pull my hat down over my ears and shove my hands into the pockets of my shorts, wishing I'd worn jogging bottoms.

Mouse seems unfazed, stopping to sniff at lamp posts, trees and gate posts as if the weather were balmy and the biting wind a soft warm breeze.

'Come on, boy – it's freezing,' I say, through chattering teeth, tugging at his lead.

He gives up his scent exploration and begins to jog alongside me, until we reach one of the pathways leading out of the village, through arable fields and patches of woodland.

My hands warm up, and I release them from my pockets, swinging my arms as we move to a sprint, ignoring rabbits and even a field of sheep. Mouse has his tongue lolling, and I find myself grinning. As well as my pleasure in our new surroundings, I'm excited about today, when I'm due to meet my volunteers for the centenary garden project.

'New place, new adventures,' I tell him, and he barks with joy.

Back at the house, Nellie has set out food and drink for Mouse, and has somehow stopped Timmy from clearing Mouse's bowls after his own.

I leave Mouse to his breakfast and head to the stairs.

'Pancakes?' Nellie calls after me.

'Ooh, yes, please,' I call back. 'Give me ten minutes.'

'No rush. I haven't started on the batter yet.'

I'm back in the kitchen in less than ten minutes, and Nellie has the batter all ready, a frying pan warming on the little stove.

'I wasn't sure what you liked on your pancakes, so I put everything out,' she says over her shoulder as she dollops the first spoonful of batter into the pan and swirls it around.

The tiny table is crammed with everything from syrup – both golden and maple – to sugar, a Jif lemon, a bunch of bananas, chocolate spread, bags of sugar – demerara and golden granulated – and even cheese with a grater.

'Maple syrup looks great,' I tell her. 'Shall I get the coffee on?'

'That would be brilliant.' She flips the pancake in the air, and it lands neatly back in the pan.

'You should be a professional caterer,' I say as I fill the kettle at the metal sink and set it back on its base to boil.

'That would be career option number three,' she says, 'after trapeze artist.' I turn to stare at her and she grins. 'Well, not so much trapeze, but I can do the aerial hoop and silks,' she says.

Sliding the first pancake on to a plate which she slips into the oven to keep warm, she paints the pan with more oil and says, 'What about you – any secret skills?'

I consider the question. 'I guess I'm pretty good at solving puzzles,' I say. 'Though I'm not doing so well at the cryptic crosswords my birth mother's got me attempting every week. They're a whole other language that I haven't quite grasped.'

'So, what kind of puzzles are you good at?' she asks.

'Murders,' I say. 'I'm good at solving murders.'

When she turns abruptly towards me, spilling the batter she'd been pouring into the pan and turning ashen, it occurs to me that I might have phrased this more delicately.

* * *

'So, you keep having to get involved in police investigations?' she asks, a little while later, after I've sat her down at the table, made and poured the coffee, and finished cooking the batch of pancakes.

I'm on my usual stool at right angles to hers, and Timmy is at her feet, hoping for scraps. Mouse has vanished into the living room, where I suspect he's gone for a nap and to avoid Timmy's high energy.

I drizzle maple syrup on to a pancake and roll it up while choosing my words. 'Pretty much,' I say.

She sips her coffee. I'm relieved to see that her cheeks have pinked up. 'So, if you hadn't been there . . .'

'. . . the cases may not have been solved.'

'That's frightening.'

'It is a bit.'

'Makes you wonder how many cases are "solved" with the wrong verdict.'

I nod. 'I think it's a known fact that there are innocent people in jail – or, at least, people who didn't commit the crimes they're actually in there for.'

She sighs and spoons sugar on to her pancake before squeezing the Jif lemon juice on top. We both watch it soaking into the grains.

'Sorry I worried you before,' I say.

'I was being daft.'

We both smile, glad to have cleared the air.

'What are your plans for the day?' I ask her.

'I'm going to visit Wrens and show the owners my roughs for the paintings they've commissioned. Hopefully, they'll love them and I can start on the canvases. I've still got that sculpture to plan and build.'

'How long will that take?'

'Normally, anything from six to eight months.' When I stare at her in alarm, she says, 'If the sculpture has to come after the rest of the garden, it can't be helped.'

I do some mental calculations. 'It's what, November now? And I'm supposed to finish by the end of April, so it might be cutting it a bit fine.'

'I'll do my best to get it done in time,' she says. ' I do have some preliminary sketches. I mean, you know I want to make sure my piece fits with your designs, but I have a good feeling about one of my ideas in particular.'

'Can I see?'

She wags a sticky finger at me. As she lowers her hand, Timmy, unable to resist, jumps up and licks her finger. He makes a horrified squawk in response to the acid taste of the lemon juice. We both laugh. 'Serves you right for being greedy,' she tells him. Looking back at me, she says, 'I don't want to show you yet; I don't want to influence your process. You collect your responses from the questionnaire and do your preliminary sketches, then we'll share our ideas.'

'Fair enough.' I reach for another pancake.

We finish breakfast, making light chat about the village, her painting commission, and the fare at the village pub, which she says is rumoured to be good, although she hasn't tried it as she had no one to go with.

'I'll take you there soon, if you like, to say thank you for all the delicious food you've been feeding me,' I tell her.

She gestures to the table, where there are only crumbs left from our breakfast feast. 'Not that I actually made your pancakes this morning.'

'It's the thought that counts,' I say. 'Anyway, that's on me – I keep trying to learn a softer approach, but somehow the blunt truth always comes out.'

10

Three volunteers turn up about fifteen minutes after my arrival at the site with Mouse that morning. I've had to wait by the fencing for one of them to bring the key, and I make a mental note to get a copy from Avery, whatever the committee may have specified about my requiring a chaperone at all times. I have a large holdall on the ground beside me, filled with secateurs and loppers.

Mouse is tired from our morning run, and he's leaning against my leg, looking ready to drop off. But he springs back to full energy at the sight of these potential new friends. Luckily, one of the women turns out to be a dog lover, and much fuss is made of my beloved hound.

'Are you going to dig some nice holes for us?' the woman asks him while ruffling his ears. He makes an affirmative rumble in response. 'You are such a clever boy,' she tells him.

'Can we go inside now?' I ask, with a laugh. 'Who has the key?' At this, they look from one to the other until I say, 'Really? No one has the key?'

'I'll get it from Avery,' says a gangly young white man who looks about sixteen, but who's already told me – rather defensively – that he's twenty-three. I'm guessing he's used to being taken for younger than his age.

'Thanks,' I say. 'Leo, was it?'

He nods. 'I'll be right back.' As he heads away, hands in pockets, long legs taking decidedly short steps, I note that, despite his words of assurance, we may have a long wait for his return.

In the meantime, I need to learn everyone's names. Turning to the woman who's still making a fuss of Mouse, I check, 'Marion?'

She nods. 'That's right – Marion Johnson. I live at Cormorants with Leo – he's my youngest. He's between jobs at the moment, so this should keep him out of trouble.'

I grin. 'I'll do my best.' I store away the family details in my mental catalogue of Greenhaven residents. 'Cormorants is one of the three big detached houses, right?'

'Yes. There's Woodpeckers – that's Stella and Jeremy Pargeter, opposite you. Then Cormorants is on Sheepcotes Lane, and there's also Wrens, on the corner of Argent Street. The couple who live there now are retired. But the people who were there before worked at the factory, so everyone knew them. They were among the hundreds who lost their jobs when Patterson's closed.'

'It must have had a massive impact on the village when the factory shut down,' I say.

'It did. I was at home raising the kids at the time, and my husband's a plumber, so we were lucky – we weren't affected in that way. But it was devastating for so many families who relied on the factory for one or even more than one income. In some cases, three generations lost their livelihood. It was like the mining districts all over again.'

'It must have been especially bad, considering some of the workers were miners who'd moved here for jobs – albeit a couple of generations back,' I say.

'Oh, you know about the history of the village?' says a compact white man with grey hair and black glasses who I remember hearing the others call Christy.

'A little,' I say. 'I looked up the village online before I came – and Avery told me some of it. I think the original Mr Patterson invited out-of-work miners from Scotland, Wales, Ireland, and I think Newcastle to come and live here, for a better quality of life?'

Christy nods. 'That's right. The lure of paid work, private gardens, and indoor bathrooms – a real luxury for the working classes at the time – attracted workers from all over.'

At that moment, Leo reappears, more speedily than expected, and we watch him wrestle with the lock.

'Done it!' comes his triumphant shout, and we all cheer as he removes the section of fencing to allow us to enter.

'Thanks, Leo,' I say as I pass him into the grounds. 'Who was meant to have the key, do you know?'

He frowns and shrugs, but Christy says, 'Norma. Not the best choice, but she volunteered.'

'Why was she not a good choice?' I ask.

'Everyone, why's Norma not a good choice to be key holder?' he asks our small assembly.

A chuckle passes around the group. At that moment, a pale woman in her late sixties or early seventies, with white hair haloing a delicate face, comes blustering on to the site, her scarf trailing behind her like the tail of a kite.

'Sorry, sorry!' she says, out of breath from rushing.

I notice that the buttons on her multicoloured checked coat are done up wrongly, and she's wearing odd socks with her ankle-length patchwork trousers.

'No harm done,' I say. 'I take it you're Norma? I'm Steph Williams.'

She shakes my gloved hand. 'I promised Avery I'd be on time,' she says with a grimace. 'But my alarm didn't go off, and then the cat had vomited a hair ball on the kitchen rug, and . . .' She trails off, and I smile.

'Take a deep breath,' I say. 'Leo fetched a key from Avery and we're all good.' Turning to the party as a whole, I say, 'So, as you know, I'm Steph Williams. I can't tell you how grateful I am to have you all here as volunteers, to help clear the space.'

'What are you planning on putting here?' asks Christy.

'Do you know, I'm not a hundred per cent sure,' I tell him. When they all look shocked, I add, 'I've typed up a questionnaire, which Stella Pargeter is kindly going to include in the next issue of *The Green Maven*. I want to be sure the garden will provide the most use to the highest number of people.'

'That sounds good, doesn't it, Leo?' says Marion in a bright tone. Her son grunts noncommittally, and it occurs to me that, despite his helpfulness over the key, he may be here through coercion rather than free will.

'Where do you want us to start?' asks Christy.

I've brought thornproof gardening gloves, which I now pass out. As they put them on, I say, 'If you could all target the brambles – of which there are many – that would be great.

Cut them off at the base for now. I want to see what the space looks like, so this is all about clearing the area above ground. We can tackle the roots later.'

'What will you be doing?' Leo asks.

I point to the ivy-covered section, where I've been told the bungalow's foundations are hidden. 'I'll be clearing ivy.'

Marion looks from the ivy to me with a concerned expression. 'I didn't think the garden was extending that far?' she says. 'I've seen the plans, and the committee only signed off on a smaller area. There's rubble in there, which might not be safe.'

I suppress a sigh. 'Don't worry,' I say, 'I'll make sure the foundations are solid, I promise.'

She's still frowning as she follows the others towards the brambles.

Mouse has found a spot beneath a willow, where he's stretched out, eyes closing for a nap. It's so bitter out here that I fish in my holdall for his blanket, which I drape over him, tucking it in around him. He blinks sleepily at me and licks my hand in thanks.

Next, turning to my task, I square my shoulders as I take in the mass of ivy. The plant itself is not an issue, but I'm a little trepidatious about what I might find beneath it. If Martin and Marion are right, and the foundations are just rubble, loose and unsafe, I will have to rethink my plan to incorporate them into the garden and will have to find a way instead to block them off.

But, as I begin to tear away the trailing vines, I find myself venturing past the rubble. In this new area, as I strip away the trailing vines, I unearth plants that I wasn't expecting. Straggly but determined stalks of purple-sprouting broccoli, Savoy cabbage, spinach and Brussels sprouts are all identifiable. These members of the cabbage family must be the descendants of cultivated plants. And I realise with a jolt that I have stumbled upon the vegetable garden belonging to Kieran Galloway's long-dead grandparents.

A couple of hours have gone by when Marion comes over. I've abandoned the vegetable garden for now, and she catches me jumping on some bricks I've uncovered from the bungalow ruins, testing their solidity.

'I won't ask what you're doing,' she says with a smile. She seems to have forgotten her earlier concern about this area. 'We're going to the café for a hot drink and possibly some cake. Do you fancy it?'

'A coffee would be amazing. Are dogs allowed inside?'

When she nods, I walk over to wake Mouse, who shakes himself off good-naturedly. I clip on his lead and we all head from the site – with Leo locking the fence behind us – and walk around to the café on the far side.

It's busy and warm inside the little coffee shop. I keep Mouse close to heel, in case anyone isn't keen on dogs – but, from the way people turn to pet him as we pass, it would appear the opposite is the case. He's in his element, and seems quite disappointed to settle at one table, rather than being allowed to rove among the guests.

Melanie, the café owner, comes to the table to take our orders. I'm told the carrot cake is particularly good, so I go for that.

Melanie sets out a bowl of water and some treats for Mouse, who holds up a paw in thanks.

'Well, aren't you adorable?' she says, smiling down at him. He barks once, and I glance quickly around, to check he hasn't alarmed anyone. But all seems calm.

I notice Nellie, at a small corner table, deep in conversation with Stella, the editor of *The Green Maven*.

'I'll be right back,' I tell the others, getting up from my chair. 'Stay,' I say to Mouse, who shoots me the baleful look he's perfected.

'You can keep me company,' Marion tells him, reaching over to stroke him. He immediately moves to sit beside her.

'Thanks,' I say. 'I won't be long.'

As I approach, Stella and Nellie are so engrossed in their conversation that it takes them a moment to notice me. I hear Nellie say, 'But you're just making stuff up.'

Stella is the first to spot me. She makes a face at Nellie, who turns to look my way, and visibly starts. 'Oh, Steph, hi,' she says, forcing a smile.

'Sorry – I didn't mean to interrupt,' I say. 'I just saw you both and wanted to say hello.'

'Have you started on the site?' Stella asks.

I say, 'Yes, the grand clearing has begun this morning, thanks to my willing helpers.' I gesture to the table I've left, where Christy, Marion, Leo and Norma are chatting.

Stella smiles and says, 'You've got a good bunch there. Thanks for the questionnaire. I've tidied it up, inserted those boxes you wanted for responses, and set it all out a bit more clearly.'

'That's great, thanks so much.'

'No, thank you. It's always good to have interactive content like that. It brings a lot more engagement from the village.'

'Oh, that's good to hear. When will it be out?'

'On Monday.'

'That soon? Fantastic.'

'The wonders of digital print,' she says. 'It's made everything speedier and more cost efficient, even for little local rags like ours. Oh, before I forget – I've added a date by which you need responses.'

'I hadn't even thought of that.'

'I'm giving them two weeks. Is that too long, though? I know you're probably on the clock.'

'No, that should be fine. There's a lot of work to be done on surveying the site and clearing and digging before I can finalise anything. I have to admit that I'm hoping my initial plans won't need much alteration for the majority of people to feel their wishes have been included in the process.'

Stella smiles. 'So, ask their opinion but hope it fits with your designs?'

Nellie raises an eyebrow. 'You sound like a politician, Steph.'

I pull a face. 'God, I hope not! I just mean that I've spent a long time coming up with designs that I believe will benefit most people in some way or another – spaces for quiet contemplation; areas for exercise; a playground with some unusual climbing equipment for the youngsters . . .'

'It sounds amazing!' says Nellie, and I grin.

'Thanks. Fingers crossed the residents agree. Anyway, I'll leave you to it. I think my coffee's arrived.'

Stella halts me with a hand on my arm. 'One more thing. I was thinking you might like to be available, in person? You could hold a drop-in session at the library the week after the paper comes out.'

'That's a great idea. What days are they open?'

'Tuesday afternoon, and Thursday and Saturday mornings.'

'Let's go for a week on Tuesday.'

She nods. 'I'm going to press tomorrow, but I've left space to add that in. I was going to seek you out if I hadn't run into you.'

'Perfect. Thanks again.'

'And don't forget to take pictures at every stage, so you can write your column for me.'

'Yeah . . .' I pull a face. 'I must admit, I'd forgotten all about that. I'll try, though. Oh – how was Sunday for the dog walk?'

'Yes, that suits us. Shall we say eight o'clock or is that too early?'

'No, that's actually later than we normally go.'

'Seven thirty?'

'Great.'

She smiles and nods, and I walk away, noting that they don't start up their conversation until I'm out of earshot. But I know neither of them well enough to be offended. My curiosity, on the other hand, is well and truly piqued.

11

After our coffee and what is, indeed, delicious carrot cake, moist and unexpectedly light with a lemony icing, I drop Mouse back at Magpies for a sleep – closing the bedroom door against Timmy – before joining the others at the site.

While they continue their attack on the invasive plants, I begin my survey of the trees, noting down the position of each one, along with its size, age and condition. I become so engrossed in the job, that I don't notice the time until Norma comes to find me, leading me back to join the others.

'Wow, you've done amazingly!' I say, taking in how large an area they've cleared in just a couple of hours.

They smile at the praise.

Then Christy says, 'The roots are probably going to be a problem.' I'm becoming aware that Christy likes to point out the potential negative aspects of any plan.

'We'll do what we can by hand,' I say. 'But, once I have the digger on site . . .'

Leo, who is lolling against a tree, hood up and hands in pockets, every inch the image of disaffected youth, says slowly, 'Do I get a go?'

I tilt my head. 'At what?'

'The digger. Do I get to drive it?'

'Oh, no! I'm sorry – you'd need a licence.'

'He can drive a tractor,' Marion volunteers.

I smile at Leo. 'That's great! Sadly, it doesn't help, though. I'm afraid the digger licence comes under a different category.'

He makes a sound that might be a scoff, and pulls his mobile out of his pocket, beginning to tap away with his thumbs. Clearly, the discussion is over.

'What's next?' Christy asks. He checks his watch. 'It's nearly two already. We should break for lunch.'

Norma, who has been disentangling her hair from a spiny bramble hanging from a tree overhead, speaks up: 'You're all welcome at mine. I've made a big pot of sweet potato soup and fresh bread.'

'That's kind, Norma,' says Christy. 'But do you have enough room for us all?'

She glances around at us, doing a tally. 'Five people, including me. I'm sure I can assemble enough chairs. And there's always the living room if people are happy to spread out.'

Christy does not look convinced. I, however, rarely say no to the offer of home-cooked fare, so I say, 'That sounds wonderful, Norma – count me in.'

Her face, which thanks to Christy's lukewarm response, was looking crestfallen, breaks into a smile. 'Good stuff,' she says. 'I'll go ahead in about half an hour, to clear some space.'

Leo glances up from his phone. 'Seems like you're doing a lot of that today.'

'Oh, very good, Leo!' she says. 'Very good!'

I decide that I like Norma. I'm still reserving judgement on the rather dour Christy.

12

Norma's house is one of the terraces I've noticed in Argent Street, featuring a white-painted brick facade with the detail I've seen elsewhere of windows protruding in a V-shape from the first floor, like a tiny tower, fronted by a miniature wrought-iron balcony.

'This is lovely,' I say as I follow her along the path to the front door.

'Wait till you see inside,' Marion says from behind, as Norma turns the key in the lock.

She pushes open the door and stands to one side so that I can enter. As I do so, I gasp. The internal walls are covered in a huge mural. Painted vines in shades of green and blue climb to the ceiling of the landing above where a skylight contributes to the impression of being in a glasshouse. I'm so engrossed in studying the white trumpet-shape waxy blooms on the vines that I don't notice the others filing in after me until Christy says, 'Well. It's something, isn't it?'

Ignoring the obvious disapproval in his tone, I meet Norma's gaze and say, 'It really is.'

We all remove our footwear and begin to shed our scarves and woolly hats, but our host says, 'I haven't got the heating on, so I'd keep your coats on for now.'

We obediently keep on our outerwear and follow her into her small dining room, where I'm struck less by the discovery of more incredible murals than by the chaos. Every surface – from the oak table in the centre to the sideboard and every one of the four dining chairs – is crammed with *stuff*.

'I meant to go ahead!' says Norma, starting to clear the chairs of sketchbooks, sweaters and partially made corn dollies.

'Can I help?'

'That would be brilliant!' She offloads the pile in her arms on to me before I quite understand what's happening. 'Just dump it all on the stairs,' she says. 'Or the banisters. Or wherever you can find space.'

Turning to address the group, she says, 'Soup and bread OK for everyone?'

There's a murmur of assent, and she's gone. I glance at the others. Christy has his arms folded and is wearing an I-told-you-so expression; Marion is busying herself collecting knitwear from the various chairs; and Leo has pushed back enough items on the table to make a perch for himself as he scrolls on his phone.

'Oh, Leo – come on,' says Marion. 'Don't leave everyone else to do all the work.'

Christy clears his throat. 'When do you think Norma last dusted in here?' He sweeps a finger over a bare patch of table and pulls a face as he displays his dust-covered digit.

'I don't know, Christy,' says Marion quietly, 'but we're here now, so let's make the best of it, should we?'

'I should have gone home for spaghetti hoops on toast,' he mutters.

Marion rolls her eyes but stops when she catches me looking. I wink and she laughs.

'What is it?' says Christy. 'What's the joke?'

'Nothing,' says Marion, grabbing a few more jumpers and leaving the room. I follow her out and we converge in the hall, taking in the fact that the banisters are already laden with garments.

'Honestly, he drives me mad sometimes,' she whispers, setting down her pile on one of the stairs near the bottom. I pile my load on top and we turn back towards the dining room.

'Christy or Leo?' I ask with a raised eyebrow, and she bursts out laughing. She's still giggling, hands over her mouth like a naughty schoolgirl, when we re-enter the dining room, to find both men forming neat piles of objects on a cleared section of a sideboard, and draping any garments over a carver chair at one end of the table.

'Gosh, how wonderful,' says Marion, as she and I stop and stare.

'It just needed someone to apply a bit of logic,' says Christy with what is already feeling familiar pomposity.

Norma bustles in, carrying a steaming tureen in mittened hands. 'My word,' she says, 'I'll have to invite you round more often.'

'Along with a cleaner,' says Christy drily. I'm not sure if she doesn't hear the snipe, or chooses to ignore it. She sets the large casserole dish on the table and says over her shoulder, 'I'll be back with bowls and the bread.'

The smell is amazing. Leo wanders out of the room, returning with two folding chairs, and we all arrange ourselves around the newly cleared parts of the table. I notice Christy surreptitiously using one of the sweaters from the pile to wipe dust from the table before taking his seat. I can't say I blame him. If I weren't used to being covered in soil, I imagine I'd be a lot less willing to sit among the grime.

The soup turns out to be even better than it smells. I devour three bowls of it, and even Christy accepts a second helping. The bread is granary, and still warm, so that the butter melts into it.

As we finish up with teas and coffees, I fill them in on Stella's suggestion that I hold a session at the library a week on Tuesday.

'What a wonderful idea,' says Norma.

'Yes,' says Christy. 'That should put paid to the idea that the committee's going behind people's backs to spend money on a garden nobody wants.'

I pull a face. 'Is there a lot of opposition?'

'Oh, not so much,' says Marion, so quickly that I'm not convinced.

Christy begins to speak but Leo interrupts, as if in response to a silent plea from his mother: 'Have you heard Martin's gone away?'

As these are the first words he's said all meal time, we turn to him in surprise.

'Yes, I knew that,' I say. 'He told me he was going.' Now, they all look at me. 'What?' I say.

Christy clears his throat – another of his mannerisms, as I'm becoming aware – and says, 'Martin Patterson spoke to you?'

'Er . . . yes. Why is that so strange?'

Norma shakes her head. 'Martin believes we are all beneath him. Even Christy, who has a PhD in . . .' She screws up her face in concentration then says questioningly, '. . . trains?'

Christy clears his throat again. 'The effect of the introduction of locomotives on the industry and export habits of the United Kingdom.'

'Yes, that,' says Norma.

I shrug. 'Martin wasn't exactly friendly, if that's what you're imagining. This wasn't some "welcome to the village" pep talk.'

'So, what did he want?' asks Leo.

I feel almost uncomfortable under their joint scrutiny. 'Erm . . . Not much . . .' I think back. 'Mainly to tell me he was the lord of the manor, and I should mind my p's and q's.'

The others share another look. 'That sounds about right,' says Marion.

'Oh, he did say I could visit his garden in his absence, if I got John to show me round.'

Christy exchanges another look with the others. 'He said you could visit his garden?' He seems astonished.

'Well, only after I backed him into a corner,' I admit.

Marion laughs. 'Good for you.'

Norma shudders as she reaches for a hunk of bread from the near-empty basket. 'That man's a bully.'

'Did he say anything else?' asks Christy.

I sigh. 'He basically told me I couldn't do anything without his say-so. That I needed his sign-off before doing any work.'

Christy folds his arms. 'And now we reach the crux of the matter.'

Marion shakes her head. 'Honestly, that man . . .'

'He doesn't have any final power of veto, as he claims?' I check.

He and Marion make scoffing sounds. 'He does not,' says Christy firmly. 'He lost all his power in this village when he sold the factory to an asset stripper and the council took on the rest.'

Leo says, 'I've got to say, I'm kind of stunned he's going to let you in his garden. Here, look.' He passes me his phone, and I scan the news story on the screen:

Local land owner reclusive and obstructive, complain villagers

It goes on to explain how Martin Patterson refused to allow the council's workmen on to his land to deal with a drainage issue. '"In his mother's day, we always had our annual summer fete in the garden at Eagles," said one resident. "Now, Mr Patterson won't even let the council carry out basic maintenance."'

'It's particularly problematic because the drainage issue's affecting the bungalows on either side,' says Christy.

I whistle as I set down my now empty coffee mug. 'Does the man have no redeeming features?'

It's clear from the ensuing silence that none of them can come up with any.

Norma claps her hands and gets to her feet. 'Right. Pile up your plates and bowls and I'll deal with them later.'

'Don't you want us to help wash up?' asks Marion, but our host shakes her head.

'It's all good. The cats can lick them clean.' Seeing our horrified faces, she bursts out laughing. 'Joking! Gosh, do you really all think I'm that much of a slob?' When all of us fail to meet her gaze or respond, she says, 'Well, I wasn't expecting that,' in such a forlorn tone that I feel a stab of guilt and say quickly,

'I'm sure none of us would have eaten here if we felt that way.'

She doesn't look entirely convinced.

* * *

About an hour and a half after our lunch, when my diligent volunteers have cleared far more brambles than I had imagined possible in one day, I tell them they can pack up. As they leave their work, I thank them and ask them to leave their gloves and tools beside my holdall.

Norma lingers after the others have left. I've noticed she's been more subdued since lunch.

'I'm afraid I can't leave you,' she says.

'Oh, right – I need chaperoning,' I say.

She pulls a face. 'I don't know what the committee think you're going to do: steal some acorns?'

'Or carve my initials into a tree?' I suggest.

She smiles but it doesn't reach her eyes. I touch her arm. 'Hey, I'm sorry if we upset you after that lovely lunch you served us.'

'It isn't you,' she says. 'You've only just met me. But the idea that those people, who I thought of as my friends, could have such a low opinion of me . . .'

'It's not about your personality,' I say. 'It's only your housekeeping.' The minute the words are out, I wish I could bite them back.

But she laughs. 'Oh gosh,' she says, 'let's be honest, here – it's only because they've hit a nerve. As you so rightly point out, I am not a born housekeeper.'

I shrug. 'Not everyone is. Could you afford a cleaner?'

'My daughter's always offering to come round and clean. She only lives up the road, in Witham.'

'So, why not take her up on it?'

'I think I might. Until now, I felt ashamed at the idea of letting someone else clean up after me. Does that sound silly?'

I shake my head. 'But we all have different strengths. And those murals . . .'

Her face brightens. 'You really liked them?'

'They're extraordinary. I'm already trying to work out if we could incorporate something similar into this garden. Would you be up for that? Perhaps we could get the school involved?'

'Oh, I'd love that!' She tucks a loose strand of hair into her multicoloured woolly hat. And then she fishes in her coat pocket and draws out a key on a plain fob. 'Here,' she says. 'It's ridiculous to think you need supervising.'

I smile and thank her, and she surprises me with a hug before taking her leave.

13

Nellie makes another delicious meal for our dinner. While we tuck into her lentil dal with warmed nan, I fill her in on my discovery at the site.

'So, the garden's still there?' she says.

I nod. 'I mean, obviously everything's looking a bit straggly and anaemic, but it's clear there was a well-tended vegetable plot there.'

'It's amazing to think those plants have been self-seeding for all this time,' she says.

'Yeah, that's what I thought. Anyway, it seems a shame not to make the most of the area. I'd like to talk to Kieran and see if he has any photos of how it looked in his grandparents' time. As it's November, not much is visible above ground. I can't tell if this was a cottage garden – meaning there was a mix of perennial flowers, interspersed with edibles – or just a veg plot.'

Her eyes grow wide. 'Are you thinking of reinstating the original garden?' When I nod, she says, 'I bet Kieran would love that.'

'I hope so. I'd like to run it by him. I don't suppose you know where he lives?'

She squints for a moment, then says, 'I *think* he still lives in his parents' old place on Argent Street. If I'm right, he's near the little church.'

'Who would know which is his house?' I ask.

She thinks for a moment, loaded spoon poised halfway to her mouth. At last, she says, 'I reckon Jeremy would know. I'm pretty sure he and Kieran are mates.'

'Perfect,' I say. 'I'm seeing him and Stella on Sunday, when we take the dogs out. I can ask him then.' I nearly suggest she come along with Timmy, but I really want to give Mouse a break from the manic tearaway. And, after seeing her with Stella in the café, I'm not sure about putting the two of them together.

As if reading my mind, she surprises me by bringing up the meeting: 'Sorry if Stella and I weren't very welcoming earlier. We were having a bit of a . . . disagreement.'

'Oh? Can I ask what it was about?'

She pulls a face and feeds a chickpea to Timmy, who seems to eat anything and everything he's offered. 'It's a bit embarrassing, to be honest . . .'

'OK, that's fine. You don't have to tell me anything.'

She meets my eye. 'Stella thinks I'm having an affair with Jeremy, her husband.'

I stare at her. 'Isn't he about sixty? And you're what . . . twenty-something?'

She nods. 'Twenty-nine.'

I clear my throat and fork up some potato from my bowl. 'So . . . why does she think that? I mean, are you?'

'No! God, no! But we've been meeting up in secret, so I guess I can see why she'd think that.'

'You're meeting him in secret, but you're not sleeping together?'

She shakes her head. 'He's . . . It's . . .'

'He's your long-lost father,' I say.

She bursts out laughing. 'Where did that come from?'

'I guess my own experiences,' I admit. 'I think I mentioned that my biological mum has me doing these cryptic crosswords every week. But I'm not sure that I told you we've only recently found one another.'

'Really? How come?'

I shrug. 'My mum felt quite threatened at the idea of me looking for my birth mother, so that put me off for a while. In the end, though, I registered on the website, and she – Verity, my birth mum – found me.'

'What's that like?' asks Nellie.

I'm aware that she's keeping me from asking more about her own secret, but I don't mind. 'It's good but also kind of surreal,' I say. 'It's like meeting someone who's a complete stranger but, at the same time, they're oddly familiar. For instance, we both enjoy solving puzzles. Having said that, she's much better at the crosswords than I am.'

Nellie says, 'I'm great at those!' then tilts her head. 'Which is kind of weird, given how scatty my brain is most of the time.'

I laugh. 'Maybe it's because your brain can go in several directions at once.'

She thinks about this, then says, 'Do you know, that actually makes some sense . . . Now, do you want seconds?'

'Always. I'll get it.'

We finish the meal and I insist on clearing the dishes. When I head into the living room later, I'm touched to see Mouse and

Timmy asleep together, curled up on a large floor cushion, the little dog fitting easily against the curve of Mouse's belly.

'Aren't they cute?' says Nellie. She's on the sofa. Although the TV is on – it's showing a period drama – she's got her sketchbook on her lap, and is drawing. Her hair has been swept up into a messy topknot and fixed in place with what looks like a crocodile clip.

I take a seat beside her, and she slides the book on to my lap. 'This is what I'm working on,' she says. 'What you said about Norma's murals made my brain start clicking.'

'Is clicking a good thing?' I ask.

'You tell me.'

I glance down and take in her sketch: a large bird in flight, trailing the entire village from its talons.

'This is amazing,' I say. 'Is it for the mural?'

But she shakes her head. 'It's a detail for my sculpture. It was just when you talked about how Norma's walls were completely covered in her art, I got to thinking what it would be like if my sculpture had detail carved all over the surface.'

I meet her eye. 'That sounds stunning.'

'I think I can get it to work, too. But timing might be an issue.'

I laugh. 'That's putting it mildly. Isn't this months of extra work?'

'Definitely weeks. But maybe I can get help from some of the people in the village. It's a surprisingly artistic community.'

'Is that why you've been meeting with Jeremy?' I ask. 'Is he artistic in some way?'

'You don't give up easily.'

I pull a face. 'Sorry. But you are the one who brought it up.'

'True. And no, that's not why I've been meeting him.'

Her expression is as tightly closed as a new bud, so it's clear I won't get anything more out of her tonight. Soon after, I whisper goodnight to Mouse, who opens one eye but chooses to stay with Timmy. And then I say goodnight to my housemate and head up to call my brother Danny, whom I've been meaning to speak to since I arrived.

14

'Let me guess,' says Danny on our post-dinner video call. 'Your new housemate's been killed and you're the suspect.'

'Not funny.'

'A little funny.'

'Not even slightly. Nellie is very much alive. How are your brood?'

He fills me in on my niece and nephews. Apparently, nine-year-old Alice, who had been struggling with some difficult emotions, seems more settled.

'That's such a relief,' I say, and he nods.

'I think it helped when you had her to stay at Beaulieu,' he says, referencing my first placement.

'She did adore Apple,' I say. This unusually named teenager took my niece under her wing.

'Not just that,' he says. 'You know she loves her Auntie Lou.'

My family refuses to call me Steph, the name I've had since my financial risk-taking ex-husband lost me my then business, making changing my name seem both practical and like a form of rebirth.

'Maybe we can do it again,' I say. 'Let me get to grips with the project here and we can reconvene.'

'Thanks, sis.'

'No worries. You know I love seeing her. How are the others?' My brother and his wife have four children, which always strikes me as too many, much as I love them all. Danny and Karen certainly seem permanently exhausted.

After he's filled me in on the kids' various antics and we've said goodnight, I drop a text message to our mum and dad. The response comes within ten minutes, while I'm cleaning my teeth:

> Dad here. Glad all good. Taking up violin as not enough to do on allotment this time of year.

I type back:

> Is Mum OK with this???

There's a long pause, and then I receive:

> This is your mum. No, I am not OK with violin. Please talk to your dad.

I respond:

> I think that needs to come from you. Sending love – and maybe earplugs? x

Once in bed, I call Mike. For once, he doesn't answer, and I remember he's at the cinema, so I type him a message before settling to sleep.

But my dreams are disturbing, featuring Martin Patterson wielding a shotgun and telling me to stay off his land. Norma appears, wearing a scarf that seems to be a plant tendril, so long it trails out of sight. She begins to paint all over Martin, who doesn't react but keeps his gun trained on me. Just as Norma's saying, 'It's all about good housekeeping,' the gun goes off. But it isn't me who's been hit – it's Nellie, who seems to have come out of nowhere. As I bend over her bleeding form, she murmurs, 'It's not me. It's the raven.'

By the time I awaken at six, in time for my run with Mouse, I'm drenched in sweat and my heart is pumping too hard.

15

Thursday and Friday pass with more of the same: my wonderful group of volunteers continue their clearing efforts, allowing me to focus on my survey. By Friday afternoon, I have a note of every tree in the hundred-metre plot, along with an asterisk beside the ones that will need to be removed, either because of overcrowding or to make space for the garden's planned areas and features.

On Saturday, Mouse and I take a long stroll around a nearby reservoir, where I have to keep him on a short leash to prevent him from chasing the waterfowl. The ground is muddy but the birds are out in force, and we're thoroughly entertained. Just as we get back to the van in the car park, Mouse lets out a curious sound, and I turn to see a murmuration of starlings reeling above the lake. We stand for so long watching the kaleidoscopic patterns against the sunset that it's dark by the time we climb back into the van.

* * *

On Sunday morning, as agreed, Mouse and I head out for our walk with the neighbours. Mouse strains at the leash as we cross the road, eager to see his new friends who are waiting on the pavement outside Woodpeckers.

The Old English sheepdogs wave their plumy tails and Greta licks his nose before we all set off. We are not far from Suffolk and the area known as 'Constable Country', after the famous landscape artist. Greenhaven is surrounded by flat arable fields and, as the dogs trot happily ahead, I admire the big skies for which Essex is known.

The day is breezy but dry, and the sun turns everything golden. I'm relaxed and happy as I walk alongside my companions, and it takes me a little while to pick up on an uncomfortable tension between them.

'How are you both?' I ask, not wanting to be too direct.

'Oh,' says Stella with a shrug. 'We've just had another row this morning.'

'I wouldn't call it a row,' says her husband.

'Shall we have an argument about whether it was an argument?' she snaps.

My Sunday morning suddenly seems less golden. 'The dogs are getting on well,' I say.

'Yes, your Mouse is a fine boy,' says Jeremy.

'Greta and Marlene are very welcoming,' I say.

'And they don't keep secrets,' says Stella.

I suppress a sigh. If Mouse weren't having such a lovely time, I'd consider calling him to head home. One of the reasons that I'm a gardener is because plants are so much more straightforward than humans.

'Do you two want me to give you some space to talk?' I ask.

'Jeremy here doesn't believe in talking,' says his wife.

'That's not true,' says Jeremy, pushing a hand through his thick grey-streaked hair. 'I just don't want to talk about this.'

'No, but you're happy to discuss it with your girlfriend.'

'For the millionth time, Nellie is not my girlfriend.'

I interject, 'I don't think that's why they're meeting.'

Stella whirls towards me with such a fierce expression that I take a step back. She sees my alarm and puts up an appeasing hand. 'Sorry! We shouldn't be dragging you into this.' She takes a deep breath. 'Let's change the subject. Why don't you tell us where you've worked before? Have you always been a garden designer?'

Relieved to be moving on from the hostility, I tell them about my previous placements, from the gated community of Beaulieu Heights in north London – leaving out all the residents' secrets, as that seems a contentious topic – to the rejuvenation of a parterre in Derbyshire, and a garden design competition at Coleton Fishacre in Devon. They seem to relax as we chat, asking pertinent questions about both the locations and the projects.

After a while, I ask Jeremy for Kieran's address. He frowns.

'What do you want with Kieran? He doesn't know anything about gardening, I'm afraid.'

'I've uncovered his grandparents' vegetable plot and I want to talk to him about the possibility of restoring it.'

He glances at Stella. 'That sounds just what he needs, don't you think?' he says, and she smiles and nods.

'Is he looking for a project?' I ask.

'Not exactly, but he's been very down recently,' he says. 'Something like this – both commemorative and forward-looking – can only have a positive impact.'

'I'm sorry to hear he's not doing well,' I say.

He nods. 'He's not had an easy time. His dad died not long after his grandparents, and his mother died last year.'

'Well, let's see if this might be a nice distraction for him,' I say.

Jeremy calls to Marlene, who has wandered away from the main path to sniff around a surprisingly unfazed squirrel. She shoots Jeremy a begrudging glance but returns to the track.

'Good girl,' he calls. Looking back at me, he says, 'I'll email you his address when we get back, or drop it through your door.'

'If he's on Argent Street, you can just tell me the number,' I say.

'Righto. It's fifty-four, next to the little church.'

'Fifty-four – perfect. Thanks.'

By the time we get back from our long circular walk – complete with a break for coffee at a tea room en route – both of my companions are smiling, and Stella gives me a hug as we say goodbye. The dogs are too tired from their exertions to object to having to part as we enter our respective homes on opposite sides of the street.

* * *

Over Sunday lunch – Nellie's gone to town, serving Yorkshire puddings, three different vegetables, roast potatoes, a lentil and nut roast and an apple crumble with custard for dessert – I bring up the tension between Jeremy and Stella.

'Can you and Jeremy not tell Stella anything?' I ask. 'Only it seems to be causing problems between them.'

She puts down her fork and pulls a face. 'Trouble is, it's not down to me. It's Jeremy that won't say anything. He's worried she'll try to stop him.'

I shake my head as I stab a baby carrot. 'Obviously, without knowing what any of this is about, I can't comment on that. But something has to give soon. I don't think she's prepared to put up with much more of his secrecy.'

'I'll talk to him again.'

'Thanks. Fab roast, by the way.'

'Cheers. It's my nan's recipe. She's the one who taught me to cook.'

We smile at one another, and our chat moves on.

Later that afternoon, I call on Kieran, but he doesn't answer my knock. As I leave through the gate surrounded by an overgrown privet hedge, I glance back and see a bedroom curtain moving, as if someone has just stepped away.

16

The next day is Monday, and there's a copy of *The Green Maven* lying on the doormat when Mouse and I get back from our run. I take it into the kitchen, where Nellie has breakfast underway.

'Scrambled eggs, mushrooms, tomatoes and eggy bread,' she announces. 'I may have gone overboard on the eggs, but the Co-op had a special on some from a local farm. Coffee's on the side if you fancy pouring.'

Timmy is chasing something around the room. 'Oh and watch out for the Tiny Terror,' she says, as I cross to the worktop. 'He's found a ball of paper and believes it to be the spawn of the devil.'

I crouch to address the little dog. 'Yeah, I never trust paper. It might have anything on it.' I move to stroke him and he growls, but I know it's because he's invested in his game, so I leave him to it.

Mouse slinks in after me, finding a space in the corner furthest from Timmy's antics.

I open *The Green Maven* and turn the pages till I reach my questionnaire. Stella's done a brilliant job, making the whole thing look more like a questionnaire by Ipsos, the market research company, than the scrappy list of bullet points I sent over to her.

'Is that the *Maven*?' Nellie asks, as she brings two plates to the table.

'Yeah. I wanted to see how my questionnaire looks.'

'Show me.' I hold it up and she says, 'It looks really professional.'

'That's all Stella's doing.'

'She's very good,' says Nellie, biting into a triangle of fried bread.

'This smells so tasty,' I say, putting the paper down on the floor so I can focus on my food.

'Don't leave it there,' says Nellie. 'Unless you want Timmy to chew it to smithereens.'

'Good point,' I say, grabbing it back. She clears a section of the table and I place it there, noticing that my questionnaire is opposite the Green Raven's column.

She nods towards the page. 'What has the Raven got to say this time?' she asks.

'I haven't read it yet.'

She picks it up and reads aloud through a mouthful of bread: '"Greenhaven's new green-fingered resident needs to cultivate more than plants if she's to make friends in the rookery. If rumours on the wind are to be believed, a mobbing may be in the wings."'

Nellie frowns. 'A mobbing?'

'Yeah. I'm guessing that's a reference to the way smaller animals mob predators. Does The Raven say if it's a literal or metaphorical mobbing?'

She double-checks the page, then shakes her head.

'In any case,' I say, feeling anxiety stir in my belly, 'I can't see why I'd be the predator in this scenario. I mean, I've not got any power, have I?'

She sets the paper down and looks at me. 'I'm sure no one's going to physically attack you. This is Greenhaven.'

'What else does it say?' I ask her.

'Oh, just some more about Ms Burberry Trench and Mr On-the-Board. I'm surprised those two are still meeting after they've been publicly outed. It's hardly a secret any more.'

'Maybe their respective partners don't care,' I say. I eat a mushroom. 'How do you get these to taste so good? They're amazing.'

'You have to cook them in butter,' she says.

'Aha. Your secret is now mine.' I grin.

She holds up her hands. 'Yeah, you got me.'

We both laugh, but I sober when I recall the Raven's words. 'Avery did tell me some of the villagers don't want the funds to go to the garden.'

'Yeah, but you've got your questionnaire in there, don't forget,' she says, pointing to the paper. 'Once people realise they have a say in what's going in the garden, they'll back down.'

'You reckon?'

'Trust me – I know these people.'

I smile at her confidence. 'I hope you're right.'

After breakfast, I walk over to the site and unlock the panel ready for my volunteers. They've proven to be hard workers and, as I walk around the site, I can already see the difference they've made. Where they've focused their efforts, whole sections of scrub have been cut back, opening up areas and, making it much easier to visualise the next stages.

Mouse has come with me, and he heads into a stand of beech trees, where I'm pretty sure he'll settle for a sleep, well out of the way of any work.

Christy arrives first, punctual as a sergeant major. I wonder what he did before he retired. Marion comes next, then Norma, her coat done up correctly. Leo arrives last, all bleary eyes and bedhead.

I allocate their jobs and we go to work.

'I don't think the Green Raven is malicious, not really,' says Marion a while later, when I raise the topic of today's column. She and I are working side by side, wearing thornproof gloves and tugging bramble stems from a group of trees. The brambles have managed to make their way up the tree and over branches, from where they trail down, forming a veil of thorns that will be at face height to any unsuspecting passerby. I want to clear as many of these as possible upfront, so that anyone working on the site isn't in danger of being scratched while going about their business.

'This is actually quite satisfying,' says Marion, leaning back as she pulls on the rope-like stems, like a competitor in a tug-of-war competition.

'Just don't lean too hard or the stems might snap and you could go over,' I say.

She straightens up. 'Good point. I don't need to fall on my backside.'

'Yeah, Mum,' comes Leo's lugubrious voice from somewhere in the bushes, 'we don't need another trip to A&E.'

Marion's face – already flushed from the physical labour – turns even pinker.

'Dare I ask?' I say.

She closes her eyes. When she opens them a couple of seconds later, she says with a grimace, 'I may have tried to move the fridge on my own and got my foot stuck under it.'

'I came home and heard her shouting for help,' says Leo, pushing aside some branches and walking into view. 'She couldn't move in case the fridge toppled over on top of her.'

Marion says in a small voice, 'It's not as though I make a habit of doing things like that.'

'One word: water butt. OK, that's two words,' says Leo.

'You just get on with your work,' says Marion.

He walks off, laughing.

'Children,' she says with a sigh.

'He seems lovely.'

'Oh, he's not so bad,' she admits with a smile.

'Shall we break for coffee in a minute?' I suggest.

'Did someone say coffee?' comes Norma's voice.

'Are you all just standing around watching us work and listening to our conversation?' I say loudly.

Now, Norma comes out of the bushes. 'Pretty much,' she says with a grin.

'Not true at all,' says Christy, joining her. 'I'll have you know that we've made a big pile of dead wood, all ready for a bonfire.'

I smile. 'That's great. Thanks so much. Shall we go to the café?'

We place our tools in the holdall, then I wake Mouse before we all exit the site. I lock up, and we head around the fencing to the café on the far side.

As we file into the warm space, its windows misted up with condensation, everybody stops talking.

'What just happened?' Leo says quietly, looking around him. 'Have we got the plague or something?'

'I don't think it's us, darling,' whispers his mum. She looks meaningfully at me. And then I realise that everybody is doing the same: every eye in the place is directed at me.

'Have I got something on my back that says "stare at me"?' I murmur. Mouse grumbles quietly, and I place a calming hand on his head.

Melanie, the café owner, comes over and squeezes my shoulder. 'Steph, good to see you,' she says. 'How are you doing?'

Her face is so full of sympathy that I have to ask, 'OK, but why is everyone looking at me like I'm dying or something?'

'Have you not seen the *Maven*?' she asks.

'Oh, right. Yes, I'm going to be mobbed, apparently.'

A murmur starts up, which is preferable by far to the silence that preceded it. It would appear that the café's clients are concerned for my safety. That, I can handle.

Smiling around the room, I say, 'If all of you don't want to see me being attacked, then I don't feel I have much to worry about. You must make up about a quarter of the village.'

They laugh and nod, and both I and the atmosphere relax. 'I hope some of you are going to come to my drop-in session. It's a week tomorrow in the library, from one till three,' I say.

'I already filled in the questionnaire and dropped it through Magpies' door,' says a man I don't recognise.

'Same here,' say several others.

'It'll need to be accessible for people like my dad,' says a middle-aged man, nodding towards the older man with him, who has a walker parked beside him.

'And have benches,' says his father.

'How about a pond?' says someone else.

I put up a hand. 'Please either put your requests on the questionnaires, or come to see me at the library, so I can write them down.'

'It's rare for anyone to ask us what we want,' says an older woman. 'Normally, they just tell us what we're getting.'

'Especially the council,' says her companion, who looks similar enough to be her sister.

'Not that *they* give us anything,' points out the first. They both nod grimly.

I shrug. 'Well, it is your garden. It wouldn't make much sense to build something none of you would use.'

There are approving nods, and then, as if on some invisible cue, everyone resumes their conversations.

'Shall we, in that case?' says Christy, gesturing to a table big enough for all five of us. We remove our coats, scarves and hats and sit down, and Melanie promptly takes our orders.

'I've been thinking,' says Leo to me, after his mocha has arrived. 'Maybe you need a bodyguard.'

His mother tuts. 'Honestly, Leo, we don't live in some dangerous metropolis.'

He shrugs. 'I just think Steph might be safer, that's all.'

'I don't really think I'm in any danger,' I tell him, despite a twinge of anxiety from my reception at the café. 'Any hostility towards me was because I represented an authority that seemed to be imposing its own agenda on the village. Now that people can see they will have a say in the end result, they don't have any reason to hold a grudge against me.'

'Unless it's the Green Raven himself,' he says. 'He might be a nutter, like a stalker or something.'

His mother tuts again, and Christy breaks in, 'We don't know what gender this Raven person might be. One thing that seems pretty clear though is that he or she enjoys causing trouble. Look how this person has stirred things up with Steph's arrival. Mark my words – this is someone who enjoys causing mayhem while remaining firmly in the shadows. They are a coward, and therefore not a threat to anyone.'

Leo doesn't look convinced, but he doesn't push his point.

Norma, who has been staring at her slice of lemon drizzle cake as if it were an oracle about to pronounce some awful truth, says, without looking up from the cake, 'I'd be more scared if I was Martin Patterson. He's the one who needs to watch his back.'

'Norma!' says Christy in a warning tone.

She shrugs and finally looks up to meet his eye. 'I'm only saying things as I find them.'

'Well don't,' he says briskly. 'We have quite enough of that with this Raven. Let's stick to the facts as we know them, should we?'

Do I imagine it, or does Norma eye him with something close to hatred before picking up her fork and attacking her cake?

17

The sun is shining that afternoon when I dismiss my volunteers early so I can visit the Eagles' garden. I find the gardener about halfway down the lush sloping back lawn. John is alarmingly near the top of a tall conifer, wearing neither harness nor head protection. I hesitate to call up to him, in case I startle him and he loses his grip.

But he glances down and spots me, promptly descending with the ease of a monkey.

Catching me staring when he lands neatly at the bottom, he smiles as he dusts the bark off his hands. 'You're thinking I'm a bit too old for tree climbing.' With his grey hair and wrinkled face, he could easily be in his late seventies. But that isn't why I'm looking concerned.

'I was actually thinking you should be wearing safety gear,' I admit.

He tilts his head as if to concede my point, before saying, 'My dad trained me in pruning and tree felling long before all those health and safety laws were ever thought of. If you do the job properly, you don't need protection.'

'I'll take your word for that,' I say, holding out a hand. 'Steph Williams.'

He nods and shakes my hand. 'You'll be wanting to see the Japanese garden.'

'Please.'

He leads me to the bottom of the long slope and gestures to the scene before us, but I'm already rapt. A large, clear pond filled with giant koi carp is traversed by a wooden bridge that's painted red. A towering grey stone pagoda provides a focal point among moss-covered rocks, surrounded by the black bamboo, *Phyllostachys nigra*, whose dark stems are as striking in their simplicity as a Chinese ink painting. A slender sculpture of a heron stands guard at one end, while the leaves of a group of mature Japanese maples have turned an astonishing flame red, brilliant against the blue sky. What's more, the as yet frost-free season means that the many clumps of *Hakonechloa macra* grass have retained much of their foliage and are already poking new, lime-green shoots up from the earth, like fingers testing the air. There's a breeze here which creates movement and sound as it rustles the bamboo and grasses and traces a shiver across the surface of the water.

I stand silently, taking it all in, until John, beside me, says, 'Pretty good, isn't it?'

I turn to smile at him. 'It's beautiful.'

'Mr Patterson said you wanted to see this, for the garden you're making over the road.' He shoves his hands into the pockets of his trousers. 'Not that he seems exactly thrilled at the prospect.'

'I got that impression. But is your boss thrilled at anything?'

He laughs at that. 'He's always been a tricky one. His dad and granddad were great employers but that one's always acted like he's doing everyone a favour just by existing.' His tone now sour, he continues, 'His big brother Charlie would never have let the factory go to ruin like he did.'

I nod. 'He can't be easy to work for.'

John shrugs. 'I'm largely left to my own devices.'

'That's all we can ask for, as gardeners,' I say. 'I'm hoping he's not going to be obstructive about the centenary garden.'

'Oh, Avery Sinclair will keep him in his place, don't you worry,' he says.

I laugh. 'Good to know.' I snap a few photographs on my phone, for reference.

Meanwhile, John lowers his voice. 'I reckon she's got something on him, though I don't know what.'

Not sure how to respond, I take a final photo of the Japanese garden as a whole and say, 'Well, thank you for showing this to me. It's stunning – and you're doing a wonderful job on the maintenance of the whole garden.' I gesture to the immaculate sloping lawn and the beautifully trimmed hedges.

John's chest swells visibly at the praise. I don't suppose Martin Patterson appreciates the astonishing amount of work his gardener must be putting into the upkeep of these grounds. It seems a shame that the villagers don't get to see them.

''Course it's not at its best right now,' he says. 'You should come back in the summer.'

'That would be great.'

As he walks me up to the gate, I say, 'Thanks again. I'm not planning an entire Japanese garden, but I'll definitely use these photos for some of my inspiration.'

He says, 'I'm guessing you'll know about the Japan-British Exhibition back in 1910?'

I nod as he lifts the latch. 'Yes. It made quite an impact on British garden design, didn't it? I do want to work in something related – I just haven't decided what, or how it will fit into the minimalist design I'm planning.'

After bidding farewell to John, I head to the Co-op to see what's available for a late lunch. There's the standard supermarket selection of sandwiches, and I opt for a falafel wrap with a packet of Quavers and a can of Coke. I pay and stuff it all into the various pockets of my jacket before walking the short distance to Magpies. I keep mulling over John's words about Martin. He doesn't seem to have any friends in Greenhaven.

18

The rest of the week passes easily, with my wonderful volunteers progressing from ivy and bramble clean-up duty to employing ratchet loppers and saws, which I've trained them to use – we've managed to round up a few more of these tools locally – to lop off the lower limbs of trees that I plan to remove. While they work in one area, I don my tree surgeon's protective gear and set up my harness and ropes to remove trees in another.

All healthy wood gets chopped into logs, which we place on the pavement outside the fence, attracting a near-constant stream of villagers with their wheelbarrows, keen to acquire free firewood. Any diseased material, meanwhile, is burnt on a bonfire that is freshly built and tended each day by Leo, who is proving surprisingly reliable and mature.

'What is it about men and fire?' Marion asks me quietly on Friday afternoon, as she watches her son enthusiastically stoking the flames with fresh branches.

'It's not just men,' I point out, gesturing to Norma, who is dancing around the fire like one of *Macbeth*'s witches.

'For god's sake, Norma,' snaps Christy as he drags a large rotten branch towards the fire.

'Stop!' I tell him, running over. 'This is perfect for the log pile, to attract insects and hedgehogs.'

He rolls his eyes, but obediently turns to tow his branch to the area I've set aside for wildlife. I hear him swearing as he goes, but I choose to ignore it.

Norma, meanwhile, sticks her tongue out at his retreating back before returning to wiggling her hips with renewed vigour while stretching her arms up to the sky as if summoning rain.

As I enter the kitchen that night with Mouse after work, Nellie points to a pile of questionnaires waiting for me on the table. 'I'm gobsmacked at how many people've taken the time to fill it in,' she says. Ever since my questionnaire appeared in *The Green Maven*, I've been receiving responses, either posted through the front door, or by email, and today is no exception.

'I know – it's exactly what I hoped would happen, but I was worried I might be being naive.'

'Are you getting loads by email, too?'

'Quite a few. I've been entering it all into a spreadsheet. Most people are only asking for stuff I was going to include anyway. I wasn't sure about a sandpit, though, and I am now – loads of people have requested one. And there's also been several parents asking for some kind of playhouse, so I'll have to see what I can do there, and if the budget will stretch.'

She nods. 'A playhouse would be brilliant.'

I grin. 'It really would.'

Nellie spends the weekend staying with relatives nearby, so Mouse and I have Magpies to ourselves. In Timmy's absence, he takes all of his toys off the shelves, and scatters them around the living-room floor. After our run on Saturday morning, I call in at the library to go over a few things about Tuesday's forthcoming consultation.

We spend the rest of the weekend dividing our time between runs, long walks, and lazing around in front of documentaries on sharks, hyenas, and a new one set in the Arctic tundra. This last features fluffy white wolves that almost disappear against the snow. Mouse is very impressed at this ability. I don't think he's ever managed to camouflage his large frame for even a second.

I have to admit to missing Nellie's presence by the end of Sunday, though, so I'm pleased to see her come through the door. Mouse even greets Timmy with a friendly lick.

* * *

My sense of unease about the Green Raven's nasty column comes rushing back on Monday morning, when I pick up the village newspaper from the mat after my run with Mouse.

Walking through to the kitchen where Nellie is whisking eggs, I say, 'The paper's here.'

She turns to me and grimaces. 'What's the Raven saying this week?'

'Let me just get Mouse sorted.' I put out his food and drink – Timmy is already emptying his own breakfast bowls – and then I sit at the table and turn to the relevant page. 'My hands are shaking,' I tell her.

'I'm not surprised,' she says, glancing over her shoulder from where she's cooking an omelette.

Skimming the column, I say, 'Nothing about me this week, so that's a relief.'

'Phew,' she says. 'Anything else of note?'

'Something about someone whose skeletons are about to be revealed. It's all very vague.'

She raises an eyebrow and laughs. 'That could refer to just about anyone in the village.'

'Really?' I shudder. 'Well, I'm only here till the end of April. Hopefully, most of the skeletons will stay put till I'm gone.'

After I've showered, we sit at the table and eat the mushroom omelettes Nellie has made. They are light and fluffy.

'Is it today you've got the digger arriving?' she asks.

'Yes. I think I mentioned that it's a local guy who's providing his services for free.'

'That's one of the things about Greenhaven,' she says, 'it's a proper community, and people are willing to help each other out.'

'Yes, from what Avery's told me, there are plenty of local companies willing to donate their time or products. And I've been really impressed with my helpers – they work so hard. What are you up to today? Are you back at Wrens?'

'No, I've got plenty of sketches as well as the photographs the owners supplied, so I'll be painting at home.'

We finish breakfast, and I leave Mouse to sleep in our bedroom with the door closed while I head to the site.

The digger operator is a local man called Graham who runs his own hire business. Although I have a digger licence myself, we've agreed that he'll drive the machine, as I want to be on the outside, directing him.

Although we've only been at work for an hour and a half, Graham has already made a dramatic inroad into clearing the roots in the area designated for the playground. He's working from left to right, with me directing him, and is quite close to the bungalow's foundations when the scoop's teeth scrape at a layer of ground and reveal something other than earth. It's a glint of white, about a metre below the surface. It's probably nothing, but I hold up a hand and shout, 'Stop!' He immediately stops and turns off the engine.

I walk over to examine the trench. Graham swings himself down from the cab and comes to stand beside me. 'What have you got?'

I point to the small area of white against the rich dark brown of the clay soil. 'I'm pretty sure it's a bone,' I say.

He shrugs. 'Probably the remains of a badger or fox. We get loads of them round here.'

I'm wearing my jacket but a sense of unease is lifting the hairs on my arms like a cool breeze. I crouch and gently wipe away soil with a gloved hand. The earth falls away like a magician's cloth, to reveal the scene beyond.

Two human skeletons, their skulls leering up at us.

19

My first encounter with the village constable, PC Hawkins, does not inspire confidence. When he opens the door of his little house in response to my knock, I can hear his TV playing the theme to *Homes Under the Hammer* or another of those generic daytime shows.

'Are you on duty?' I ask him. As he's in uniform, this is intended as a reproach.

He fails to notice, surveying me with curiosity. 'Are you the gardener?'

'Garden designer,' I correct him. Relenting, I add, 'And gardener.'

'What happened? Your wheelbarrow run away from you and mow someone down?' He seems to find this hilarious. When I don't join in with the laughter, he sobers and clears his throat. 'Is there something I can help with?' he asks.

'You can come with me,' I say. 'The digger has just unearthed two skeletons.'

Panic strikes him as visibly as a runaway wheelbarrow. I manage not to voice this observation.

'Skeletons?' he checks, clearly hoping I'll slap my forehead and say, 'No! I meant dandelions!' When I don't, he pales and says, 'Let me go get my hat. And my notebook.'

I wait, and he emerges a moment later, wearing his hat and tucking a notebook and pen into his pocket.

'Shoes?' I suggest, glancing down at his slippered feet.

He smacks his forehead and vanishes again, reappearing a minute or two later wearing black lace-ups. He closes the front door behind him and accompanies me across the street and around the fencing to the opening on the far side of the garden site. Once inside, he slows as we near the spot where Graham is standing guard.

'Who's that?' he asks.

'That's Graham Tanner, the digger operator.'

'And he just happened to be here when two skeletons turned up?'

We are near enough for Graham to hear, and he and I share a look before Graham deadpans, 'No – I came here last night to bury the people I bumped off, just so I could dig them up again today.'

'We don't have murders around here,' says the PC, in an accusatory tone.

'Well,' says Graham, continuing his sarcasm, 'maybe these two just dug their own grave and obligingly lay down in it.'

I decide to intervene: 'Come and see,' I say to the constable, leading him over. He peers down at the two skeletons, then draws out his mobile phone and dials 999.

'I could have done that,' I say. 'Don't you have a line to a big police station?'

But the call handler is already answering, and he ignores me. 'Police,' he says. A moment later, he gives his name as 'PC Edward

Hawkins,' and says, 'Yeah . . . I thought it was quicker this way. There are skeletons buried in Greenhaven, CM8. They've just been dug up on some wasteland.'

He says, 'Yes, I see,' and then hangs up. Catching my eye, he says, 'It's standard procedure to call 999.'

'I didn't know that,' I admit.

Graham has lost interest and is walking back to the digger. I see him swing himself up and open a thermos. I have a sudden craving for strong coffee.

'Do you need me, or can I come back later?' I ask the PC.

The panic reappears on his face before he says, 'I need to ask you some questions.' I'm pretty sure that what he really wants to say is, 'Don't leave me here alone with the dead people.'

I humour him. 'Sure. Of course. Shall we sit down?' I gesture to a flat area of bricks where I've cleared the ivy, and we sit side by side.

Drawing out his notebook and pen, he says, 'What time did you start work today?'

I take him through the morning, from my run with Mouse – who is now at home, dozing by the radiator – and then the hour or so for which Graham and I worked before making our unwelcome discovery.

'I know the Galloway grandparents died in a fire here,' I say. 'Can I just check – their bodies were definitely recovered?' I am hoping he will say no, so that all of this, including their skeletons, can be put to rest. There is selfishness in this desire, as I know from experience the extent to which a police investigation can interfere with the creation of a garden. So, it's with a sinking feeling in my gut that I take in his response.

'Fran and Albert were dug out of the rubble and buried at the time. Horrible business. My dad was the village constable back then. I had nightmares for weeks afterwards, about dying in a fire. I'm pretty sure all us kids did.'

As I shudder at this image, I can't help wondering if being the Greenhaven PC is like royalty, one family member inheriting the throne – or, in this case, the police house and duties – when the other retires or dies.

'Have you called the station?' I ask him.

'Oh!' he says, scrabbling for his phone, which he's put back inside his jacket pocket. He takes longer than seems plausible to scroll to the number he needs and hit the call button.

While he is placed on hold and then put through to a department, I feel the cold begin to set in, scaling my legs and torso from my brick perch.

Just as I start to shiver, Graham climbs down from the digger cab and brings me a steaming mug. 'Mind reader,' I say, peering at the brown liquid. 'What's in it?'

'It's a hot toddy,' he says, then laughs when he sees my sceptical expression. 'Not really – just tea.'

I'm not keen on tea, but I take it gratefully, feeling the warmth as I hold the mug in both hands and begin to sip. 'Thank you,' I say. 'I needed that.'

'You were starting to turn blue,' he says. 'Here.' He holds out a West Ham football scarf and I wrap it around my neck, revelling in how it's retained the warmth from his cab. I'm about to thank him again but, at that moment, the PC ends his call and stands up, addressing Graham:

'I need to take your statement.'

'Sure,' says Graham. 'But I don't have much to tell you. I was operating the digger from the cab. Steph here told me to stop. I turned off the engine and came over and she showed me a bone . . .'

'Slow down,' says Hawkins, scribbling in his notebook.

'I . . . turned . . . off . . .' begins Graham slowly.

'Don't take the mickey,' says Hawkins with a scowl.

Graham shrugs. The tea is leaving a bitter coating on my tongue and I wonder if either of the men would notice if I slinked off home to Magpies for a strong mug of coffee and a cuddle with Mouse.

'How long before the station sends someone?' I ask Hawkins.

He checks his watch. 'A detective should be here in about fifteen minutes.'

'I think I might head home,' I say. 'You can call me on the mobile if they want to talk to me – or you can send them over to Magpies.'

This time, the PC lets me leave. I offer a bright smile in response to Graham's imploring look. The way I see it, he managed to escape to his cab and leave me with Hawkins for a while – I don't see why he shouldn't also have to spend a little time alone with the charming village constable.

Nellie is sitting at the dining room table when I get back, Timmy curled on a cushion in one corner. 'Hello!' she calls. 'I know I said I'd wait till I'd seen your plans, but I've been doing some new roughs for the sculpture and I'd really like to get your thoughts.'

'Hold on,' I say through the open door. 'I want to check on Mouse first.'

I run upstairs to the bedroom, where Mouse wakes as I push open our door. 'Hey, boy. Do you want to come down? I'm afraid Timmy's there, though he was asleep just now.'

He yawns and stretches his long back before picking up Mr Rabbit and walking towards me. He stops for a moment for me to stroke him, then we head out of the room and down the stairs.

Upon our arrival in the dining room, Timmy wakes up and begins to zoom around the room, dragging a cushion with him and making growling sounds. He keeps bringing the cushion over to Mouse, clearly hoping he'll join in the game, but Mouse just sits very upright, Mr Rabbit between his feet.

'I don't think much of that cushion's chances,' I say.

'Don't worry – it's one I bought for him,' says Nellie. 'I don't know if you've looked inside the cupboard at the end of the landing, but it's full of all the soft furnishings I didn't want Timmy to eviscerate.'

I laugh. 'Good plan.'

My laugh must sound weak because she stands up with a frown and touches my arm, saying, 'What's wrong?'

I shrug. 'Oh . . . we've just dug up a pair of bodies.'

Her eyes grow wide and she takes a step back. 'What? You mean at the garden site?' I nod. 'So . . . what did you do? Were they fresh? I mean – I don't know what you're meant to ask . . .'

She runs a hand through her hair, leaving her curls knotty and dishevelled.

'I'm not sure there's an etiquette guide to the discovery of corpses,' I say, not mentioning that I could probably use one, given how often I seem to stumble upon them and have to break the news to people.

She manages a small smile and I continue, 'But no, not fresh. In fact, they're skeletons. I reckon they've been there a while, but we won't know for sure until the police and coroner have done their investigation.'

'Who do you think it is?' she asks, regarding me intently.

I frown. 'How would I know? I've only just got here.' I take a deep breath and say, 'Sorry – that came out more sharply than intended. It's been pretty stressful.'

'I'm sure,' she says, giving me a hug. 'Shall I make you a chamomile tea?'

'I'd rather have coffee.'

She laughs. 'Of course you would! Only Steph Williams would ask for strong coffee after a fright. Most people are trying to lower their blood pressure. At least say you'll have some biscuits for the shock.'

'I never say no to biscuits. What have you got?'

'Actually, I couldn't sleep last night, so I made chocolate-dipped shortbread.'

'I love living with you,' I tell her, as I follow her through to the kitchen where I sink on to my stool at the table and Mouse comes to put his head in my lap, Mr Rabbit dangling from his mouth. 'And I love living with you, too,' I tell him, stroking his soft ears and under his chin. He makes an approving rumble in his throat.

Nellie makes up the cafetière and brings it to the table with two mugs and a plate of shortbread. 'I'm guessing they won't let you do any more digging there for a while . . .' she says.

'It's likely to be out of bounds for some time,' I say, reaching for one of the biscuits and taking a bite. It melts on the tongue like a Viennese whirl. 'These are amazing!'

She grins. 'The secret's in . . .' She stops, raising one eyebrow. 'Why do I keep telling you my cooking secrets? You don't cook!' She pours us each a mug of coffee.

'Why would I, when you do such a good job?' I pull a face. 'Do I sound like one of those 1950s' husbands?'

'A little. But provided you don't talk to . . . Mike, is it? . . . like that, I think you're good.' She sighs. 'This is going to delay everything, isn't it? I've blocked out until the end of June for this commission, before I head out to the Bahamas.'

'The Bahamas?'

'Yeah. I know it sounds amazing, but it's for my mum's third wedding. It's hard to get excited.'

'I can understand that. Do you like the person she's marrying?'

She shrugs. 'He's younger than I am. Seems nice enough, though. I don't know what he sees in her – she's kind of full on.'

I suppress a smile. 'Full on' is exactly the phrase I'd apply to both Nellie and her little dog.

'Coming back to the skeletons,' says Nellie, surveying me over the rim of her mug, 'how long do you think it will take to get a . . . whatever they do?'

'You mean DNA test results?' I ask. When she nods, I consider. 'I think it's down to how busy the labs are. I get the impression all British police are overloaded, so I'm guessing the labs will be, too.'

Timmy – who has left the room without our noticing – starts barking upstairs, and she gets to her feet with a sigh. 'I hope he's not attacking my duvet again. I'm sure I shut my door.' She leaves to investigate.

At that moment, Mouse barks and heads into the hall, and I'm summoned by a ring at the front door. When I open it, two smartly dressed people are standing on the doorstep. One, a forty-something black woman with cropped purple hair, shows me an ID card.

'DS Stacey Timpson, looking for Steph Williams,' she says. She has one of those accents that are hard to place, as if she's moved around.

'That's me.' I hesitate, and Mouse looks up at me questioningly. I've had more than one unfortunate run-in with police detectives, and I consider insisting they interview me on the doorstep. But, remembering that Nellie is in the house if I need support, I relent. 'You'd better come in.' I tug Mouse's collar and he and I step to the side to allow them access. She introduces the bald middle-aged white man with her as DC Zack Wright. He nods and shows me his own ID card, then they follow me through to the living room, where I gesture for them to take a seat.

'It's nice in here,' says the DS, looking around her at the big windows and the brightly coloured rug as she takes a seat in one of the armchairs. The DC lowers himself on to the sofa, but he's very tall – around six-seven, at a guess – and the low furniture looks too small for him, so that his knees end up bent at a sharp angle, like a grown man on a child's bike. He draws a small tablet out from his inside pocket and poises with the stylus.

'Tea or coffee?' I ask, but DS Timpson holds up a hand.

'Nothing, thanks. We've just had a takeaway coffee from the little café.'

'Oh, it's a great place,' I say as I sit in the remaining armchair. Mouse comes to sit at my feet. 'The carrot cake's amazing.'

'So's the lemon drizzle,' she says.

'Good tip.'

She smiles but then her face turns serious. 'I understand you and . . .' She glances to her DC, who supplies,

'Graham Tanner.'

She nods, then addresses me again, 'I understand you were the ones who found the skeletons. How are you doing?'

'I'm fine, thanks.'

'Really?'

I shrug. 'I've seen worse.' I notice DC Wright make a note on his tablet.

The DS narrows her eyes. 'Why is that?'

She clearly hasn't looked me up yet on the police database. I hesitate before saying, 'I'm an itinerant garden designer. Unfortunately, each place I've worked at has had a body. I think it's all the digging . . .' Remembering the grave I stumbled upon with Mouse at a previous placement, I stroke his ears as I continue, 'And this lovely fellow here is very good at sniffing out trouble, so we're often the first on the scene.'

She catches the eye of her DC. 'We could do with a police dog like that. The old one at Colchester only seems interested in sniffing out food scraps.'

'Salome,' he says.

'That's right – Salome!' She seems delighted. 'My New Testament's a bit rusty, but didn't she present John the Baptist's head to her mother on a plate?'

DC Wright smiles. 'That's right.' His voice is deep and local.

'A police dog named after a vengeful woman,' she muses. 'An interesting choice.' Her gaze moves back to me, and she seems to remember her mission. 'Where was I?'

The DC clears his throat. 'Ms Williams was telling us about her and her dog, and how she's . . .' He consults his tablet and reads, '. . . "seen worse".'

'Oh yes, that's right,' she says.

Nellie appears in the doorway. 'Oh! I didn't realise we had guests.' She's holding a squirming Timmy.

'It's the police,' I tell her. 'They've come about the skeletons.'

'Right. I'll keep this little terror shut away. We'll be in the kitchen if you need us.'

'Thanks. Can you leave this door open?'

Nellie shoots me a curious look but she nods and does as I ask.

'Who was that?' asks DS Timpson after we've heard the kitchen door shut.

'My housemate, Nellie. She's the village's artist-in-residence.'

'You get that, Zack?' When he nods, she turns back to me. 'We're currently waiting for the CSI team to finish at the site, but are you telling us you make a habit of finding dead bodies?'

I nod. 'I guess so.' When she and the DC exchange a look, I say, 'Not on purpose! I mean, Mouse and I don't go looking for them. I'd be quite happy to never find another one.'

'Me, too,' she says. 'But, as long as there are humans, there will be murders.' She must feel she's said too much, because she adds, 'Not that we know cause of death in this case, yet.'

'Two skeletons, though,' I say, 'buried on wasteland ... It doesn't look like suicide or accidental death.'

She exchanges another look with her DC but they say nothing.

'So, please can you fill us in on when you arrived in Greenhaven, and how you unearthed the skeletons?'

I run through the same information as I shared with the village constable, adding in details to further questions, such as what made me believe they weren't animal bones – to which I reply that I hadn't been sure, until I uncovered them further; and what I know about Graham, the digger operator.

'Very little,' I say. 'He lives in the village, and Avery, the chair of the Heritage Society committee, passed on his details. He's giving his labour for free.'

Further questions follow, including why I focused on that area of the site for today's digging, and whether we touched or moved the skeletons.

I consider this. 'I dusted them off with my gardening gloves. But I didn't alter the positions they were in.' She studies me, saying nothing. I shrug. 'I needed to check they were human skeletons before calling the police.'

This appears a more satisfactory response, as she nods before moving on to queries about my background, including my recent residencies.

'How did the Heritage Society committee select you for the job here?' she asks.

'They came across my website, where I've posted various design jobs. After a video call, they seemed satisfied that I had the necessary skill set.'

When I've answered all of her questions, there's a long silence. From the way she fixes her gaze on me, it feels as though she's trying to form an opinion of me.

I eventually break the silence, informing them, 'If you look on the police system, you'll see that I've helped with a few investigations. As I said earlier, it's usually because, with Mouse's good hearing and sense of smell, we're often first on the scene. However, in this case, it's simply that the committee hired me to create a garden, and the allocated site turned out to house an unmarked grave.' I hesitate, then add, 'I am not unmoved by the discovery of two bodies, in case that's the impression I've given. But for once I don't know the victims, and I have to admit that's a relief.'

She nods. 'I can understand that. We generally aren't allowed to get involved in cases where we know the victims. It must make things a lot harder when you've had a personal relationship with them.'

'It does,' I say.

This seems to be the end of the conversation. They get to their feet and thank me for my time.

I see them to the front door. 'Thanks again,' says the DS as the pair of them step outside. There's a curious sparkle to the grey sky, as if it's full of ice crystals, making me wonder if it's going to snow. I have to remind myself that this is the southeast of England, where snow is rare.

'Who lives in the big house over the road?' asks the DS.

'That's Woodpeckers, the home of Stella and Jeremy Pargeter. Stella's the editor of the village paper, *The Green Maven*.'

'Beautiful building.'

'It really is. The whole village is special,' I say.

'Just a shame about the skeletons,' says Wright.

'Please excuse my DC,' says Timpson, with a glare at him. 'I'm afraid the force breeds a certain type of dark humour.'

'It's OK,' I say. 'It's a coping mechanism. I get it.'

I nearly make the tongue-in-cheek suggestion that the discovery of the bodies might bring down house prices in the village, if she's interested in living here. But two people have died, I reprimand myself. Two people who were no doubt missed by their families. Perhaps they still are.

And then it occurs to me, with a rush of sympathy, that my finding of the bodies might bring peace to someone who's been missing them for years.

20

'So, how'd it go with the police?' asks Nellie as Mouse and I enter the kitchen, narrowly avoiding tripping over Timmy as he hurls himself towards us. 'Timmy – no!' she shouts.

The little dog rolls on to his back and sticks out his tongue. He is definitely grinning. Mouse steps pointedly over him and walks up to Nellie, seated at the table. She pats him on the head and says, 'You show him how to behave, 'eh, boy?' He licks her hand.

I take my usual seat, at right angles to her at the little table. 'It was fine,' I say. 'They were a bit bemused when I told them these weren't my first dead bodies, but they don't seem to think I bumped them off at least.'

She raises an eyebrow. 'Is that something you've been accused of in the past?'

I pull a face. 'There's pretty much always the suggestion that, if you found them, you might have killed them.'

'Like finders keepers but for murderers?' she muses.

'Something like that.'

'But they don't think you did it?'

'Who knows what they really think? They're keeping it close to their chests. But hopefully the fact that I only just came to the village pretty much rules out my having bumped off people who were clearly buried some time ago.'

'Unless this isn't your first visit to Greenhaven,' she says with a raised eyebrow.

'Well, there is that.' I slap my forehead. 'Oh! I'm so sorry, officers: I thought you were asking if I'd killed two people in the past couple of weeks. Now, if you're asking about previous years . . .'

We both laugh, though there's a hysterical quality to it. Then she says, 'Actually, I'm scared now. I'm going to be locking my door tonight.'

'I'd suggest doing that in any case, to keep Timmy from breaking out.'

She looks around. 'Where is he? Oh, no . . .' She runs from the room, and I could swear Mouse shoots me a look.

'I know, boy. He's a lot. You're doing great.' He comes to my side and drops Mr Rabbit into my lap. 'Thank you,' I say, making a show of cuddling the beloved toy. 'He's lovely.' Mouse makes his rumble of agreement.

Nellie reappears in the doorway, wide eyed. In her arms, a happy Timmy is chewing on something familiar.

'Is that one of my trainers?' I ask.

'I'm so sorry! I'll buy you a new pair.'

I get up to inspect the footwear. It's been mangled. 'I don't know how he managed that so quickly,' I say.

'I suspect he's had it for a day or two,' she says. 'He steals stuff and hides it away to chew on when I'm not looking.'

'Not to worry,' I say. 'It's an old pair. The ones I wear for running are safely in my room. It's my own fault for leaving these out where he could get to them.'

'No, let me pay.'

I roll my eyes. 'You've been cooking for me twice a day since I got here. You don't owe me anything.'

She sinks on to a seat. 'If you're sure . . .' Holding Timmy in front of her face, she says, 'What am I going to do with you?' He pants happily and continues to chew.

With a sigh, she sets him down on the floor, where he begins to roll around with the trainer, growling softly. Mouse surveys him with the indulgent look of an older sibling who has grown out of such childish pastimes.

'Coffee?' suggests Nellie.

'Yeah. I'll do it.'

'No, you stay there.' She gets up and fetches the biscuit tin. 'Help yourself to more shortbread while I get the coffee on.'

'You're spoiling me – you do realise that?' I say as I open the lid to take a biscuit. 'I can never be independent again.'

She laughs. 'I'm amazed you've survived this long. What do you eat when I'm not around?'

'Beans on toast mostly.'

She pulls a face. 'That's not food.'

'Protein and maybe iron and vitamin C?' I suggest. 'To be fair, I've not had to fend for myself much. Most of my placements have been at least partially catered. And, in the breaks between jobs, I often spend time at my brother and sister-in-law's, and they both cook.'

'So, what . . . you're never going to learn?'

I help myself to another biscuit and grin. 'Not so long as other people seem happy to feed me.'

Mouse barks at that moment and runs into the hall, so we're not surprised when the doorbell rings.

'I'll go,' I say. Mouse's tail is wagging before I even open the door, so I'm expecting one of his new friends, either Avery or Marion. It turns out to be the former. Avery is dressed in an elegant cream winter coat which ties at the neck and goes out in what I have heard described as an 'A-line' shape. It reminds me of a campanula's bell-shaped flower, and looks as though it would billow out if she twirled.

Mouse has pushed past me to the doorstep, where Avery has bent to stroke him. Now, she straightens up. 'Steph, are you OK?'

'Sorry – was I staring? I was just thinking that you ought to be a dancer.'

'I am. But that's for another time. I meant are you all right after your traumatic experience?'

'Oh! Yes, I'm fine, thanks. Do you want to come in? Nellie's just making coffee.'

'If I'm not intruding.'

She follows me to the kitchen, where Nellie has already set the cafetière on the table to brew. 'Avery, hi!' she says, fetching a third mug.

'Hi, Nellie. I was just checking on Steph after her and Graham's distressing discovery.'

We all squeeze in around the three sides of the table. 'I'm OK, really,' I say, wondering how many people I will have to reassure on this front. 'I mean, it's not like I witnessed anything. And the bodies were . . .' I pause but then, figuring that Avery is not the type to beat about the bush, I finish, 'fully decomposed. Skeletons are somehow a lot less disturbing than bodies with the flesh still on.' I regret my bluntness the moment both sets of eyes turn on me in evident discombobulation. 'Sorry, sorry,' I say. 'As Nellie already knows, I've been involved in other murder investigations. It's much harder when you know the person.'

Avery's expression softens, and she nods. 'I can imagine. I'm so sorry you've had that.'

I shrug. 'It's far worse for their families and loved ones.'

'Can we change the subject?' asks Nellie.

'Of course,' says Avery. 'Steph, I was impressed with the questionnaire you put in last week's paper.'

'Thank you. Stella improved on it. I'm hoping some people will turn up to the drop-in session.'

'That's at the library?' When I nod, she says, 'You've cleared it with the team there?'

'Stella has. Apparently, they're being really supportive.'

She smiles. 'Yes, Fleur the manager is always quick to back local initiatives. We're very lucky.' She surveys me for a moment before asking, 'Did you read the Green Raven column?'

I pull a face and nod.

She says, 'I was a bit concerned that our not-so-friendly Raven might have alarmed you.'

'With the reference to a "mobbing"?' I say. She nods. 'It's not like I'm running for government here,' I say. 'I'm not really sure what a mob would be objecting to.'

'I'm sure you're right.' She tuts. 'Honestly, I wish this Green Raven would come out from the shadows. It started harmlessly enough but it's close to bullying now. I have talked to Stella about it, but she seems to think the villagers enjoy the scandal.'

Nellie takes a biscuit. Timmy, who has been happily chewing away on his spoils, suddenly becomes aware that food is being consumed without him. He arrives at Nellie's feet and sits, looking up at her as if he hasn't been fed for weeks.

'Honestly, Timmy, you're incorrigible,' she tells him, nonetheless breaking off a corner of her biscuit to feed him. He wolfs it down and returns to his pitiful staring.

Looking over at Avery, I say, 'Do you have any idea who the skeletons might be?'

'Do you remember my telling you about Martin Patterson's brother, who was meant to run the factory, but ran off with one of the factory girls?'

There's a long silence. 'You think it's them?' says Nellie at last.

Avery nods slowly. 'It never made sense to any of us, Charlie running off like that. He had too much of a sense of duty.'

'You really think it's him and his girlfriend?' says Nellie.

'I think it's the most likely explanation. Various teenagers have run away over the years – Greenhaven does not have a lot to offer energetic young people – but they've all been back in touch at some stage. Charlie is the only one who never contacted his family again.'

'Neither did his girlfriend, according to Vera in the Co-op,' says Nellie.

'His girlfriend Megan, too,' agrees Avery. 'Both sets of parents died, never knowing what happened to them.'

'That's awful,' I say.

'I think it broke her mother,' says Avery. 'She died about a year later.'

We lapse into silence again. Some things are too tough for words.

21

'If it is Martin's brother and the brother's girlfriend, who do you reckon killed them?' says Mike, having adjusted to the news of bodies more easily than I expected.

I've come upstairs to call him after a cheese toastie for dinner. (Poor Nellie has a headache, and couldn't even face eating one of those.) Mike is wearing a chunky green sweater and sitting beside his flaming log burner with Edward the cat on his lap. The scene is so cosy, it looks like a knitwear advert.

Our own scene is not so bad – the vibrant red curtains with their retro print, the bed with its matching spread, and Mouse beside me on the little bedroom sofa, his head on my lap as he stares at the cat on the screen. Thankfully, for once he's not blocking my view.

I pull a face. 'I did wonder if the Patterson parents intervened, not wanting their son to marry beneath him.'

'What? You're thinking they killed their own son?'

I hesitate, then say, 'No, not really. And, if they had, wouldn't they have buried them in their own grounds, so no one would disturb the bodies?'

'True. But you reckon they weren't happy about the match?'

'They definitely disapproved, which is why some people believed the runaway story. It would have been the only way the two could be together.'

'Classic Romeo and Juliet,' says Mike.

'Right down to their deaths at the end it seems,' I say sadly.

'When will the police have a conclusive ID?' he asks.

'I get the impression Essex police are really overloaded at the moment, so I doubt long-dead victims will be a priority, but we'll see.'

He frowns. 'I know two people are dead, but I'm wondering . . .'

'. . . how this will affect the centenary garden build,' I finish.

'Yup.'

'The police have cordoned off the area around where we found the bodies, and I have permission to work outside that.'

'That's something, I guess. Can you manage?'

'I think we'll just have to.'

'Oh, my phone's ringing and it's Celine. Speak tomorrow?'

Celine is his teenage daughter, whom I've yet to meet. 'Sounds good.' We smile and end the call. Mouse looks up at me with big eyes. 'Sorry, boy. Edward will be back soon. Bedtime?'

Although he gets down from the sofa, he heads over to his ball and nudges it with his nose. This favourite toy has some form of friction built in, so that it takes itself in unexpected directions when rolled.

While he amuses himself, I take a look at my next clue in the cryptic crossword:

6A – Swallow this. Sounds fine for a chest complaint.

For once, I come up with the answer almost immediately: coffee. The first syllable 'coff', sounds like a c-o-u-g-h – in other words, a chest complaint. And the second syllable, 'fee', sounds like a fine or a charge. With a smile, I fill it in and message Verity, my birth mother:

Did you get 6A yet?

She messages back:

Yes. And I thought of you ☺

I laugh at the thought that she already associates me with coffee.

In bed a little while later, I think through the day's discovery. It seems probable that Avery's right, and the skeletons are those of Charles Patterson and his girlfriend, Megan.

So, who killed them and why?

And then I remember this morning's Green Raven column, and the reference to 'skeletons'. What if the writer is also the murderer – or knows the killer's identity?

22

There's a queue outside the library on Tuesday morning when I turn up just before 1 p.m. for my consultation session. I head to the front of the line and knock on the door, and one of the librarians kindly admits me, assuring the waiting villagers that the building will be opened shortly.

'How are you doing?' asks Fleur, the manager, after closing the door behind me. She's a tiny black woman with the kind of neat, quick movements that remind me of a wren. Today, she's even dressed in a brown flecked dress, which enhances the effect. My response to her enquiry is drowned out by her two assistants greeting me as if I was a celebrity author, rather than someone tallying responses to a questionnaire.

Fleur leads me to a table they've set up, with a chair behind it, and two chairs in front, presumably for my visitors.

'Oh, this is great,' I say.

She surveys me, her head tilted in her bird-like way. 'You still haven't told us how you're doing.'

The other two staff members join her, all displaying sympathy. 'You mean because of finding the skeletons?' I say, and she nods. 'At least they appeared to be long dead,' I say, hoping that doesn't sound callous. 'Has there been confirmation of their identities?'

'There are rumours,' says one of her staff, a tall, white seventy-ish woman, whose name I can't remember – and her name badge is facing the wrong way.

I'm about to question her about these rumours, to see if everyone agrees with Avery's theory, when her boss says, 'As they're just speculation, I think we should wait for the police to check the DNA, don't you?'

Her staff member doesn't look happy at being shut down, but she doesn't push the matter.

Keen to ease the tension, I say, 'Do you always have such a big turnout on a Tuesday?' They all start to laugh. 'What?' I say.

'They're here for you,' says the tall staff member.

'For me?' I check. When they nod, I feel my stomach muscles clench like a carnivorous plant snapping closed. 'I guess I'd better get started in that case.'

I settle myself at the table, take out my notebook and a pen, and prepare myself for the onslaught.

Thankfully, the villagers turn out to be in good spirits. Far from the arguments I was dreading, they mainly want to chat or offer free plants. One has potted up cuttings from his prize roses; another offers me an oak tree she's been growing in a pot. A third tells me about her pile of original Crittall windows, which she suggests I could incorporate into a shelter or gazebo. Although I keep note of all of the plant offers, I reluctantly reject the windows, which will not be safe in a park, where young people are bound to climb on the structures.

'Can I have a note of your details, in case I think of some other way to use them?' I ask her.

'Sure but I work at the Co-op, so you can always come by there. I'll give you my info though, in case it's handy.' She writes in the notebook: Vera Carlow, with her phone number underneath.

'Thanks so much,' I say.

She leans in and whispers, 'Is it true about the bodies?'

I hesitate, not wanting to give away too much so early in the police investigation. But the discovery of the skeletons seems to be an open secret, so I nod.

'I've never found a body,' she says. 'Unless you count the cat I dug up at the end of the garden after we'd just moved here.'

Not sure how to respond, I nod again.

'Do you have pictures?' she asks.

I stare at her. 'No. I don't have pictures.'

She deflates with disappointment, then takes her leave.

But she seems to have set the tone for the session. I can only assume that gossip has travelled across the village like *Fallopia baldschuanica*, the invasive 'mile-a-minute' Russian vine, speeding along a fence. All of the assembled party now want to talk more about the skeletons than the garden.

After about twenty minutes of these frustrating interactions, I rise and ask everyone waiting to listen. Explaining that I have nothing to add about yesterday's discovery, I suggest that people stay only if they would like to contribute to the discussion around creating a centenary garden that will benefit the entire village.

A knot of at least six people leaves, muttering discontentedly among themselves. At least this means that the four people remaining genuinely wish to talk about the garden.

I smile brightly and say, 'Would you all like to come over together?'

The tall library worker kindly brings over more chairs and supplies hot drinks, and we settle in for a proper discussion of what is and is not doable at this stage.

It transpires that the group contains both a retired structural engineer and – I fail to hide my excitement here – a former gardener at Farleys House in Sussex, which was home for thirty-five years to photographer Lee Miller and her husband, the painter and art patron Roland Penrose. The place is known as 'the home of the Surrealists' and, although I've never visited, I've read a lot about it.

She laughs at my enthusiasm. 'You really should get over there,' she says.

'When I get a gig near there, I will,' I say. 'In the meantime, you must have some ideas around design for here.'

She shakes her head. 'Actually, I'm here on my father's behest. He's busy this morning but he's keen to make use of the garden, preferably with his best mate who also lives in the village. They were wondering if there might be a way to incorporate a chess table as a permanent feature.'

'I love that idea,' I say.

The structural engineer, whose name I have yet to ask, says, 'I've seen double-sided outdoor games tables, where you can have another board on the underside, and it rotates and locks into place as needed.'

The gardener says, 'Oh, so there could be a backgammon board as well.'

'This is all great,' I say. 'Would either of you be able to look into sourcing one of those tables? I'd need to know where it was coming from, and how much it would cost.'

'I can do that,' says the engineer.

'Brilliant, thanks. You know, it's making me wonder if we shouldn't also have a giant chessboard marked out on the ground, for kids. We could have giant pieces.' I make some sketches and add some notes.

'Was there anything else?' I ask the group.

An older woman who hasn't spoken yet sets down her mug of tea and says, 'Please could we have a rose garden?'

I nod. 'I was thinking of a sensory garden, which would have tea roses, star jasmine and honeysuckle for scent, along with some textured plants, plus grasses for the sounds when the wind runs through them. Oh, and do you know the witch hazel, *Hamamelis*? It has spidery flowers on bare branches in winter, which give off a lovely scent when not much else is going on.'

She seems happy with this answer, so I turn to the remaining member of the party. 'I don't think we've heard from you,' I say, smiling at the young woman, who has refused a drink and seems to be retreating as far as possible inside the hood of her coat.

'Oh, there's nothing,' she says softly.

The older woman clearly knows her. She squeezes her arm and says, 'Come on, Eloise, no one will bite.'

'It's just . . . I was wondering . . .' She takes a deep breath and blurts out, running the words together, 'I didn't put my name down in time to be a volunteer but I want to be a garden designer, and I was wondering if I could help out with something even if it's just a little job.'

I smile again. 'Of course!'

It's a joy to see the relief on her face. She even moves forward in her hood. 'Really?'

I nod. 'I'd love some help. And I'll be happy to show you some of the tools I use for designing, if you're interested?'

She nods so enthusiastically that her hood falls off, much to my delight. 'That would be sick . . . amazing,' she corrects herself, blushing.

'Are you in school?' I ask.

'Only college. It's just Mondays and Thursdays. I'm doing a foundation course in Colchester.'

'Great. We can work around that. How old are you?' I say.

'Eighteen.'

Next, I show my visitors some of my preliminary sketches, and we discuss where would be a good place to work in a games table and the grid for giant chess.

As they get their coats on, preparing to leave, I address the older man. 'Sorry, what's your name?'

'Mally McDonald.'

'And you're a structural engineer?' When he nods, I say, 'Could you help me with something for the build?'

'Of course – I'd be delighted. What do you need?'

I find my sketches for the miniature building I'd like to erect. 'It's this,' I say. 'I need to know if the foundations still in the ground from the bungalow are strong enough to support a little house for the children to play in.'

'What a wonderful idea,' he says, taking the sketches from me. 'I can come over now, if you like?'

Noticing that Eloise is trying to catch my eye, I say, 'How about tomorrow afternoon, at two thirty? Would that work?'

He puts on a flat cap and says, 'Perfect. I'll see you then, at the site.'

I thank him and say goodbye to him and the other two older people before turning to Eloise. 'Was there something else?' I ask her.

'I have ADHD,' she says. 'Sometimes I forget appointments, and I say the wrong things sometimes too.'

I say, 'Well, I'm quite straight-talking myself, so let's make a deal not to worry too much about offending one another, should we?' I slip my materials back into my bag and thank the library staff before walking out with the young woman.

Once outside, I stop walking and say, 'As for the appointments, I'm sure you've thought of this, but could you set an alarm on your phone, to remind you?'

'I always mean to set alarms,' she says. 'Mum and Dad go on at me about it. But I always get distracted by other stuff when I pick up my phone.'

'Ah, OK. Well, I could remind you and make sure you set the alarms for working with me, if that won't feel like I'm interfering?'

She shakes her head, so I say, 'Why don't you set your first alarm now? It's Tuesday, so you don't have college tomorrow. Does that mean you're free?' She nods, and I say, 'Shall we say we'll meet at nine thirty tomorrow, at the site? Do you know where that is?'

We're standing on one side of the rectangular island allocated to the garden. She points to the far side. 'I've seen a padlock on the fencing over there.'

'That's it. Great. Set that alarm now, then.'

She does as I suggest, holding up her screen to show me, then beaming before saying goodbye. There's a definite bounce in her walk as she strides away.

23

'I forgot to ask this morning – how's your headache now?' I ask Nellie. She and I are sharing a margherita pizza from the Co-op for dinner. She's looking pale, and has turned down my offer of wine.

She frowns. 'Headache?'

'Yeah – you know how you couldn't even face my cordon bleu cooking last night?'

She laughs but it's not her usual hearty sound. 'Are your cheese toasties that good?'

'So good that Gordon Ramsay keeps emailing me for my secret ingredient.'

'Wow. Well, I'll have to try them next time.'

I set down my slice of pizza. 'Look, are you OK?'

'I'm fine.'

Raising an eyebrow, I say, 'You know you can talk to me.'

She gazes at her plate and says, 'Thanks.'

When nothing more is forthcoming, I change the subject: 'Do you have any idea who the Green Raven is?'

She reaches for a slice of pizza and takes a bite while she considers my question. Timmy is on the floor beneath her chair, face tilted, in anticipation of donations or crumbs. Mouse is dozing on the floor, beside the still-warm oven, enjoying the break while Timmy is distracted.

'Do you know,' says Nellie, 'I haven't a clue. When I first got here, I thought it must be Mrs Harris. She lives in one of the bungalows near the village hall.'

'Why her?' I ask, picking up my pizza slice and taking another bite.

'At that point, I'd never heard her say anything nice about anyone. But now her daughter's moved in nearby, and she's like a different person. I feel bad, cos maybe she was just lonely.'

'That makes sense. Is there anyone else it might be?'

She narrows her eyes to the ceiling for a moment, then shakes her head. 'It's got to be someone who doesn't work – or at least has a lot of time off. They've got to be around enough to see all the stuff they talk about.'

'That's true. So we're looking for someone who doesn't leave their house, maybe?'

She shakes her head. 'They spot stuff on different roads, so they're getting around. Well, unless they've got spies out there, doing their work for them. Why'd you want to know, anyway?'

I finish my slice and reach for a second. 'It just doesn't seem fair, writing about people and exposing their secrets, but keeping their own identity hidden.'

'It is kind of cowardly,' she agrees. 'Are you planning on taking them down?'

I laugh. 'Not really my job.' I raise an eyebrow and add, 'But, if I knew who it was, I might tell Stella.'

She frowns and dusts off her hands. 'Doesn't Stella know? I mean, she must be commissioning whoever it is.'

I shrug. 'She claims the piece is delivered anonymously in time for every issue.'

Nellie narrows her eyes. 'I think she's bluffing. There's no way she's paying them without knowing who they are.'

'I doubt Stella has a budget for paying contributors,' I say. 'It's only a local rag.'

'Don't let her hear you calling it a "rag",' she says with a grimace.

'Good point. I didn't mean to be derogatory.'

We sit in silence for a moment and then she says softly, 'I keep thinking about those skeletons. There's something awful about them lying there for all that time, without anyone knowing.'

'Well, someone knew,' I say.

'You know what I mean. Everyone's just gone about their business, without any idea there were two dead bodies buried in the middle of the village.'

'Sorry – I didn't mean to trivialise it,' I say. 'It's even worse when you realise that their families probably didn't know they were there. If it is Martin's brother and his girlfriend, I wonder who started the rumour that they'd run away.'

'I've been wondering that,' Nellie says. 'But I think I heard that Charles left a note, so maybe they were murdered before they could run.'

'It makes you wonder if it was his father who discovered them trying to elope,' I say. 'Eldest son, set to take over the family business – I can imagine emotions might run high if it looked like he was sneaking away from his duties.'

'What kind of father would kill his own son?' she says. 'Especially if he wanted him to inherit the business.'

We fall quiet again for a moment, and then I say, 'If there was a note, it could also have been forged after the event.'

'If so, it would have to be someone who knew his writing,' she says.

I know both of us immediately think of Martin again. The younger brother, possibly resentful of his older sibling. Might they have had an argument, and Martin attacked Charles? Perhaps Charles's girlfriend was a witness, or got in the way . . .

It's a horrible thought.

24

My young volunteer Eloise is waiting for me when Mouse and I arrive at the garden site the next morning. I've told the other volunteers I won't be needing them today, because I want to give her all my attention this morning. In the afternoon, of course, I have Mally, the engineer, coming for his inspection.

'Morning!' I say approaching the young woman. 'The alarm worked, then?'

She nods. She seems to have retreated inside both her shyness and her hood.

'Great to see you,' I say. 'This is Mouse.'

'He's gorgeous,' she says. 'Can I stroke him?'

On cue, Mouse trots over to her and licks her gloved hand. 'Oh, you're lovely,' she tells him, taking off her glove to pet him while I unlock the fence panel and move it to the side.

'In we go,' I say.

Once we're inside, I replace the panel and lead the way. Police tape clearly marks off the area where the skeletons were found.

'Are they still there?' she asks, staring at the tape.

'The skeletons? No, they've been removed. We're not allowed back in that section yet, but I want to show you something right next to it. Come on.'

I lead her over to the foundations. 'With garden design, it's important to be adaptable as you discover things about the site – such as water pipes, meters, electricity cables and so on. You might need to cover up something for safety, or disguise an eyesore – and you might sometimes find that something you've turned up can be incorporated into your design. These foundations were already here, and . . . hold on . . .' I rummage in my holdall and draw out my sketchbook, turning to the relevant spread. 'What do you think?'

I pass the book to her, and she stops stroking Mouse to take it from me. Looking from the sketches to the bricks and then to me, she says, 'Are you going to build this?'

I nod. 'Well, I'm going to see if there's a bricklayer in the village who can build it. But first, Mally, the structural engineer we met yesterday, is going to come this afternoon to check the base is safe and can hold the weight.'

'Oh my god, I would have loved a playhouse like this when I was a kid.'

'Do you think there's a risk it might just become a place for teenagers to hang out and smoke?' I ask her.

She frowns in concentration. After a moment's thought, she says, 'You need to make the ceiling really low, so only kids fit in.'

I smile. 'That's a great idea.'

Her face lights up.

'Let me walk you around the site,' I tell her. 'I'll show you what I've got planned so far for the different areas, and you can tell me any ideas you have for improving things.'

'Where's the giant chess set going to go?' she asks.

'I'm not sure. I don't want to take down more trees than I have to. I've done a survey, and some are diseased or rotten, or just growing too close to others. But it feels like we might need to clear a couple to make space for the games room, as I'm going to call it.'

'Won't people expect it to be indoors if you call it a room?'

'That's a good point. In garden design, "rooms" do tend to be more formal, with very definite boundaries. What do you suggest?'

She squints while she considers. 'The games zone.'

'Sounds good.'

As we walk towards the area I've allocated for the sensory garden, I have an idea. 'Hold on . . .' I duck between two rhododendrons to assess an area I spotted previously, before calling for Eloise to join me. 'What do you think?' I ask, gesturing to the hidden clearing. 'We'd need to open it up, but I reckon it could be just the spot for our games zone.'

'It's perfect,' she says, stroking Mouse's ears. He hasn't left her side since they were introduced.

'I'll have to measure the space, but it seems big enough,' I say, making a note. 'We'll need to incorporate level paths so people in wheelchairs can access it easily. And the giant chess set will need a flat base.'

'Is this still garden design?' she says.

'What do you mean?'

'Well, chess tables, giant chess, playhouses . . . Where are the plants?'

I laugh. 'Good point. But yes, designing a garden means taking into account the needs and wishes of your client, so that might include a swimming pool with changing rooms; a tennis court; a miniature stream . . . It's all still about designing an outdoor space, so it's all part of our job as garden designers.'

She nods, gently running a hand along Mouse's tail. He doesn't seem to mind.

After we've completed our tour of the site, avoiding the taped-off area, I take Eloise to get a hot drink at the café. She orders a hot chocolate with cream on top; I get a black coffee with an extra shot; and we each order a slice of cake.

While we wait, I ask about her home life. Apparently, she has three older brothers.

'I'm not allowed a dog,' she says wistfully, gazing into Mouse's eyes. 'Mum says I'd forget to feed it.'

'Would you?'

She shakes her head. 'I mean, I forget lots of things but I could never forget to feed a doggy like you, could I, Mousey?' She talks to him in a baby voice, and he licks her hand. She sounds so certain, I believe her.

'Maybe seeing as you're eighteen, so a grown-up, you could make your case again?'

She shrugs. 'Maybe.'

The café owner brings over a tray and offloads our drinks and cakes; we thank her before she heads back behind the counter.

Eloise stirs her hot chocolate with the long spoon and says, 'I had an idea . . .'

'For the garden?' I ask. When she nods, I say, 'Go on.'

'How about keeping an area like a wood, where kids and their grown-ups can make dens out of branches?'

'Ooh, I like that. So we'd need a steady supply of willow or hazel – something quick growing and flexible . . . There's already some willow and hazel in the park, so we might not even need to plant anything new, just make sure someone is in charge of keeping the pile stocked with new branches that are the right size. You have a brilliant imagination,' I tell her. 'I think you'll be a natural as a garden designer.'

She flushes with pleasure. 'Can I put you in charge of that?' I ask her. 'If I show you where the trees are, do you think you could cut the first branches when we finish the garden, and either take on sourcing new ones, or find someone who's happy to do it?'

She nods.

'Fabulous,' I say, sipping my coffee. After we've finished our drinks and cakes and fed some treats to Mouse, I settle the bill before we don our coats and hats and make our way back out into the chilly day.

'You can head home if you like,' I tell Eloise.

She hesitates, so I say, 'Do you want to come to the site around two thirty, when Mally should be coming over to assess the building base, to see if the kids' playhouse is doable?'

'Can I?'

'Of course.'

'See you in a bit,' she says, waving goodbye and heading off at a jaunty pace.

25

Once again, Eloise is waiting when I get back to the site at twenty past two. In the meantime, I've popped home for a sandwich and left Mouse to doze in our room.

As I reach Eloise, who's leaning against the fence, hood up, and thumbs tapping on her phone, I ask, 'Did you have some lunch?'

She looks up. 'I had a Twix.'

'That's not lunch.' She flushes inside her hood, so I soften my tone as I continue, 'If you want to be a garden designer, you need to fuel your body for the work. Think about including protein with every meal.'

She nods, and I drop the subject, unlocking the panel and letting her inside.

Mally turns up bang on two thirty and the three of us walk over to the foundations.

'So, there was a bungalow here?' he checks.

'That's what I've been told. Apparently, it burned down years ago.'

He takes his time, first walking around the area – being careful not to step past the police tape – then crouching to examine the state of the remaining bricks, measuring their depth, first with a metal tape measure he draws from a pocket, and then with a laser measure he conjures from another. He finishes by walking all over the bricks.

At the end of his inspection, he nods. 'All looks pretty sound to me.'

'So, we can go ahead and build on top of it?'

'Provided you choose the right materials, it should be able to take the miniature building you're proposing. Two and a half metres high by three wide, was it?'

'About that, yes. I'd ideally like two floors, each with a low ceiling.' I smile at Eloise, to acknowledge that this was her idea, to deter teenagers.

'If you let me know what materials you're using, I'll provide more formal calculations. You can excavate any extra rubble – it might be useful as hardcore for your remaining builds. Let me know if you need help finding a decent builder. There's one in the village, plus a couple of others I know in the Colchester area.'

'Brilliant, thanks so much.'

He stands, looking thoughtfully at the foundations for a moment, before turning to me and saying, 'Is this where Kieran Galloway's grandparents lived?'

'That's right. Do you know him?'

'I only just made the connection. He's in my chess club. I get the impression he's never got over what happened to his grand-parents. Did you hear they never charged anyone with the arson?'

'Kieran suggested there was a cover-up,' I say.

Mally looks sceptical. 'He's a bit of a conspiracy theorist,' he says. 'He also thinks the moon landings didn't happen.'

'In this case, he believes that someone in power paid off the local constabulary.'

He's silent for a moment, crouching to re-examine a brick that's slightly higher than the others. When he straightens, he turns to look at me and says, 'Let's be honest here – Martin Patterson is not a popular man.'

I stare at him. 'He thinks Martin killed his grandparents?'

Mally winces as if he's revealed more than he intended. 'Oh – I assumed you were referring to the Pattersons.'

'I wasn't, but I can see where power would come in if it was Martin.'

Eloise says, 'Mum says she's surprised he's still living in the village. Apparently, he's had death threats.'

'Really?' I say. 'Do you know who sent them?'

She shakes her head. 'But Mum reckons it's someone who lost their job when the factory shut.'

'I wasn't living here then,' says Mally, 'but, from what I've heard, it does sound as though it was mishandled. I reckon better management might have stopped the business from going under. It's no wonder people here are still smarting.'

'Where was the factory?' I ask.

'Haven't you seen it?' says Eloise. 'It's the building behind the big gates on Hogs Green Road.'

'Oh, that's the road I'm staying on, in a house called Magpies,' I say.

Mally says, 'Oh yes – one of the old management houses. If you pass your house on the right and continue along Hogs Green, cross over Tabernacle Street, and you'll come to the works on the right. It has a keep out sign. It's an interesting building – worth a look through the gates.'

'I'll have to wander over.'

'Did Mr Galloway lose his job, too?' asks Eloise.

'Kieran?' says Mally. 'I believe both his parents did. He does something in finance, and works from home.'

Eloise says, 'So he must really hate Mr Patterson, if both his parents lost their jobs because of him.'

Mally doesn't answer, so I say, 'As you've both said already, I imagine a lot of villagers feel resentful towards Martin Patterson.'

'I'd move away if I was him,' says Eloise.

I laugh. 'You seem very keen to see Martin move away.'

'No, I mean Kieran,' she says. 'Imagine having to keep seeing the man who might have killed your nan and granddad, and then lost your parents their jobs.'

We are all silent for a moment, before Mally turns to me and says, 'I'll be in touch with some details for possible builders for the playhouse.'

'Brilliant. Thanks so much.'

We shake hands and he strides away, hands in pockets and coat collar turned up against the wind which is picking up as the day goes on.

'Can I come back tomorrow?' asks Eloise while I lock up.

I click the padlock into place, then turn to her and say, 'You'd be very welcome. Thanks for your help today.'

She smiles and I watch her start for home.

And then I cross into Argent Street, which leads to my own place of residence.

Remembering Mally's recommendation to view the factory, I turn on to Hogs Green Road and pass Magpies, continuing on until I reach the metal gates. It's three thirty and starting to get dark, but I can make out the silhouette of the old building.

My first thought is that I've never seen so many roofs on one edifice before. It's a long, low rectangle, set at right angles to the road, and bearing small, triangular roofs along its length, like the bony plates on the spine of a stegosaurus.

My second thought is that the whole site – from the main building to its surrounding hardstanding – seems deserted and neglected.

I shiver and turn for home. But, at that moment, a movement near the far left-hand end of the factory catches my eye. It's a pair of figures in dark coats coming out of a door. They're too far away to identify – not that I know many people in Greenhaven – but it seems strange that they are hanging around here just before twilight. I'm about to call Avery, to check they aren't intruders of some kind, when a silver Audi Q4 approaches, stealthy as a spider with its near-silent electric power. It slows on the approach to the factory, and I move out of the way. I see Avery at the wheel, involved in what is clearly a heated conversation with her passenger. I squint into the car, and make out her companion. It's Martin Patterson.

They don't spot me, and I don't wait to greet them: whatever their disagreement, I don't want to find myself in the middle of it. I start walking home, glancing back just once, to see Avery climbing out of the car, presumably to open the gates.

On my short walk along Hogs Green Road, past the former managers' houses that are nearly identical to Magpies, I mull over the fact that the supposedly out-of-bounds factory appears to be in use by a group of people. And then I wonder why Avery and Martin would choose to drive, rather than walk the short distance from their respective homes of Herons and Eagles.

It seems to me that the only reason for them to travel by car would be if they didn't want to be seen.

26

'So you reckon they're meeting in secret?' says Nellie over dinner that evening.

I shrug. 'It looks that way, but what do I know?' I fork up a piece of fried tofu, which is golden and crispy. 'You might have to teach me to cook at this rate,' I say. 'Otherwise, I'm going to be in withdrawal from your food when I leave Greenhaven.'

She laughs and raises an eyebrow. 'Do you want it enough, though? I'm happy to teach you, but you have to want to learn.'

'Are you going to make me polish your car for days?' I say.

'Oh, I get it!' she says, '"Wax on, wax off" like in *The Karate Kid*.' She tilts her head. 'Hmm. I might. Or I'm sure I can devise some devilish tasks of my own for you.'

'Thanks a lot.'

She grins, then turns serious. 'So, if you saw Martin Patterson with Avery, chances are there's some clandestine deal going on, where they're trying to get him to agree to . . .' She thinks for a moment before saying, 'If he's used up all the money, I can't see what they could want from him. Maybe they want him to give up his house.'

'Why would he do that?' I ask.

She shrugs. 'To make amends. Like the Nazis having to give back the art they stole from the Jews.'

'Whoa! That's a pretty extreme comparison.'

'What about the people in Greenhaven who lost everything? The ones with family members who killed themselves?'

'There were suicides?' I ask in horror.

She nods. 'I've heard of at least two people who were made redundant when the factory went under, and who couldn't get work because they were considered too old or infirm.'

'What work had they been doing?' I asked.

'Did you know the original Mr Patterson made a point of hiring injured soldiers from the First World War?'

'He sounds a pretty impressive man,' I say.

'If you overlook the whole control freak thing I mentioned – you know, how he made a village that his workers would never have an excuse to leave?' She continues: 'Yeah, so old Mr P made it so one whole area of the factory focused on making small pieces of furniture that would mean the workers didn't need a lot of strength to build them. They produced things like the stools we're sitting on now, Formica tables like this one, and small side tables – that kind of thing. He was quite into the Arts and Crafts movement, and he bought into the idea that, instead of each worker only making one section of something, they'd work on the whole thing. It meant they had more of a connection with what they were making. It was meant to be better for their mental health. So a worker could make an entire stool, for instance.'

'Do you know, I like the sound of Grandfather Patterson.'

She nods. 'Yeah, I know I keep saying he was a control freak, but it seems like he did really care. As the injured soldiers retired and were replaced with younger models, the factory started making more of the bigger pieces of furniture, like sofas and armchairs. But they always made sure there were jobs for disabled workers. One of the women who applied the Formica laminate sheets to the tables was blind, apparently.'

'How do you know all this?'

'Ohhh.' She stabs a piece of green pepper and examines it as if it might reveal something in its glossy surface. 'I've talked to a lot of villagers while I've been here.' Looking up, she adds, 'I'm creating a kind of . . . oral experience project – you know, what people think about living here.'

'I've not known you long but you keep surprising me,' I tell her.

'Once this place gets its talons into you, it doesn't let go easily,' she says, putting the pepper in her mouth. 'You'll see – you'll end up wanting to know everything. I think it's why the Green Raven manages to have such a strong presence. People who live here talk about the village like it's a part of them rather than just a place, you know?'

'They do seem pretty devoted,' I say, thinking of the fact that the village has its own Heritage Society; the way Norma has painted the walls inside her house to resemble a fantastical greenhouse; and how in Avery's house, Herons, plus Stella and Jeremy's place, Woodpeckers – and, indeed, here at Magpies – the furniture either is original or has been kept as faithful to the period as possible.

'It's a beautiful place,' says Nellie. She pauses and adds, 'But it has a lot of pain.'

'Not so much a haven as the name suggests,' I say, and she nods, looking sad.

'Wine?' she says suddenly, pushing back her stool. 'I forgot I got another bottle at the Co-op earlier.'

After the wine has been poured, our conversation lightens, until we're talking about her obsession with *Bridgerton*, and how she wants to make herself a dress with a low-cut bodice.

'Do you make your own clothes?' I ask.

'Nope. But how hard can it be?'

'Maybe start with something simple,' I suggest. 'You know, like a tea towel or a cushion cover.'

'You're probably right. I do have a tendency to dive straight in at the deep end.'

I shudder as this expression brings back an unwelcome memory from my last placement – a body, floating in a pool.

'You all right? You look like someone just walked over your grave.'

'It wasn't my grave,' I say. Then, not wanting to dwell on unwelcome reminders, I change the subject: 'How's your painting of Wrens coming on? Was it a series?'

'Yeah: four paintings of the house at different times of the year. The owners supplied me with photos that show the cherry tree in flower with loads of crocuses for spring, a mass of orange, red and yellow flowers in summer – I think they said they're dahlias? – then the cherry tree with gold leaves in autumn, and finally snow on the ground plus berries on the holly tree in winter. It's all nearly done, just a few finishing touches to 'winter'. They seem really happy with it all. After that, I want to do a series of paintings of well-known local characters.'

'Really? That sounds brilliant.'

She nods. 'I keep asking Avery to pose for some sketches, but she's proving elusive.'

'She is a greyhound,' I say, without thinking. When she stares at me in bemusement, I laugh and explain my observations about Avery's sinewy build.

'Right, so what kind of dog am I?' she asks.

'Oh, it's not as if everyone's a breed of dog,' I say. 'It's just that Avery struck me that way the first time we met and I can't shake the impression.'

'I think I'm a Jack Russell,' she says. 'You know – little and a bit manic.' I don't point out that she's just described Timmy, who mercifully has worn himself out and is asleep in the living room with Mouse. Studying me for a minute, Nellie says, 'I reckon you're a lurcher, maybe? Or a wolfhound? Something lean and strong, but mysterious.'

I laugh. 'Mysterious?'

'Well, compared to me.'

'I don't know,' I say. 'I reckon you've got secrets of your own.'

When she doesn't answer, instead licking her finger and becoming intent on removing a spot of soy sauce from her polo neck, I feel a clench of concern. I find myself wondering what Nellie is hiding, and hoping it won't affect me along the way.

27

'Does anyone use the old factory?' I ask Norma on Thursday morning.

Pulling on a pair of gardening gloves, she says, 'Not that I know of. Why?'

'Oh, I just thought I saw somebody there last night.'

'I hope not,' she says. 'There's been some vandalism at the site – and someone's stolen the sign from the gate. I hope they haven't caused any more damage.'

'Is it going to be renovated or demolished?'

'It's a piece of architectural history,' she says. 'I keep saying we need to turn it into an arts centre, with studios and a gallery.'

'That sounds amazing, but is there enough call for it here?'

'The village has plenty of artists,' she says, echoing what Nellie told me. 'And I'm sure we could attract more – we're not far from Braintree and Colchester.'

'You're not on about that arts centre again are you, Norma?' comes Christy's voice from close by.

'I'm not "on about" anything, Christy,' she says crossly. Lowering her voice, she adds: 'Just because he's about as artistic as a piece of chewed gum.'

I hold up my hands. 'Now, now.'

'Well, it's true. Right, where do you want me?'

Norma arrived late as usual, and everyone else is already at their tasks. I send her to work with Eloise, who's measuring up the area for the wooden car that will be 'parked' outside the playhouse.

I want to get the digger back in, but the police have made it clear I'm not allowed machinery until they've finished with the skeletons' trench. Instead, I'm ensuring we get as much as possible done manually in the meantime. Leo and Christy are digging up ivy roots, while Marion is attacking various buddleia shrubs with my wonderful ratchet loppers. I'm following her path, digging up the buddleia roots once she's cut the plants to the ground. It's hard work, and I'm sweating by the time Avery comes by in the afternoon.

She's dressed in a dark knee-length coat with a rounded collar, a toque pulled low over her grey bob. There's something 1920s about the look, which suits her lean frame. 'I just thought I'd pop by to see how you're getting on,' she says.

'Not bad, thanks,' I say, pushing my fork into the ground and wiping my forehead on my sleeve.

Catching sight of Avery, Norma comes over. 'Steph thinks the vandals might have been back at the factory.'

Avery frowns. 'Really? What did you see?' she asks me.

'Oh . . . nothing, really. It's Norma who thought it might be vandals. To be honest, I thought there was a meeting of some sort.'

'When was this?' asks Avery, frowning.

'Yesterday, late afternoon.'

There's a moment's pause before she says, 'Oh, don't worry: I know what that must have been. I just went to check on the site – make sure everything was still locked up tight and so on. I do it from time to time, since the vandals broke in. Anyway, what were you doing at the factory at night?'

'It was hardly night. I'd only just wrapped up here. I was just passing by.'

'In the dark?'

'Like I said, it wasn't dark yet – not that it would have deterred me if it had been. Sometimes I enjoy an evening stroll. Mouse usually comes, too. And our morning runs often start in darkness, with me wearing a head torch, so we're used to a lack of light.'

'You must have been eating your carrots,' says Norma with a smile.

Christy's voice comes booming over: 'You do know that isn't really a thing?'

Norma sighs loudly and rolls her eyes. 'I think I'll get on,' she tells me, walking off to join Eloise near the rubble, where they are trying to work around the police tape to establish the shape of the playhouse, and how far it needs to extend.

Avery turns back to me. 'I do hope we haven't made the wrong call, hiring you.' She gestures to the site. 'As far as I can tell, very little progress has been made.'

I'm taken aback by her sudden change in tone and manner. 'It's deceptive,' I say.

She raises a sceptical eyebrow. 'How so?'

'Christy and Leo have done an amazing job on the bramble clearing, and they're now digging out ivy roots. Marion and I are clearing unwanted buddleias. We can't start the build until we've got the ground prepared. And, of course, we're hampered by the discovery of the skeletons – it means we can't just bring in machines to do all the heavy work.'

'Poor Charlie and Megan,' she says with a sigh. I'm relieved to see her diverted from her criticism.

'So have their identities been officially confirmed?' I ask.

'They have, according to our indiscreet village policeman,' she says. 'Not that anyone doubted who they were. Such a waste of young lives.'

'Is anyone being charged with their deaths?' I ask tentatively.

This proves a mistake: she draws herself up and says, 'I'm sorry – is there some way in which you are involved in this matter? Did you know Charlie or Megan? Were you related to either of them?'

'No,' I say, attempting a meek tone. I really want to stay to finish this job.

Shaking her head, she says, 'Steph, are you under the impression that your role here is anything other than to create a garden for the village to use and enjoy?'

'No, I just . . .'

She holds up a hand. 'No, I'm sorry. We have a village constable, and a sterling detective sergeant with her own team. I know you've got away with playing Nancy Drew, or whatever your own generation's equivalent might be, at one or two of your previous places of employment. That will not hold here, do you hear me?'

There's only so much lecturing I can take. 'Avery,' I say slowly, 'I'm not sure what your own previous employment entailed, but you seem to be under the impression that I am a small child whom you can hector and control. I am a grown woman and an experienced professional, accustomed to managing my own time. With my input, Greenhaven will gain a wonderful garden, both beautiful and useful. It will benefit many generations. But I unearthed those skeletons and, as such, it's only natural that I'm curious as to their identities and why they were killed.'

Her mouth has dropped open, in a manner that suggests Avery Sinclair is not accustomed to having people talk back to her. I feel a sense of satisfaction at going against the tide in that respect. Until today, I rather liked the woman, but she needs to know that I am not a pushover.

Her lips thin with disapproval, she says stiffly, 'If you're quite finished, then I have somewhere I need to be.'

'Enjoy the rest of your day,' I say.

She nods and leaves without another word, and I set to work digging out buddleia roots, not stopping for a break until I've burned off my rage.

28

'She's lying,' I tell my brother Danny later that day on a video call, after filling him in on my lecture from Avery.

'About how you should keep your nose out?' he says. 'Only, I think she's got a point.'

I roll my eyes. 'About it just being her at the factory. I saw two other people moving about – and she pulled in with Martin in the car.'

'I refer you to my previous comment.'

'Thanks for your support.'

'Come on, sis. She hires you to make a garden, and you're sniffing around after skeletons . . .'

'. . . which *I* found,' I point out.

'. . . which you found, yes, but whom you didn't know.'

'True,' I say grudgingly.

'And then isn't it this Avery woman's business who she meets in the factory? Isn't she like the head of the NIMBY committee?'

I laugh. 'That is what the committee's called, yes.'

He smiles. 'So, maybe, for once . . . could you focus on making a garden?' There's a long pause, then he says, with a sigh, 'But you're not going to do that, are you?'

'Unlikely. So, tell me about my niece and nephews.'

'Frankie is currently a horse.'

'Really? Are you keeping him in a field?'

'Apparently, he's a special type of horse that subsists largely on Coco Pops and chocolate milkshake.'

'I think I want to be that type of horse.'

He laughs. 'Don't we all?'

'How's Alice?'

'She's won another prize for her creative writing.'

'Ah! That's great! Tell her well done from me. And send over the winning piece, when you have time. I'd like to read it.'

'Will do.'

'How about Luke and Stevie?'

'Stevie's started walking, so nothing's safe, especially him. And Luke still climbs on everything, especially stuff that we haven't got round to tying down.'

'Argh!'

'Exactly. He's got some serious thrill-seeker gene that he didn't get from me or Karen.'

'Can you wrap him in padding of some sort?'

'Karen came up with a rule where we don't take him to the playground unless he agrees to wear a bike helmet.'

'Wise woman.'

'That she is.'

'Have you heard from Mum and Dad?' I ask. 'I haven't told them about the skeletons.'

'Probably sensible. Did you hear about Dad's new passion?'

'You mean the violin?'

'Oh gawd, the violin! That's a sore topic, as you can imagine. I think Mum would handle it better if he was getting lessons, at least. But he's insisting he can learn to play from this book he picked up in the library sale. He inflicted a fifteen-minute concert on us last weekend. But I'm not even talking about that. He's also growing a forest of those insect-eating plants. Some of them look big enough to swallow a grown man.'

'Where's he doing that? I thought he was in trouble with the allotment board, after that guerilla planting he was doing on other people's plots.'

'Kitchen windowsill, living room windowsill, dining room windowsill . . . Mum keeps complaining cos she can't shut any of the blinds.'

'I wonder why he always has to find a project that winds Mum up,' I muse.

'Maybe that's part of the selection criteria.'

'That would explain it.'

'Are you and Verity still doing the crosswords?' he asks.

'Well, I'm attempting to. She's definitely better at it than me, but it's a nice way to keep in touch without too much pressure, you know?'

He nods. 'I'm glad it's working out, sis.'

I smile at him. 'Me, too.'

'Right: I can hear a battle breaking out in the bathroom over who gets to play with the squirting octopus, so I'd better get up there before they take their mother hostage.'

I laugh. 'What a knight in shining armour you are.'

He sticks his tongue out at me and we end the call.

My mind is swirling with information and the lack of it, so I grab my notebook, take my seat at the curved wooden dressing table, and spend a few minutes making notes. I write:

1. Skeletons confirmed as Martin Patterson's older brother Charles and his girlfriend, Megan.
2. Who killed the above? Was it Martin? Why were they murdered?
3. Why was Avery so defensive about last night's activities at the disused factory?
4. Who is the Green Raven?

Although I have no answers, I feel a bit lighter for laying it all out on the page.

And then I run downstairs, to join Nellie for hot chocolate and homemade lemon drizzle cake in front of her choice of television, while the dogs snooze beside the radiator, bellies exposed in a bliss of relaxation.

* * *

Friday passes slowly, as – in the absence of machinery – we're having to excavate root-impacted areas manually, using forks and spades. I'm so grateful for my volunteers' uncomplaining approach to the physical labour that I treat them all to coffee and cake for afternoon tea, and send them home early after wishing them a good weekend.

I don't get a chance to talk to Nellie that night about the identity of the skeletons, as I find a note from her when I get home, telling me that she and Timmy have gone to her relatives' again and won't be back until Sunday night.

'Just you and me again, boy,' I tell Mouse.

He does not seem as sorry as I am about this news, and I can't say I blame him.

29

On Monday, after another quiet weekend filled with explorations of the area, Mouse and I return from our run to find his bowls already stocked with food and water, and a stack of pancakes sitting on the table for the humans. Nellie is at the table, holding a wriggling Timmy on her lap.

'He keeps trying to eat your food,' she tells Mouse. 'You'd better get in there quickly.'

Whether he understands or not, Mouse does not need encouragement to eat, and trots straight to his bowls.

'This looks good,' I say, taking my usual stool at right angles to Nellie. She has the *Green Maven* newspaper open on the table, and I realise it's the new edition.

With more than a little dread, I say, 'What does our resident corvid have to say this week?'

'What's a corvid?' she asks, placing Timmy down on the floor at last. He gives her a disgusted look before slinking into the corner to chew on my – or perhaps I should say his – trainer.

Assuming my best nature voiceover impression, I say: 'A corvid is a member of the crow family, such as the rook, the jay, the jackdaw, the magpie – and our neighbourhood oracle, the raven.'

'Right,' she says, laughing. 'I haven't looked yet. Hold on . . .' She turns to the page and begins to read. '"The largest bird in any community is not necessarily the most powerful. As your feathered correspondent can attest, where eagles fly, crows also may gather."'

She frowns. 'What do you think that means? The Raven's normally a bit less cryptic – like you can usually work out who they're talking about.'

I frown as I work it out. 'Eagles must be a reference to Martin Patterson, as that's the name of his house. But who are the crows that are gathering?'

Taking a pancake from the stack and putting it on her plate, she begins to pour a spiral of maple syrup on to it. Once satisfied, she rolls the pancake and takes a big bite. Syrup comes dripping out at the bottom, spilling down her polo neck. She rubs at it with her spare hand, which only rubs it further into the fabric. With her mouth still full, she looks up at me and says, 'I reckon pretty much anyone in the village could be a crow, with their sights on Martin. He's not exactly anyone's favourite person, is he?' She swallows hard and takes a gulp of coffee.

I sip my own coffee and place a pancake on my plate before reaching for a banana.

'So, it's a threat?' I say, as I peel the banana and start to slice it.

She shrugs. 'I don't know if threats are the Raven's style . . . More like a warning, maybe.'

'Do they say anything else?' I ask.

'Nothing else about eagles, but you get another mention.'

I groan. 'What now? Am I going to be pecked to death by a gaggle of geese?'

'Actually, it's a nice one this time:

'"Flocks migrated to the library on Tuesday, where this feathered reporter has it on good authority that our new introduction is acclimatising well. The outcome remains to be seen, but this bird, for one, is cautiously optimistic."'

'Why do I feel like you're reading me my horoscope?' I say. 'Except that, while I don't believe in astrology, I do have an underlying fear that the Green Raven is somehow controlling things, do you know what I mean?'

'Timmy, no!' says Nellie. I hadn't noticed, but the little dog has been using Mouse's tail as a toy, jumping on it and batting at it like a kitten with a ball of wool. She gets up and grabs Timmy, placing him in the hall and shutting the kitchen door. Almost immediately, he starts up a pitiful whining and scrabbling on the other side. Mouse comes to sit beside me, grinning and looking for all the world like he's won a prize. I study him for a moment but, as I can't see how he could have set out to get Timmy into trouble, I decide that he's simply relieved to be free of his tormentor.

'Is that it from the Raven?' I ask Nellie once she's settled back to her breakfast with the paper on the table beside her.

She scans it. 'Something about a lack of bird seed?' she says.

'Read it to me,' I say, biting into my banana and chocolate spread-filled pancake.

'"The current near-seedless state means this little bird may soon be starved. Do share your titbits with your feathered friend, if you can spare the time."'

'Oh!' she says, 'They've just found a new way to say they want people to share gossip.'

'Seems like it,' I say.

'Clever,' she muses.

'If a bit totalitarian,' I say, 'encouraging people to tittle-tattle on their friends and neighbours.'

She shudders. 'I hadn't thought of it like that. I'm starting to wish . . . I mean, I thought the Green Raven was a force for good at the start. But now . . .'

'I know what you mean. There's something distinctly sinister about the column, isn't there?'

'It's like it's polluting the village,' she says. She surprises me by standing.

'You've only had one pancake,' I say.

'Two. You just weren't paying attention. But I have to get this sweater in the wash before the syrup stains.'

'Sure. Thanks so much for this. I'll clear away when I'm done.'

'Just put any leftover pancakes in the fridge.'

'Will do.'

She downs her coffee and leaves the room, narrowly managing to prevent Timmy from zooming in as she leaves. 'No,' she says from the other side of the door. 'Leave poor Mouse in peace.' The whining starts back up, but thankfully recedes as the little dog presumably follows her upstairs.

After clearing away the breakfast things and setting the dishwasher, I go for my shower. Mouse accompanies me upstairs, settling in the bedroom. I make sure the door's shut as I head for the bathroom. Passing Nellie's door, I can just about hear her talking to someone, above the sound of Timmy's growls. He must have found new prey.

I'm surprised that she's on the phone, when I thought she was in such a hurry to get her jumper in the wash. But perhaps the other person rang her.

I stop for a moment when she starts shouting. 'This is not what we agreed.'

Deciding it's not my business, I continue on my way. I wish Nellie would confide in me, as something is clearly troubling her.

Once I'm dressed, Mouse and I head over to the site, where the volunteers and I spend another day at manual labour. At my request, Eloise and Norma have started to mark out the different areas in chalk, although most of these are still in need of major root removal.

I've had an email from Mally, the structural engineer, with information on sourcing an outdoor games table for chess and backgammon, so I add the details into my budget.

By the end of the afternoon, things have progressed to a point where I really will have to get on to the police about letting in the machinery for more digging and prepping. But, knowing how overstretched the force are, I'm not holding out much hope.

Nevertheless, I call DS Timpson when I get home. She takes my call, but it's clear she's in a hurry. When I explain my business, she says, 'Not until we've sent a team for a final inspection of the pit, to make sure we've not missed anything.'

'When will that be?'

'I can't say for sure. Was there anything else?'

I run through all of the things I'd like to ask her about her investigation, but I know she won't tell me anything, so I say, 'No, that's it.'

'Right. I'll let you know when it's clear for you to go ahead.'

'Thanks.'

* * *

Over dinner that evening, I ask Nellie, 'Did you hear about the skeletons? I completely forgot this morning, with all the Green Raven stuff.'

She puts down her fork. 'What? Do you know who they are?'

'The village grapevine was right – it is Martin's brother Charles and his girlfriend, Megan.'

Nellie meets my eye. 'And this is definite?'

I shrug. 'It came from Hawkins, so . . .'

'So Avery was right,' she says quietly.

'She was. But I get the impression most people who were around back then assumed it would turn out to be Charles and Megan.'

'It's so awful,' she says. 'I mean, I only know stuff about the village from what people have told me, but that disappearance was the stuff of legend. Some people made it sound dead romantic, you know? The whole star-crossed lovers malarkey.' She pokes at her bowl of mushroom stroganoff with her fork. 'Really, they were there the whole time, dumped in a makeshift grave.'

'Who do you think killed them?' I say.

She meets my eye. 'It's got to be Martin, hasn't it? I mean, who else would've had it in for Charles? He was the golden boy.'

'That kind of person does tend to attract jealousy,' I say. 'There might have been other people who resented him.'

She pulls a face. 'Yeah, but everyone else in the village wanted him to take over running the factory. He'd had the education for it, and was mature and thoughtful – not like Martin, who was always getting into trouble.'

'What kind of trouble?'

'Oh, from what I've heard, he was a right hooligan, up to all sorts of thieving and vandalism, and getting into fights and stuff. Mummy and Daddy kept having to bail him out.'

I raise an eyebrow. 'In other words, about as charming and delightful as he is now.'

We both huff a laugh. Then she says, 'I'm glad the Raven didn't lay into you again this week.'

'Me, too. It made me quite uneasy the last time.'

'I don't blame you. It upset me, too, to be honest.'

She sets down her fork again and I look at her in surprise.

'Are you done? You've barely touched your stroganoff, which is delicious, by the way.'

She shrugs. 'Maybe I'm going down with something. Do you mind if I turn in?'

'Of course not. I hope you're OK. Message or call me if you need anything.'

'Will do. Thanks.' She gets to her feet and leaves the room, and I hear her rounding up Timmy before ushering him upstairs – no mean feat, given his distractible nature.

I'm left with my own musings. My mind moves from the sad deaths of the two young people to my progress with the centenary garden. Whatever I may have maintained to Avery last week, things are not going as quickly or smoothly as I'd hoped. I finish dinner and clear away, then head up to bed early, worn out from all the digging. Mouse is already snoring in his corner.

It's only when I climb into bed that I recall that a 'gathering' of crows is known as a 'murder'.

30

My second encounter with PC Hawkins is, if possible, more frustrating than the first.

Although he's in uniform when he opens his door to me at three thirty in the afternoon, his hair is in disarray and he's unshaven. Against a blaring background of what even I recognise as the theme from *EastEnders*, he pulls a face and says, 'You again! Not more skeletons, I hope?'

'No, but I'm concerned . . .'

He holds up a hand to stop me. 'Just a minute.'

He vanishes back inside, and the television thankfully goes quiet.

'Can I come in?' I ask when he reappears in the doorway.

He glances behind him, presumably assessing the state of his home, then turns back to me. 'Best not.'

'OK then. Well, I'm concerned about the Raven's latest column.'

He frowns. 'What raven?'

This is going to be a long one. Taking a deep breath, I say slowly, 'Have you seen this week's *Green Maven*?'

'I have, yes. I thought your questionnaire was a good idea.'

'Thanks. But that was a couple of weeks back.'

'Oh! Are you talking about the Green Raven?'

'I am, yes.'

'Seems to be all nonsense as far as I can tell,' he says.

I shake my head. 'It's word play, hints and riddles.'

'If you say so.'

Suppressing a sigh, I say, 'Have you got your copy to hand?'

Again, he glances inside. I find myself picturing untidy piles of newspapers, paperwork and detritus. 'Not to hand, as such . . .' he says slowly.

'Right, well I've taken a picture, so . . .' I find the image on my phone and pass it to him.

He glances down at the screen, then back to me, holding out my phone. 'Right. Thanks for showing me that. Still none the wiser.'

I don't take my phone. 'Can't you see it?' I say.

'See what?'

Pulling teeth, I think. 'There's a threat to Martin Patterson.'

He makes a scoffing sound. 'Where d'you get that from?'

I recite from memory, '"where eagles fly, crows also may gather."'

'Like I said, nonsense.'

'Where does Martin Patterson live?' I say.

'At Eagles. What's that got to do . . . ?' His voice trails off as he looks down at my phone. After a long pause, he looks back up. 'So, who are these crows, then?'

'I'm not sure, but I think it's a threat, or possibly a warning.'

'What kind of threat?'

'Martin's very unpopular in the village, isn't he?'

'I wouldn't say that. He's the lord of the manor, so there's bound to be resentment – jealousy, you know? – but Mr Patterson's not a bad one, as they go.'

'Listen,' I say. 'As I'm sure you know, a gathering of crows is called a murder.'

He makes a scoffing sound. 'Are you suggesting someone wants Mr Patterson dead? Look, Ms Williams, I'm sure you mean well, but Greenhaven is a quiet place. We don't have murders here.'

'Except for the two skeletons over the road.'

His face turns red and he hands my phone back. 'Now, look, I don't know where you come from, but here we don't go around throwing allegations about the place.'

'Peterborough,' I say.

'What?'

'That's where I'm from. And we don't throw allegations about the place there, either. Believe me, I wouldn't be here if I wasn't genuinely worried.'

I see the door close in Hawkins' face before his literal door closes in mine. What next? Glancing towards the large white form of Eagles, I realise I will have to go direct.

* * *

Unfortunately, Martin Patterson seems no happier than Hawkins to find me on his doorstep. And that's before I even state my business.

He's looking especially smart, in a checked tweed suit with a maroon handkerchief in the breast pocket. He greets me with, 'Did John not show you everything you needed?'

'He did, yes, thank you. I'm not here about that. Can I talk to you for a moment?'

He makes a show of checking his watch. And then, with a sigh, he opens the door wider. 'You'd better come in. But I haven't got long.'

I step into a large hallway with quite a grand staircase. He leads me through a door to our right, into a sitting room. When he gestures for me to take a seat, I perch on the edge of an armchair and he takes the one opposite. I don't have time to take in my surroundings, because he launches straight in:

'So, Steph, isn't it? What can I help you with?'

I take a deep breath. 'Did you read the latest Green Raven column, the one in yesterday's paper?'

He frowns and gets to his feet. Striding to an oak magazine rack, he takes *The Green Maven* from the front of a stash of newspapers and walks back to me. 'It's here. Why?'

Here we go again. 'The Green Raven . . .' I prompt, and he turns to the column and begins to read. I am expecting – perhaps even hoping for – a sudden paling of his skin. Instead, he sits back down, scans the piece, then sets it on a coffee table beside him. 'Well?' he says.

'"Where eagles fly, crows also may gather,"' I prompt.

He shrugs. 'That's true enough.'

'You don't think it's a direct warning to you – possibly even a threat?'

He makes a scoffing sound before getting to his feet, hands in pockets, the most casual of stances. 'Hardly! My word, you gardeners clearly have too much time on your hands. Now, if you'll excuse me, I really do need to get on.' He gestures for me to leave.

As he sees me out of the living room and tries to usher me through the front door, I turn and make one last attempt to get through to him: 'I think you should be on your guard, at least,' I say. 'The Green Raven chooses their words carefully. If "eagles" and "murder" are in one sentence . . .'

'Where on earth did you get murder from in that?' he asks.

'A gathering of crows,' I say. When he still looks blank, I add, 'The collective noun for a group of crows is a murder.'

'Oh. Is that all? Right, well, I appreciate your concern, but this is Greenhaven.'

Once again, I find myself on the wrong side of a closed door. With a sigh, I head for home.

31

'Did you hear about the statue?' Norma asks me the next morning.

She's just arrived on site – late as usual – and she's clearly eager to impart her news.

'What statue?' I ask.

Christy comes over from a nearby beech tree, where he's been lopping off dead branches. 'Norma, what are you starting now?'

She bridles. 'I'm not starting anything, Christy. I'm just asking Steph if she has heard about the statue.'

'Steph has more important things to be getting on with than becoming embroiled in village gossip,' he says.

She puts her hands on her hips. 'Honestly, Christy, you can be such a bore at times. Why don't you toddle on back to your work and let Steph decide for herself if she wants to hear what was discovered *buried with the skeletons*.'

'I definitely want to hear,' I say.

Christy and his loppers return to their tree, though not before he's muttered that caring about doing things the right way is not the same as being boring.

Norma gestures for me to take a seat on a large tree stump, which I do, and she sits beside me, patting her gloved hands together for warmth.

'Do you know the story about the missing statue from Eagles?' she asks.

'Is this the one the housekeeper was accused of stealing?'

She nods. 'Poor Nancy O'Donoghue was fired over it. She always swore she hadn't touched it, except when she was dusting. It was one of a pair on the mantelpiece.'

I frown. 'If it was one of a pair, why would the family think she'd stolen it? Surely anyone stealing it would take its mate as well?'

'That was one of the things she kept pointing out, first to her employers and then to anyone who'd listen. But the Pattersons were adamant. You see, she was the only one outside the family with keys to the house.'

'And you're saying it's turned up now, buried with the skeletons?' I say.

'That's right.'

'Sounds like the murder weapon,' I muse.

'But there's no way Nancy murdered anyone,' says Norma.

'Did you know her?'

'I was friends with her daughter, Olivia. She was only fifteen when her mum killed herself. She emigrated to the States as soon as she was old enough. She said there were too many reminders round here. I can't say I blame her, though I was devastated when she left.'

'It all sounds awful.'

She nods. 'And now the statue's turned up, buried with Charles and Megan.'

'How did you hear about the statue?' I ask. 'About it being buried with the bodies, I mean.'

'Eddie,' she says. When I look blank, she says, 'Eddie Hawkins, the village bobby.'

I frown. 'I think Avery said something about him being indiscreet, but surely he's not allowed to reveal important details of a live investigation?'

'Oh, Eddie's a law unto himself. He goes drinking at the Feathers, and all sorts of things spill out. My next-door neighbour was there last night, and she overheard him talking to Sam, the barman.' She sighs, and I see a tear on her cheek. 'It's all so horrible. I think we all wanted to believe the two youngsters had got away and started a new life. But they've been dead this whole time. Such a waste.'

I squeeze her shoulder. 'I imagine the whole village must be in shock.'

'Some more than others. Many have moved here since it happened, so they won't know much about it, whereas this is where I grew up, so I remember it all.'

Thinking about Nancy getting the blame for the statue's disappearance, I say, 'I can't get my head around the idea that the family refused to believe Nancy was innocent. I mean, if Charles went missing at the same time, why didn't they assume he'd taken it, to get some cash?'

'I think it took a couple of weeks before anyone noticed that the statue was missing, so they didn't link the two events,' says Norma. 'They were very caught up in the search for Charles.' She shivers. 'I'm getting cold, sitting here.'

I stand. 'Let's get the blood pumping. Are you OK to help Christy over there? He's digging out ivy and bramble roots.'

She pulls a face. 'Really? You want me to work with Christy?'

His voice reaches us, 'I can hear you, you know, Norma.'

She sighs and calls brightly, in an accent like something out of *Little House on the Prairie*, 'And I'm just *itchin'* to work with you, Christy!'

'Even though I'm boring,' comes his lugubrious response. If Christy was Eeyore from *Winnie the Pooh*, Norma would be Tigger. And the two don't mix.

I find myself mulling over the new information, while I'm digging out ivy roots near a holly tree. If Martin's brother was murdered and the weapon taken from Eagles, then either Nancy the housekeeper was guilty of both the theft and the killings, or someone else was. And, if it was someone else, surely Martin, as next in line to the family fortune, must rise to the top of the suspect list?

32

Nellie nearly chokes on her dinner – a sumptuous macaroni cheese (the secret's in the mustard, apparently) – when I tell her about the statue.

'How did Norma get to hear about this?'

I raise my eyebrows. 'You'll never guess.'

'I bet I will.' She squints while she considers the options. Timmy, at her feet, is fixing her with a look so beseeching that food ought to leap into his mouth of its own accord. She offers him a cheesy tube of pasta, and he wolfs it down before returning to his woebegone stance.

'You'll get fat and farty,' she tells him.

'Fat seems unlikely,' I say. 'I've never met a more energetic dog.'

She rolls her eyes. 'If cats are autistic and dogs have ADHD, Timmy has whatever the most hyperactive form of ADHD is.'

'That sounds about right.'

'Eddie!' she shouts without warning, making me jump.

I've already forgotten what we were discussing, so she supplies, 'I bet that's the person who told Norma – PC Hawkins.'

'Ahhh. Is he known for this, then? I was quite shocked when Norma said he gets careless when he drinks. Although, come to think of it, Avery also mentioned that he could be "indiscreet".'

'Everyone knows Eddie can't keep a secret. I dunno how he's managed to keep his job.'

'Me neither. He didn't even seem to know what he was doing when I showed him the skeletons.'

She nods. 'But it's probably true about the statue,' she says thoughtfully. 'Hawkins is a shit policeman but he'll just be reporting what the detectives have shared with him.'

'I agree. What do you make of it?'

'How'd you mean?' She forks some pasta into her own mouth before feeding another morsel to Timmy.

I order my thoughts. 'Did Charles Patterson and his girlfriend Megan steal the statue, get caught in the act, and end up murdered for it?'

'That doesn't make sense,' she says.

'No, I realised that as I was saying it. If they were murdered in the act of stealing the statue – perhaps by a member of the household who mistook them for intruders in the night – why bury the statue with them?'

'Unless the statue was the murder weapon,' she says.

'Yes, that's what I think, too. But you don't kill someone for attempting to steal a statue, and then bury them with said statue. You give the statue a good clean and then put it back on the mantelpiece, so no one realises it was the murder weapon.'

'You're assuming the killer was clever.'

'True – and that they were in a fit state to think clearly,' I say. 'I guess, if the murder was unplanned, they're likely to have been in a state of panic afterwards.'

'Why kill both of them?' she wonders.

'My thought was that they murdered one of them, and the other witnessed it, so they had to kill them as well.'

She shakes her head, gazing at Timmy. 'Humans, eh, boy?' He puts up a paw and she feeds him another piece of penne. She explained when she dished out that she always uses penne rather than macaroni for this dish as she finds it better at absorbing the sauce. It certainly has a lovely smooth, al dente texture.

Focusing back on the matter in hand, I say, 'Who do you think did it, though?'

She scrapes the last of the sauce from her bowl with her fork before sitting back and saying, 'What do you know about Charlie P and his relationship with Megan Hughes?'

'Only that Charles's parents disapproved of the match. I imagine it had to do with snobbery, as she was "just" a factory girl, and Charles was set to inherit?' I perform air quotes around 'just'.

'Ah no, there's more to it than that. You see, Megan's dad, John, was trying to form a trade union at the factory. His issue was with low pay for the women workers. He'd realised women were receiving twenty per cent less than their male counterparts for the same jobs. Simon Patterson – that's Charlie and Martin's dad – claimed that, as the men were sometimes the sole breadwinners in their households, they needed the higher earnings. But John – who'd managed to get his hands on the company accounts – insisted Patterson's could easily afford to pay the women the same as the men – and that many of the women were the only earners in their families.'

'I like the sound of John.'

'He was one of the best, by all accounts.'

'Did he get anywhere?'

'He managed to rally the workers in a strike. But Simon Patterson called in the police. It was a time when money still bought power.' She raises an eyebrow. 'What am I saying? Like that's changed. Anyway, the workers who were picketing the factory were arrested, many of them acquiring mysterious injuries that nobody talked about afterwards. John walked with a limp from then on. A few days after the strike, all but John returned to their jobs. He was fired, and there was no more talk of increasing the wages for women.'

'That's outrageous,' I say.

'I know. I mean, this was the late seventies, so he didn't stand much chance of changing things.' She sighs. 'Anyways, it means that John Hughes and Simon Patterson hated each other. But, while John was willing to overlook his antipathy for the sake of his daughter, Simon did not reciprocate. He made it clear that Charlie had to end things with Megan.'

'So, that's why everyone was so ready to believe the story of Charles and Megan running away together,' I say.

She nods. 'It made sense: star-crossed lovers, like I said.'

Reflecting on the bodies in the grave, I say, 'But now it's clear that, even if they'd intended to run away, they never made it.'

'And that they were killed by someone who had access to the house,' she says gloomily.

'. . . And who probably acted on an impulse – grabbing the nearest heavy item – rather than it being a premeditated act,' I say.

We look at each other for some time. I know we're both thinking that the arrow of incrimination is pointing pretty directly at Martin Patterson – the younger brother who, with Charles's death, stood to inherit everything.

As if thinking of him has summoned him, I receive a text on my way to bed that night:

> Martin Patterson here. Please come to Eagles at 8 tomorrow morning. We need to talk urgently about the centenary garden.

I wonder what could possibly be urgent about the garden. He certainly didn't want to talk to me earlier, when I tried to draw his attention to the Green Raven's warning.

What if the reference to the garden is a ruse? Perhaps he has somehow heard that I've linked him to the skeletons – that I suspect him of fratricide? But that's ridiculous: it's not as though I have any proof that he killed his brother and Megan.

I hope he hasn't discovered some long-buried legislation, ruling that the land can't be developed. Recalling that there used to be a dwelling in one section of the grounds, I discount this. And then I remember my first encounter with Martin – and how he tried to convince me that he owned the land. Was this because he was the one who'd put Charles and Megan in that hole, after murdering them?

It occurs to me that I don't have to turn up – just because the man has delusions of grandeur, it doesn't mean I have to play along with them. But my curiosity has been aroused, and it won't be satisfied until I know why he wants to see me.

I message back:

Sure. See you then. Hope all's well.

He does not reply.

* * *

'So, the lord of the manor has summoned you?' says Mike on our evening video call, when I tell him about the message.

I shrug. 'It does feel that way.'

'This is the guy who destroyed the family business?'

'Yep. And more than half the village seem to have lost their jobs as a result.'

'Damn,' he says slowly.

'Said the beaver,' I say automatically before grimacing. 'Sorry! It's just something my nephew Frankie says when anyone says "damn".'

Mike groans, then says, 'Maybe Martin's read that you're a super sleuth.' He strokes his cat Edward, who has just jumped on to his lap and is purring loudly as he swishes his tail in front of the camera.

Mouse, ever hopeful of befriending Edward, leaps from his bed in the corner and comes running, making an excited sound in his throat when he spies the black and white cat. He jumps on to the sofa beside me, his nose so close to the screen that I have to lean around him.

Mike laughs. 'Well, who needs to see their girlfriend, anyway?'

I try to gently push Mouse to one side, but to no avail. At last, giving up, I sit back and we continue our conversation through a screen of dark fur.

'You think he's calling me for something to do with the investigation?' I ask Mike.

'It's possible. I mean, your crime-solving antics aren't exactly a secret.'

'Hey, I take objection to "antics".'

'All right, then, shenanigans.'

'Just so you know, I'm sticking my tongue out at you right now.'

'That seems fair.'

There's a moment's silence, while we both consider the implication of Martin Patterson wanting my help for a criminal matter, rather than something horticultural.

'I suppose he does have a gardener,' I say after a minute.

'So he's unlikely to require your advice on the best time of year to mulch his wotsits,' he agrees.

'Plus, I'm not sure I'd be able to advise him on wotsit mulching. They're famously tricky to grow.' Mike laughs. I love the sound, which is full of warmth and good humour. 'Why are you so far away?' I ask.

'Because there's a large dog blocking our way.'

'You know what I mean.'

He sighs. 'I know what you mean. I'll try and get over to see you in a few weeks. I've got Celine this weekend.' This is his teenage daughter.

'You know, I'd like to meet her, when you feel the time's right,' I say softly.

'I want that, too. Except, I kind of don't. She's at the age where she thinks everyone is evil and every aspect of her life has been designed to torture her.'

'I remember that age,' I say.

'I can't believe you were ever that bad.'

'I left home at sixteen and my parents didn't try to stop me,' I point out.

'I forgot that,' he says. 'Were your mum and dad really unbearable?'

'Probably not. But I bet I was,' I say with a laugh. 'I got better, though.'

'You got a lot better,' he says in the tone of voice that makes me extra sorry he's hundreds of miles away.

I clear my throat and say, 'Well, I'll let you know what the deal is after my trip to the big house tomorrow.'

'Remember to doff your cap,' he says.

'Always.' I nearly tell him about my and Nellie's theory that Martin may have murdered Charles and Megan. But why worry him for nothing?

As I get ready for bed shortly afterwards, however, I can't help reflecting on what Martin Patterson could want to see me about. A little voice in my head keeps asking if I'm sure I'm not walking into some kind of trap.

33

Mouse and I get back from our run at seven the next morning. We've been exploring the wider countryside, and today's track took us through woodland and open common land. When we set off, I wore my head torch against the dark, and I could see my breath in its beam, a cloud of warmth in the surrounding cold darkness. Now, a hazy light has dawned and I've turned off the torch. Mouse's and my breath is still visible, puffs of warm droplets suspended in the cold air.

Back in the house, there's no sign yet of Nellie, though we can hear Timmy scrabbling upstairs, behind her bedroom door.

'You OK if I let Timmy out?' I ask Mouse. He doesn't look thrilled at the prospect, but it feels cruel to leave the little dog shut in.

Timmy is delighted to be liberated. He hurls himself down the stairs, and I'm worried he's going to hurt himself, but he lands neatly before charging at Mouse, all happy yaps and wagging tail.

Mouse lies down, offering a good-natured lick when Timmy approaches him head on.

'Good boy,' I tell Mouse. 'Come, Timmy.' I walk through to the living room, where I open one side of the French windows.

Although he follows me, Timmy hesitates when we reach the open door, looking back to see if his big friend is going to join him.

'Out you go,' I say, picking a ball from a basket of toys beside the door and throwing it for him. He runs out at once, and I leave the door open, so that he can return when he's run off some steam, and hopefully done a wee. His excited yaps can be heard throughout the ground floor. Returning to the kitchen, I set out breakfast for both dogs, fill the cafetière and run upstairs for my shower.

When I come back downstairs, dressed in my gardening clothes and with my hair in a ponytail, I can't hear Timmy.

Mouse has eaten his breakfast and emptied his water bowl, and is curled up on the floor cushion in the living room, Mr Rabbit beneath his jaw.

'Where's Timmy, boy?' I ask him, striding to the open French window and peering out. It's obvious as soon as I step into the garden that the little dog has gone. With a clench of my stomach, I run up to Nellie's room and bang on the door.

'Who is it? What's happening?' comes her muffled voice from inside.

'I'm coming in,' I say loudly, before opening the door. 'It's Timmy.'

She's immediately awake and sitting up. 'What? What's happened?'

'I let him into the garden and he's not there now. I'm really sorry!'

'Not again,' she whines.

'He's got out before?'

She climbs out from under the covers and grabs a pair of dungarees from the floor before pulling them on over her fleecy pink rabbit-print pyjamas. 'I can't find where he does it,' she says. 'I've been all round the garden, checking the boundaries, and I can't see a gap.'

Glancing at my watch, I say, 'I know this is on me, but I'm meant to be having a meeting over at Eagles in a few minutes.'

She shoos me with one hand as she reaches for a pair of discarded socks. 'Go, go.'

'Are you going out to look for him?'

'Yeah, but don't worry – he'll be fine. The roads are quiet here.'

I feel a shiver of fear at the thought of the little dog running out in front of a vehicle. But Nellie's right: the roads are quiet in Greenhaven.

'All right. Take Mouse. His lead is by the door.'

'Will do.'

Back downstairs, I wake Mouse and say softly, 'I'm sorry, boy, but Timmy's missing. Can you help Nellie look for him?'

He surveys me dolefully. I'm pretty sure that, even if he understands, he can't fathom why anyone would want to find Timmy, having managed to get rid of him.

Nellie appears moments later. She steps into sparkly pink wellies in the hall and reaches for a red duffle coat.

'OK, I'm off,' I say. 'I'll help you look when I get back if you haven't found him.'

'We'll have him back by then, won't we, Mousey?' she says, clipping on his lead; my generous dog gives a little rumble of assent.

'Mouse might be able to sniff him out, or hear him from far away,' I say, pulling on my gardening boots and jacket. I wish them luck before stepping out of the front door and closing it behind me.

Although I keep an eye and ear out for Timmy on my brisk walk to Eagles, there's no sign of him.

What's more, there's no answer to my ringing of the doorbell at the big front door, even though I push the button three times and wait several minutes. Each time, I hear it ringing throughout the house.

Eventually, I decide to check the back garden, just in case there is something there that is the reason for Martin's summons. Maybe John needs a hand with some muscle work. For a moment, I remember last night's concern that it could be a trap. But it seems more likely that his nibs simply wants another chance to berate me for having the audacity to build a garden within his kingdom.

The side gate is unlocked and I walk through to the grounds. A host of brown leaves are still clinging to a trio of beech trees, but most of the other trees are bare and stark against the lead-grey sky. There's an icy wind on the exposed garden slope. Shivering, I zip up my jacket and plunge my hands into my pockets.

I call, 'Martin! Are you here?' but there's no response. The lawn is in need of a mow, which surprises me, given how beautifully the garden was maintained the last time I was here. But then I suppose the autumn weather has hardly been conducive to mowing.

I'm about to leave when I notice a flattened track in the over-long grass, as if something heavy has been dragged along it. Unable as ever to resist satisfying my curiosity, I follow the track down to the lower part of the garden.

And here, my breath stops for a moment.

Because Martin Patterson is lying on his back beside the koi pond at the bottom of the slope, arms and legs spreadeagled like he's practising his snow angels. As my own breathing resumes, forming a misty haze in front of my face, I am only too aware that the man on the lawn has no such proof of life. And his grey skin is the exact shade of the lowering November sky.

34

My third encounter with the village bobby is the toughest trial of my patience so far.

'So, you just found him like this?' Hawkins gestures behind him, to the spot where the lord of the manor is lying dead on the lawn. Since his arrival at the scene, he's been keeping his back firmly turned to the sight.

'That's right,' I say, clearing my throat and keeping my own gaze turned away from the puddle of vomit that was the PC's immediate reaction upon seeing the corpse. 'Is the same detective coming as last time?' I ask.

'As soon as Colchester can spare a detective, they'll send one,' he tells me. 'I don't know who yet. They've got a lot on.'

I want to ask Hawkins if this is his first corpse with the flesh still on. He was bad enough with the skeletons but he seems even more panicked by the responsibility here. Deciding to take pity on him and proffer some information, I say, 'I received a text last night, asking me to come this morning. Here.' I pass my phone to him.

'So,' he says, looking up at me after reading the text, 'Mr Patterson was alive at nine thirty last night.'

'Not necessarily,' I say.

He frowns. 'But he sent you this message . . .'

I shrug and say, 'Somebody texted me from his phone. That doesn't mean it was him.'

His face displays confusion – and then I see understanding dawn. He removes his woolly gloves to take his notebook out of an inside pocket. He opens it and makes a note.

'Do you not have a tablet?' I ask – regretting it immediately when his expression again shows befuddlement. 'I mean a hand-held screen,' I say slowly.

'Oh! No – they haven't issued me with one of those. Tell the truth, I'm not sure I'd know how to start with one.'

'Fair enough.' My phone pings in his hands, and he frowns again, reading the screen. 'I think this is for you,' he says, handing it back.

I see it's a message from Nellie:

Timmy found safe and sound! Mouse is a hero! X

'Is it something to do with Mr Patterson?' asks Hawkins.

I smile and send a thumbs up before looking up and telling him, 'No, it's nothing to do with this. It's just my housemate.'

We stand in silence for a moment, then I say, 'Let me give you my statement. The detective will probably take it again, but I'm sure you want a preliminary one.'

He clears his throat. 'I was just about to do that. Can you tell me what happened when you arrived at the house this morning? What time was it?'

I tell PC Hawkins about my arrival at the house at 8.00, the lack of response to my ringing of the bell – and then my coming around the back and following the drag marks to Martin Patterson's body.

'Drag marks?' he queries, looking up from his notebook. He has such an air of concentration when he writes, I half expect him to poke his tongue out of the side of his mouth, like Charlie Brown in the old *Peanuts* cartoon.

'Yes,' I say, pointing to his left, where the flattened trail can be seen in the still dew-damp grass.

He follows the trail down with his eye – and I see him blanch when he reaches the corpse.

'It's never pleasant to see a dead body,' I say, wondering if this is the understatement of the year. Am I becoming inured, or is it just that, for once, I didn't have time to form a relationship with the person who's died?

He frowns again. 'You've seen a body before? Apart from the skeletons, I mean.'

Deciding not to tell him how many cadavers I've had the misfortune to behold, I simply say, 'Yes, sadly.' I also refrain from sharing the observation that at least the smell of death is less pervasive out here than indoors.

The PC clears his throat, and asks in a brittle tone, 'About these drag marks . . . Are you suggesting Mr Patterson might not have just had a heart attack?'

Suppressing a sigh, I say gently, 'I don't believe he dragged his own body down the slope, do you?'

I could swear he considers this option for a moment before making another note. Then he says, 'He might have walked down and then dropped dead.'

'He might,' I say, not pointing out that drag marks form an unbroken trail, in a way that footprints do not.

'So, why did he ask you to come here, do you think?'

I don't bother repeating my suggestion that his murderer might have sent the text. Instead, I say, 'Your guess is as good as mine.'

He lifts his gaze from his notebook. 'Were you sleeping together?'

I burst out laughing. 'Where did that come from?'

'It's a standard question: were you and Mr Patterson having a sexual relationship?'

'I met the man twice,' I say. 'And no, we didn't sleep together. The first time, he didn't even take his coat off.'

From his expression, he's clearly trying to picture us having sex with our coats on. I consider offering to draw him a diagram. Instead, I say, 'The first time we met was outside the site for the centenary garden. I was on a run with my dog, and Mr Patterson must have seen us from his house and worked out who I was – Greenhaven's a small village, and I was an unknown face, I suppose. He came over to tell me that John would be happy to show me his garden while he was away.' I don't tell him Martin's real motive for talking to me – I can save that for the detectives. Knowing Hawkins, he'd assume I'd murdered Martin to stop him interfering in my garden-building.

The constable writes everything down in his painstaking way. He seems not to know any form of shorthand. When his pen finally stops moving, I say, 'The second time was when you refused to believe Martin was in danger, so I came over here to warn him. He also refused to listen.'

The PC's face flushes. 'That newspaper piece was just stuff and nonsense.'

'Right,' I say, refraining from pointing at the evidence to the contrary currently stretched out on the grass behind him. I take a deep, calming breath and say, 'Do you want me to stay with the body, so you can take a look at the murder scene?' When he frowns again, I say gently, 'Martin wasn't murdered here – which means he was killed somewhere else, probably inside the house. There are no footprints that I can see – the grass is too lush for that, and the murderer or their accomplice clearly kept to the drag trail when they walked back up. It would be helpful to the detectives if you could locate the spot where Martin was killed before they arrive.'

I witness his hesitation. Should he leave me – the possible murderer – alone with the corpse? Deciding to make things easy for him, I say,

'Actually, why don't I leave? You have my details, and you've taken my statement. If you can find the key, you can lock the gate behind me, so that no one can tamper with the body.'

'I have the keys,' he says, drawing a fob from his pocket with two keys attached. 'Mr Patterson liked us to keep spares at the police house, in case there were ever problems while he was away.'

'Good. Come and see me out, then.'

He draws back his shoulders. 'Look, Ms Williams, not being funny, but you're acting like you're in charge. Let me remind you that I am the police officer, and you are a civilian, as well as a suspect in a possible murder.'

A definite murder, I think, but choose not to say.

* * *

It's a relief to get back to Magpies, where Mouse is lying in a corner of the living room while Timmy performs zoomies. I can't tell if Mouse is genuinely managing to sleep through Timmy's frenetic activity, or just pretending. Either way, both dogs seem OK. There's no sign of Nellie, so I make a pot of coffee and settle at the kitchen table with my notebook.

I want to write down all my observations around Martin's murder, before the detectives summon me for their enquiries.

The trouble is that the number of suspects I know of is already excessive. It occurs to me that, if I take into account all the people in the village with any grudge against Martin Patterson, the investigation could go on for years.

I hope Colchester sends DS Timpson again. She seemed bright and on-the-ball, in striking contrast to our village constable. Perhaps Timpson can find a way to narrow down the suspects from a field to a flower bed – or an analogy that is less delightful, and better suited to murder than gardening.

35

'Mouse is an absolute star,' says Nellie, entering the kitchen and pouring herself a coffee from the cafetière. 'He got straight on Timmy's trail when we left here.'

I stop writing in my notebook. 'Thanks for letting me know he was back safely. Where did you find him?'

'Like I said, Mouse found him. He'd got into the cemetery, and was digging up some snowdrops.'

'Oh no!'

She pulls a face. 'Don't worry – I put them all back, but he'd made quite a mess in a short amount of time.'

'Well done for replanting them,' I say.

'So, what did our lord and master want with you?' she asks.

'Hard to know,' I say. 'Given that he was in no fit state to tell me.'

She frowns. 'How do you mean? Like he was drunk? Sick?'

In the past, when I've had to announce a death, it hasn't always gone well, so I decide to try a different tack. I meet Nellie's eye and say nothing, waiting for her to work it out. It doesn't take long.

'Ohhhh,' she says. Tilting her head, she asks, 'Is it bad that I don't feel much?'

'Did you even know him?'

'Only from afar. He didn't exactly stand around chatting with us commoners.'

'Then it's perfectly fine to feel very little,' I say.

'Bit of a shock for you, though, I imagine?'

'Again, not as much as if I'd known him well. But yeah: not my most enjoyable experience. Plus, it's always sad to see a life ended that way.'

She frowns. 'What way? Oh, my god – did he kill himself?'

I hesitate, not wanting to give away too much before the police have investigated. 'I don't think so, but Hawkins was still waiting for the detectives to turn up when I left, so I don't know much.'

'Was there a lot of blood?'

'No blood.'

'What sort of state was Hawkins in? I bet he was in a right tizz. He was bad enough this one time when he had to tell off a kid he'd caught graffitiing on a bench outside the Co-op.'

I decide not to mention the constable's unfortunate purging upon seeing the body, and just say, 'Yeah, he didn't seem too confident. I tried to give him some pointers, but I'm not sure he took them on board.'

'I love the idea of you training a policeman,' she says. 'Is that part of your job description while you're here?'

I laugh and grimace at the same time. 'It's just hard to stand by and watch Hawkins messing things up.'

'I get that. So, what happens now?'

'The police detectives will visit the scene of the crime and bring in a CSI team, who'll inspect the site and take photos, and the body will be taken away. I'm guessing the coroner will want a post-mortem, to see how he died. Oh – and the detectives will want to talk to everyone who's had contact with Martin in the past few days, I should think.'

'And you,' she says.

'Definitely me, as I found the body,' I say glumly.

'Oh – I just remembered what you said last time, about how they always suspect the person who found the body.'

I nod. 'Yeah. They tend to go on the attack at the start.'

'You want me to be there as your attack dog?' she says. 'I can growl if they're getting too aggressive.'

Mouse has wandered into the kitchen and come to my side while we've been talking. With a smile, I stroke him and say, 'I'm sure this one will provide that service if necessary, thanks.'

He makes his rumble of agreement, and I feed him a treat from the jar that Nellie has left on the table.

'How long before they turn up?' she asks.

'No idea. I think I'm going to head to the work site to meet everyone. I'm a bit late, but they all started jobs yesterday so they know what they're meant to be doing, and hopefully they'll have got a key from somewhere.'

'I thought Norma was meant to be the official key holder,' she says.

'She gave her key to me, as she's always late.'

Nellie shakes her head. 'Artists and cats. Can't herd either of them.'

I laugh, picturing a 'flock' of artists, with Nellie and Timmy attempting to herd them in a straight line as they stumble off in various directions, pencils and paintbrushes in hand.

'Right,' I say, 'no rest for the wicked. You coming, boy?'

Mouse barks once and fetches his lead, and we leave for the site.

36

The detectives track me down at three o'clock that afternoon, while I'm underneath a wild rose, attempting to saw through its thick trunk without getting my woolly hat or curls snagged on the thorns.

'We need to interview you,' says DS Timpson as I come crawling out from the undergrowth, picking dead leaves and twigs from my hat and hair.

Mouse, ever alert to potential threats, shakes off his nap nearby and jogs over. Surveying the officers, he makes a low grumble, so I place a hand on his head to reassure him. I guess he's no more trusting of the police than I am. 'It's all right, boy,' I tell him. 'We've met them before, remember?' Addressing the DS, I say, 'Is it OK if we talk here? I've got a lot to get on with.'

She glances at the volunteers, who all stopped working the minute they saw the police officers arrive, and have congregated around us, looking concerned.

'She didn't do it,' says Leo.

The DS looks amused. 'What didn't she do?'

He falters. 'Whatever it is you're here for.'

Eloise adds, 'She's only been here for like two weeks.'

I'm touched by their loyalty.

The DS addresses the two young people, 'No one is accusing Ms Williams of any crime at present. We are merely hoping she might have some interesting observations to share with us.'

This seems to appease my defenders.

The DS says, 'We'd rather interview you in private. Can we go elsewhere?'

I check my watch. 'Do you need me to come right now?' I'm aware that I'm being close to obstructive. *You've had them in your house and it was fine*, I remind myself.

'That would be best, while it's still fresh in your mind,' says the DS.

Addressing the still-assembled volunteers, I say, 'If you all want to pack up, that's fine. It'll be dark in about an hour, in any case.' Handing the key to Marion, I ask, 'Do you mind locking up, and opening up tomorrow?' She takes the key with a nod.

'Shall we go to your house?' DS Timpson suggests, once we're out on the street.

'Sure.' I clip on Mouse's lead and we walk in silence the five minutes to Magpies, where I let us all in. Mouse accompanies us into the living room, where we all take seats, and he takes up his post beside me, Mr Rabbit also on guard at his feet.

'We just wanted to get a statement from you, while it's fresh in your mind,' says the DS again. 'So, if you could talk us through everything, starting with why you were at Mr Patterson's property this morning.'

I nod and begin my account, starting with the message I received last night – which they ask to see – and finishing with the moment when I took my leave of PC Hawkins, and he locked the gate behind me.

'Did you find the murder scene?' I ask.

She raises her eyebrows. 'What makes you think this was a murder?'

'Well, he was probably dead before his body was dragged down the lawn.' I maintain eye contact with her and keep my voice level.

She eyes me, as if trying to gauge whether I'm mocking her. 'Again, where are you coming up with these theories?'

I don't manage to hold back an eye roll before responding, 'It's not rocket science, is it? There were drag marks leading to the body. He didn't drag himself.'

She's still watching me, as if I'm giving away insider knowledge, thus proving my guilt. 'I don't know how he died, or who did it,' I say. 'But it looks like a pretty obvious murder.'

'Do you believe the message you received on your phone came from Mr Patterson?' she asks.

I think for a moment. 'Well, I'd rather believe it came from him than someone else – like the murderer, luring me there to find his body. Plus, the tone sounded like him.'

'The tone?'

'Yes: the way he pretty much ordered me to turn up at his house. At first, I did wonder if it might be a trap.' When she tilts her head questioningly, I explain, 'Everyone believes Martin murdered Charles and Megan – the skeletons found on the garden site. So, getting a text summoning me to the home of a possible murderer . . . Well, it seemed like it might be a trap of some kind.'

'I see.' From her frown, I'm not sure she does. 'How well did you know Martin Patterson?'

'Not well. We'd only met twice – once when he stopped me on my morning run and told me not to do any work without his sign-off, and once when I went to warn him . . .' I trail off, realising I haven't yet mentioned the Green Raven's column.

She sits forward, hands on her knees. 'Go on.'

'Do you know about the Green Raven?' I ask. She glances at her DC, who looks up from his tablet to shake his head. 'OK . . . Well, Stella – you remember, I mentioned her the last time you were here? She lives over the road, in the beautiful house, Woodpeckers. Well, she publishes the village paper, *The Green Maven*, every Monday, and it contains a gossip column by an anonymous source, calling themselves the Green Raven. This Monday's column contained a pretty clear threat – or possibly a warning – to Martin Patterson.'

'Can we see?' she asks.

'Yes, of course . . .' I leave the room, Mouse at my heel as if held in place by an invisible magnet. I find the paper on the side in the kitchen and bring it back, folded open to the Green Raven's column.

DS Timpson takes it from me and scans it, before passing it to her DC. He photographs it on his tablet.

When Mouse and I return to our places, she asks, 'What made you suspect that this column contained a threat to

Mr Patterson?' I explain my thoughts on eagles and gatherings of crows but, once again, I'm met by a blank face. She says, 'And you say you went to warn the victim?'

'That's right. I called on PC Hawkins yesterday morning, but he dismissed my concerns, so I went from there to Eagles, to talk to Martin directly.'

She frowns. 'You say PC Hawkins dismissed your worries?'

I know I'm probably getting the village bobby into trouble, but a man has died. 'That's right,' I say. 'Hawkins felt the column was . . .' I pause to recall his words, '. . . nonsense. He also said something along the lines of "murders don't happen in Greenhaven".'

She stares, and I feel as though I might finally be breaking through her cool facade. '"Murders don't happen"?' She raises an eyebrow at DC Wright. 'Does he think those two skeletons buried themselves?'

'That's what I wanted to know,' I say.

She shakes her head. 'So, you went to the local police officer with your concerns, and he sent you away with a flea in your ear, and now the man whose safety you were concerned about is dead?'

'That's pretty much it.'

'And you say you went straight from PC Hawkins to the house – Eagles – to see Mr Patterson?'

'That's right. It was after I finished at the garden site on Tuesday, around three thirty.'

'Can you run us through the conversations with both men?'

I do as she asks, and she and her DC both take notes.

'At least you tried,' she says when I've finished. 'It's just a shame you were dealing with the kind of men who can't be told.'

Although this smacks of sexism, I let it pass. Her male DC can object if he wants.

She takes the newspaper back from him. 'Can we keep this?' she asks me.

'Sure.'

'And can you forward that text message to this number?' She hands over a card, and I do as she asks.

And then she says, 'It does seem strange, Ms Williams, that there have been three deaths in Greenhaven, and you were found at the scene of each one.'

'It's only two sites,' I point out. 'And I wasn't *found*. I mean, it's not like I was hiding – I'm the one who reported them.'

'True,' she says. 'But you've been in the village, what, three weeks?'

'That's right. It'll be four on Monday.'

'Right,' she says. And then she just looks at me. As I'm pretty sure this is a tactic designed to make me crack, I return her gaze with a smile.

She tires first. Glancing at her DC, who nods, she sighs and gets to her feet. 'I think we've got everything we need for now. Thanks for taking the time to bring us up to speed.'

At the living-room door, she turns back. 'Please let us know if anything else occurs to you. You can reach us on the number you used to forward Mr Patterson's message. And, Ms Williams, we will get to the bottom of this, and find out who killed Mr Patterson.'

I show them out, wondering if her last words were designed as reassurance or threat. She can't really believe I killed a man I barely knew?

After we've seen them off, Mouse and I go for another run. I have adrenaline to burn off, and he is always happy to oblige.

37

'Did you hear John's been arrested for Martin Patterson's murder?' Norma drops this into conversation the following morning as airily as a poppy dropping its seeds.

We're at the site, in the section I've allocated to the children's play area. I've asked the volunteers to help me map out this area, so that I can get an overview on my design for the space. We are, of course, banned from the gravesite, where the police tape is making a flapping sound in the biting November winds.

I stop in the middle of measuring distances with my laser, to take in Marion's news. Frowning, I say, 'John? But he seemed so zen when I met him.'

Leo chips in, 'And he's about a hundred and two.'

'Don't be ageist,' says his mother, but without much conviction. She adds, 'We all thought John's patience was limitless, but perhaps even he had his tipping point.'

Christy appears uncharacteristically quiet – until I realise he's still engrossed in the measuring task I set him, for a sandpit that will mimic the Japanese pond in the grounds of the Patterson house. There will be an 'island' in the sandpit, bearing a pagoda-style tower, designed for climbing. Christy is doing calculations on an old-fashioned calculator before making notes in a little notebook, both of which he must have brought along for the purpose.

'Are you sure John's been arrested?' I ask Norma.

She tucks wisps of white hair into her multicoloured hat as she considers this. At last, she says, 'Maybe he was just taken in for questioning.'

'Ah,' I say. 'That doesn't mean anything, except that he may have been the last person to see Martin alive.'

'But they did have a big row,' she says.

This gets my attention. 'Martin and John? When was this? You saw it?'

'Oh, it wasn't me,' she says. 'Vera at the Co-op was walking the dog and she witnessed the whole thing.'

'So, you had it from her?'

She shakes her head. 'Vera told Nick.'

'Who's Nick?' I ask.

'The postman.'

'So, Vera overheard the argument and she told the postman, and he told you?'

She hesitates. 'Actually, I think Vera told old Samuel who lives in one of the prefabs on Cross Street, and he told Nick, who told me.'

The chain of reporting is getting longer and weaker the more I question her. 'How long ago was this argument?'

'Last week, I think,' she says.

Christy stops his calculations to come over. 'It stands to reason John would snap eventually,' he says. 'I don't know how he bore that man for as long as he did.'

'The man was an arse,' says Leo.

'Language,' says his mother mildly.

'Well, he was. Look at what he did to Dad.'

Frowning, I turn to Marion for an explanation. 'I thought your husband wasn't affected by the factory closure,' I say. 'Isn't he a plumber?'

'He didn't pay Dad for plumbing work,' says Leo, before his mother has a chance to respond. 'Dad did weeks of work for him over at Eagles, and Patterson never paid up.'

'Pretty typical, from what I gather,' says Christy. 'He had the money but, like so many wealthy people, he preferred to hold on to it.'

Eloise nods. 'My nan used to clean for him, but she stopped going when he didn't pay her for three weeks in a row.'

'I keep wondering why he didn't sell up,' I say. 'It seems no one wanted him in the village.'

Norma shrugs. 'You know what the landed gentry are like about their estates.'

'Hardly gentry, Norma,' says Christy, and she scowls at him.

'You know what I mean. He inherited land and a grand house, and he thought that made him better than everyone else.'

'Do you know what the argument was about?' I ask her.

'Apparently, John was furious because Martin had cut back one of the Japanese maples without checking with him first.'

'Why would he do that himself, rather than get John to do it?' I ask.

'Why did Martin Patterson do anything?' says Marion. 'He was a law unto himself.'

'Was he keeping up with paying John, does anyone know?' I ask.

They all shrug. Then Christy says, 'I think he must have been, or John wouldn't have kept working for him.'

'I don't know,' says Marion. 'Free housing, don't forget.'

'True,' says Christy. 'That bungalow wouldn't be cheap to rent.'

I consider what they've told me, before saying, 'Cutting one of his own trees hardly seems like the crime of the century.'

'Quite,' says Marion. 'But John is very precious about that garden.'

'So, why didn't Martin check with John first – before cutting the tree, I mean?' I ask again.

Norma says, 'John was laid up with the flu, and Martin said he didn't want to bother him.'

At least this explains why the lawn was so long: I'd have expected John to do his final pre-winter mow by now.

Norma continues, 'Martin said the maple was blocking his shot when he was practising his golf swing.'

I pull a face. 'Did he do a bad job of the pruning?'

'According to John, it was a "massacre",' says Norma. 'Nick said old Samuel said Vera said he turned almost purple with anger. He loves those trees.'

'Arboricide,' I say, and she laughs.

'Very good.'

'But not really a motive for whatever the word is for killing your boss,' I say.

'Tyrannicide?' suggests Christy. 'The killing of a tyrant.'

'We all have our triggers,' says Norma darkly.

I wonder what her triggers might be, and decide to be extra nice to her from now on.

38

'I'm sorry you're going through this again,' says Mike on that evening's video call. 'How are you holding up?'

'Yeah, OK, thanks. I'm trying not to feel somehow responsible.'

'Of course you're not responsible! He's the one who summoned you there – it's hardly your fault he was dead when you arrived.'

'I guess.'

'And it sounds like he wasn't exactly a lovely human being,' he says.

I raise an eyebrow. 'That's for sure. I've yet to find someone with a good thing to say about him.'

'So, do you think the skeletons are linked somehow to Martin's murder?' he asks.

'It seems too much of a coincidence otherwise,' I say. 'Maybe the skeletons turning up proved something to somebody.'

'I like a woman who doesn't rely on speculation,' he says with a raised eyebrow, 'just good, hard facts.'

'All right, I know it's a bit vague at the moment. But now we know the skeletons belong to Martin's older brother Charles and his girlfriend Megan, which is proof they didn't run away after all – and that someone killed them. What if that someone was

Martin – and one of Megan's relatives suspected him? They may even have confronted him after the skeletons were ID'd.'

'From what you've told me about his murder, it doesn't sound like a spur-of-the-moment thing.'

'No, that's true. There was no obvious sign of injury, so I'm thinking poison, which would be proof of premeditation.'

We're quiet for a moment, the only sounds being Mouse's eager panting at the cat on the screen and said cat's oblivious purrs.

After a short time, Mike says, 'I don't suppose you have any suspects yet, do you?'

'Only Martin for the bodies in the grave.'

'Remind me what makes you think he would have killed his own brother?'

'To inherit, maybe,' I say. 'At first, I did consider that it might be a joint suicide, covered up by the Pattersons. But now I know about the statue that was buried with them, it's pretty clear it was a murder and the statue was the weapon.' I continue, thinking aloud: 'As for Martin's murder, while it seems plausible from the timing that it was one of Megan's relatives who targeted him, there are also any number of villagers with a grudge to bear. You can't destroy the livelihood of an entire village without making enemies.' Remembering the meet-up at the old factory, I add, 'Then there's Avery and whatever she and Martin were doing at the factory with at least two others.'

He whistles softly. 'Do you think they threatened him?'

'It's possible they gave him an ultimatum on something. Or maybe they tried to get him to confess to the murders.'

'For a small place, there's a lot of intrigue.'

'I know.' I sigh. 'I thought this was going to be a chance to focus on my work.'

'You really should know better by now.'

I sigh and nod before adding, 'As far as Martin's popularity goes, it doesn't help that it seems like he never expressed any remorse for the loss of all those jobs.'

'Sounds like a charmer,' says Mike.

'Put it this way: I don't think many people will turn up to his funeral,' I say.

He frowns. 'Has his body been released already?'

'Oh no, not yet – I was just thinking ahead. What I'd really like to know is whether poor John has come back from the police station. I don't believe for one minute that he killed Martin.'

'Especially if he'd just got over flu when they argued last week,' says Mike. 'It seems unlikely he'd be strong enough to drag a body.'

'Agreed. I hadn't even thought of that. To be honest, even at peak fitness, I doubt John would manage to wrangle Martin's weight. John's lean and strong, but he's small, and Martin was a big man. I'll mention that to the police if they are keeping him – though I'm sure they'll have thought of it.'

We move on to more general topics, including a course in hedge laying that Mike's signed up for.

'You be careful with that bill hook,' I tell him. 'They're vicious things.'

He smiles. 'Always good to know you care.'

'Of course I care.'

We grin at each other like love-struck teenagers. I'm glad we have no witnesses to our soppiness, aside from our furry companions.

After our call, Mouse slinks off to bed with Mr Rabbit as consolation for the loss of Edward the cat's company.

After changing into my pyjamas and cleaning my teeth and face, I prop myself up against the pillows in my bed and tackle another crossword clue:

7D – Unoccupied, I start organising group holiday.

But I drift off to sleep before making headway.

My dreams are typically invaded by both the crossword clue and current events, so that I find myself on a minibus with my group of volunteers, plus Avery and Nellie, all heading off on holiday, via a memorial for Martin Patterson. Nellie is busy making something out of discarded rubbish at the back of the bus. After a while, she shouts, 'Ta-da!' and steps back to reveal a giant sculpture of a green raven with glowing red eyes. The bird turns its head and lets out a loud caw.

Avery says, 'Well now, isn't that lovely?' And everybody smiles and claps.

39

When I wake at six the next morning, to the reassuring sound of Mouse's snoring from the corner of the room, my heart is beating too hard and I'm drenched in sweat.

Sighing, I reach for my phone and take another look at the crossword, trying to make headway with the clue of the night before.

I type a message to my birth mother:

Unoccupied is . . . what – vacant?

A response comes almost instantly:

That's right! Almost there 😁

I find I'm constantly amazed by the extent to which Verity has embraced emojis. I avoid using them with my mum and dad, who otherwise get confused. Once, I sent Mum a laughing/crying emoji in reply to a funny message, and she responded:

Why are you crying? Are you OK?

I lie in bed, mulling on what I can do with 'vacant' that would fit the rest of the clue – as well as the grid. A group holiday is a . . . But I can only think of places like Butlin's holiday parks, and I'm pretty sure that's not right here. A resort? But that's not a group holiday, just a place for a holiday.

With a sigh, I roll out of bed and start to dress for the morning run. It's Saturday, so we have more time than usual, and Mouse and I stop to check on John at his little cottage during our loop. He takes a while to come to the door, and we're just turning away when it opens.

'Oh Steph, hello. Is everything all right?'

'I hope I didn't wake you.'

'Us gardeners are early risers,' he says with an attempt at a smile. He has an air of sadness, plus a slight stoop that I don't remember noticing before.

'We certainly are,' I say. 'I just wanted to see how you were doing, with all that's going on. I heard you were questioned by DS Timpson yesterday.'

'That's right. They'd heard about a disagreement I'd had with Mr Patterson, and wanted to know a bit more. And then they asked when I saw him last. It's a bad business, isn't it? Do you know, I worked for the family for more than forty years?'

'I'm so sorry; it must be really hard. Can I ask . . . Did you see him on the day he died?'

'No. I'd arranged to have the day off, to help my daughter move house, and I stayed over near there.' He sighs and rubs his face. 'I wish I'd been there – perhaps I could've seen off whoever did this to him.'

'I doubt it,' I say. 'I reckon they planned it for a day when they knew you'd be out of the way.'

His pale eyes grow wide. 'Do you know, that hadn't even occurred to me?' He shudders. 'It turns my stomach to think about it.'

'Me, too.'

'I rate that DS woman though,' he says. 'I reckon she knows her stuff.'

'I think so,' I say with a smile. 'I'm sorry for your loss, though.'

As I take my leave, I can't help wondering what will happen to John, now that his employer is dead.

40

On Sunday morning, I can't find one of my running trainers.

'I'm sure they were both here,' I tell Mouse, holding up the solitary remaining shoe.

Standing by the bedroom door, he makes an impatient noise in his throat, so I let him out while I search under the bed, in case I've kicked it there by mistake.

Mouse returns a minute or so later and barks once. It's clear he wants me to accompany him, so I follow him along the landing, past the bathroom, and to a set of shelves with doors built into an alcove at the far end of the floor. Mouse tries to fit inside, but he's too big. I get the idea, though, so I coax him out, allowing me to crouch for a closer look. Sure enough, amid empty crisp packets, shuttlecocks, tennis balls, a shredded towel and what might once have been a sweater, I find my trainer.

'Timmy's a hoarder, isn't he?' I say as I grab my shoe. 'Great work, boy – thank you.' I pat his head and turn to walk away, but Mouse doesn't budge. 'Is there something else?' I have an awful thought that Timmy might have got hold of Mr Rabbit and stashed him here – until I realise that Mouse is far too calm for this to be the case. When he nudges a crumpled piece of paper with his nose, rolling it towards my feet, I at first think he just wants to play. But when I throw the paper ball along the landing, he shoots me a look that I recognise as his version of an eye roll. I reach to unfold it, and realise it contains some of my gardening notes – fortunately only ones I've disposed of in the recycling.

'Clever boy,' I tell Mouse. 'You're quite right – this is mine.' Out of curiosity, I sift through the detritus while he watches. I discover several more sheets of paper, some of them typed. Smoothing out one of them, I find myself sitting down on the floor with a thump.

Because the text in front of me, although faded in places from Timmy's toothy attentions, is clearly a draft of the Green Raven's column.

41

Staring at the crumpled piece of paper in my hand, I try to process its implications. If Nellie is the Green Raven, why has she been lying to me? I thought we were close enough for her to treat me with kindness and respect. I blink back sudden tears at my housemate's betrayal, and Mouse, sensing my distress, pushes his nose on to my lap. As I take deep breaths while stroking his soft muzzle, my mind clears enough for me to realise that Nellie is the only one who can answer my questions.

I push Mouse gently from my lap and, a moment later, throw open my housemate's door, incriminating sheet of paper still in hand.

If I'd been less preoccupied with my discovery, I'd already have known she wasn't there. Instead of a yappy dog, plus a lump beneath the bedclothes, there's a neatly made bed and an absence of inhabitants.

'Where are they?' I ask Mouse, who looks up at me bemusedly.

I grab my trainers and we trail downstairs, but it's obvious there's no Tiny Terror about.

'We might as well go for our run, boy,' I say, pulling on my shoes and clipping on his lead.

As we reach the front door, I discover a note taped to it bearing my name.

Half expecting it to be an apology – despite Nellie's having no idea I've uncovered her duplicity – I remove it and open it up. It's another sheet of white paper, this time bearing Nellie's curly writing, in a purple pen:

Morning Steph and Mouse!

I forgot to say last night that Timmy and I are in London all day today. Mum's booked me a fitting for my bridesmaid's dress . . . Wish me luck . . . XX

Despite a twinge of sympathy, the anger and hurt remain as I place the note carefully on the hall table and step outside with Mouse. We turn right along Hogs Green Road and begin to jog, quickly falling into a comfortable rhythm.

As we reach a now familiar footpath through fields and pick up speed, I find myself wondering over and over again how it can be possible for Nellie to be both my kindred spirit and my antagonist.

* * *

Still smarting from the revelation that Nellie is the Green Raven, I consider waiting up to confront her that night. But, by the time I've checked in with Mike, my parents and my brother Danny, and exchanged brief messages with Verity, my birth mum, I'm ready for bed.

Mouse is already snoring softly in his bed with Mr Rabbit tucked beneath his chin, and I slide gratefully between my own covers.

My phone starts ringing almost as soon as my head rests on the pillow. Reaching for it, I see Caroline's name on the screen, and I groan.

Caroline is my ex-husband Ben's whiny girlfriend. I consider letting it go to voicemail, but the memory of Ben's recent disappearance for over a year has me answering.

'The man's a moron,' comes her nasal voice with her usual lack of greeting or enquiry as to the state of my affairs.

I pull a face. 'What's he done now?'

'He's only gone and bought back one of those bloody records – you know, the ones I sold to pay for his expensive lawyer?'

'The John Lennon?' I guess.

'Yeah. Bloody waste of money.'

'Where did he get it? The money, I mean.' I immediately regret asking this, as I don't want to know the answer. But she surprises me:

'He's got a job. Like a real one. And it pays OK. I mean, not spectacularly, but it's honest dosh.'

'Well, that's good.'

'Yeah. He does like these tours for a posh chocolate factory. And he's a natural – they love him.'

I laugh, thinking of Ben's innate charm and showy nature. 'Why doesn't that surprise me?'

She laughs, too, then says, 'So, how are you?' I'm so taken aback by her straying from her inherent self-absorption, that I'm silenced for a moment. 'Lou?' she prompts.

'It's Steph,' I say, in a tone reflecting just how bored I am by my various family members – including a certain ex-husband and his partner – still calling me Louise. I've been Steph ever since Ben destroyed my previous business with his financial shenanigans.

'Oh, yeah,' she says. 'You all right?'

'Yes, I'm fine, thanks. How about you?'

This thoughtful version of Caroline is so unnerving that I ought to be prepared for her next words: 'I've got a favour to ask.'

I close my eyes for a moment. When I open them, I say, 'If it's money—'

'No, it's not,' she interrupts. 'I already told you – he's earning money. And we've got my salary, too, so that's all good.'

I can't remember what she does, but she continues, 'It's about that, actually. My manager wants to make a garden out the back. The office has this really ugly paved courtyard surrounded by high walls. It's like one of those prison yards you see on TV, but much smaller. It's dead claustrophobic.'

'Right . . .' I say.

'So, do you think you could do us something?'

'Oh! You want me to redesign your work garden?'

'Yeah. What do you say?'

'What's the budget?' There's a long silence, which I interpret as, *You mean you won't do it for free?* 'There is a budget?' I check.

'Thing is, Lou . . . Steph, I told my boss you were a mate.'

I manage not to point out that even that claim is taking the mickey: my 'mates' do not contact me only when they want something. 'Sorry, Caroline, but I have plenty of paid work, and no time to take on anything gratis. But I'll send you a link to an online directory of qualified garden designers, so you can make sure you get someone legit. If you choose someone local to you in Newcastle, you won't have to worry about travel expenses.'

There's a long silence. At last, she says, 'Couldn't you just do a plan, and then we can get a builder in and buy the plants ourselves?'

'It doesn't work like that. Garden designing takes weeks or more.'

'Well, thanks for nothing,' she snaps.

She hangs up and I'm left staring at my phone. With a big sigh, which has Mouse turning in his bed, I call up the website for the Society of Garden and Landscape Designers, and share the link with Caroline.

And then I settle down to sleep.

I don't have an ounce of energy left; confronting Nellie will definitely have to wait until tomorrow.

42

Mouse and I go for our run at the usual time on Monday morning, managing not to disturb Nellie or Timmy. I hope they got home safely last night. As Mouse and I run along frosted country trails, our breath suspended like speech bubbles in the cold air, it occurs to me that my anger towards my housemate has already softened. These twenty-four hours apart should mean we can now have a less emotional discussion about her intentions behind the Green Raven's apparent malice.

'Nellie wouldn't do anything to hurt me,' I say, trying to convince myself, and Mouse barks his agreement. His tongue is lolling from his mouth, and his happiness is so apparent that I find myself grinning in response.

My phone rings and I draw it out to see my ex-husband Ben's name on the screen. With a sigh, I stop to answer, much to Mouse's disapproval.

'It's Ben,' I tell Mouse, and he woofs a hello.

'Is that my buddy Mouse?' comes Ben's confident voice.

'It is. I hope you're ringing to apologise for Caroline's behaviour yesterday.' The long silence tells me he is not. With a sigh, I ask, 'What do you want, Ben?'

'Nice to talk to you, too!' he says with a laugh. 'Really, Lulu . . .' I close my eyes and wait until he finally catches up: 'I mean Steph. Sorry. Is now a bad time?'

'Kind of. Mouse and I are just out on our run, then we have to get to work.'

'I won't keep you. It's just that I wondered if you'd reconsider your decision about helping Caro.'

'Why would I do that?'

'For old times?' he suggests in a wheedling tone.

'The old times where you lost me my home and business?'

He laughs but he has the grace to sound less certain. 'All right, not old times. How about new ones?'

'Sorry, Ben – I don't have time to take on another project, and certainly not one where I won't be paid. I sent Caroline a link to a database of designers. Please tell her to either hire someone from that – and be prepared to pay them – or to find an untrained person with some plant knowledge, who is happy to volunteer their time. Goodbye.'

I hang up before he can object. Glancing down at Mouse, I say, 'Right, boy, let's run off that conversation, should we?'

He makes his rumble of agreement and we set off for the remainder of our run. But I don't have long to fume over Ben and Caroline's selfish behaviour.

When we get back to the pavement outside Magpies, my van has police tape across the side doors and rear access, and a uniformed officer is standing guard beside it.

'What the hell?' I murmur.

Mouse begins to growl at this travesty towards his beloved vehicle, so I draw him close and murmur to reassure him. The PC eyes him warily, and I say, 'He's fine. He won't hurt you.' The man nods but looks unconvinced. 'Why is my van taped off like it's a murder scene?'

'This is your van, ma'am?' He draws a small notebook from his breast pocket, flips it open and checks, 'Ms Louise Williams?'

'That's me. What's going on?'

'We're just waiting for your van to be collected. I believe DS Timpson would like to interview you, about the death of Martin Patterson.' He uses his radio to alert the call handler of my presence, all the time keeping me firmly in his gaze.

'Where is DS Timpson?' I ask, when he comes off the radio.

'She's currently back at the police station in Colchester.'

I tilt my head questioningly. 'So, can I drive my van over there?'

'I'm afraid not, ma'am.'

'I can't drive my van but I'm expected to somehow get to Colchester to be interrogated?'

He draws out his phone and checks something. 'There's a number thirty-eight bus that goes to Witham train station. It should be leaving from the Co-op in about fifteen minutes. You can get the train from Witham to Colchester.'

With a grudging acceptance of my fate, I head towards the house to change out of my running gear. It takes me a moment to persuade Mouse to stop glowering at the PC and come inside. I suspect he's worried the officer might steal the van if he turns his back. I have to promise Mouse treats, which I dole out quickly the moment we're both in the hall, with the front door closed behind us. I wonder if the police officer would respond as positively to the offer of a treat: the use of my van in return for one of Nellie's amazing biscuits. *Probably best not to try*, I tell myself.

'Wait there, boy,' I tell Mouse, dashing upstairs to apply a lick of deodorant, pull on clean clothes, and make it back down in time to head over to the bus stop, where I send Avery a text, asking her to unlock the garden for the volunteers. I'm relieved when she sends a thumbs up in response.

* * *

It takes us an hour and a quarter to reach the police station on Southway in Colchester. I try not to dwell on the fact that it would have taken about twenty minutes by van. During the journey, my brain keeps turning over what on earth the police might have found, and how it might be linked to Martin's death. I can't think of anything in the van that could incriminate me.

Whilst the rational part of my mind is happy to point out that I haven't killed anyone – and that DS Timpson seems very professional and thorough – a more disquieting element appears to enjoy reminding me of the times when I've witnessed police incompetence or even corruption. What if someone is trying to pin Martin's murder on me, and the officers don't do their due diligence, to uncover my innocence?

In between these concerns, others pop up, such as whether there might be some mistake about Nellie – whether she could have somehow picked up the Green Raven sheets from someone else. And, if this isn't the case, why she would choose to feature me in the malicious column – and why she claimed not to know the Raven's identity. It's this lie that hurts the most.

Thankfully, Mouse is entertained by first the bus and then the train, appearing not to notice my distraction. He also seems to have forgotten the Curious Incident of the Man and the Van in the excitement of new travel, interesting smells, and attention from friendly strangers.

As we walk from the vehicular station to the law-enforcing one, I realise we are not going to see any of the ancient part of Colchester. It's a city I've wanted to visit for a while, boasting among its many antiquities an old castle set in a large sloping garden. I had not intended for my first visit to the city to be to the police station for an interview about a murder.

When we reach the police station, I am summoned almost immediately by DC Wright. A kind desk clerk offers to mind Mouse, who is delighted to make a new friend and check out a fresh supply of treats.

I, meanwhile, follow DC Wright into an interview room, where I take my seat on the other side of the table from him and DS Timpson. She greets me and explains that the interview is voluntary and I am free to leave at any time – before, rather confusingly asking if I'd like to consult a lawyer.

'Do I need a lawyer?' I ask.

'As I said, this interview is voluntary, so that is your decision.'

'I'll leave it for now,' I say, hoping I'm not making a mistake.

She nods before speaking our names for the recording, and launching in with her first question:

'Can you explain why the same formula of organophosphate pesticide that we found in Martin Patterson's blood was discovered inside your van?'

I stare at her. 'I'm sorry. Can you say that again?'

She just watches me while I no doubt display every emotion as I feel it – flicking through objection, denial, confusion and then, for a moment, mistrust. I have to remind myself that this is a police officer who has done nothing to make me doubt her.

I take a deep breath. 'You're saying Martin Patterson was killed with pesticide, and you found the container in my van? So that's why there was police tape, with an officer standing guard?' Her face is inscrutable. I continue, 'I don't use pesticide. I garden organically, wherever possible.'

'"Wherever possible",' she repeats, folding her hands on the table. 'So, you admit that you do resort to chemicals on occasion?'

'I can't think of the last time I used a chemical pesticide,' I say. 'It's just not something I do. I mean, not since the research came out more than a decade ago, proving that they harm humans, pets and beneficial insects.'

'To clarify, you're saying you were not aware that there was a container of pesticide in your vehicle?'

'There can't have been. I would have known.' With a frown, I say, 'Can I ask what made you search my van?'

'We received an anonymous tip-off.'

Feeling like I'm stuck in a Kafka novel, I say, 'But . . . like I said, I don't even use pesticide.'

She reaches for a transparent evidence bag and places it before me. 'And yet, a container of pesticide was found.'

'You found this in my van?' I say, staring at the container. I'm aware the conversation is becoming circular, but what can I do other than maintain my innocence and ignorance? I stare at her, trying to order my thoughts. 'How did you get access to my vehicle anyway?'

'A Ms Sinclair let us into the house so that we could retrieve the van key.'

So Avery went behind my back. But perhaps she had no choice. 'Are you allowed to search my vehicle without telling me?' I ask the DS.

'We are if we've obtained a warrant – which we had – and if we believe that the search might be helpful to our investigation – which as you can see, it was.' She folds her hands on the table and says, 'Ms Williams, you can see how this looks, can't you? Not only were you the first on the scene after Mr Patterson's murder, but you were in possession of the same poison as was used to kill him.'

It's my turn to scrutinise her. But she's still not giving much away. At last, I say, 'Are you charging me?'

She clears her throat. 'Not at present, no.'

'OK . . . so I'm guessing that means you don't have anything on me. I mean, the mere presence of pesticide in a gardener's van wouldn't make for a very tight case, would it – especially as I'm sure you haven't found my fingerprints on the container?'

She glances at DC Wright, who shrugs. Looking back at me, she says, 'Our lab is still examining the evidence.'

'So, what am I doing here?'

She frowns. 'Ms Williams, I'm not sure you appreciate how serious this is.'

I laugh, albeit sardonically, and she raises an eyebrow. I explain: 'It's just that I'm aware you're doing your job. But it also feels like a waste of both of our time. You know I have no connection to Martin Patterson . . .'

'We are still verifying that,' she says.

I hold up a hand. 'OK, so, as I was saying, you have to go through the motions. But really, you both know I'm not the murderer. If you let me, I can help you find out who did kill Martin.'

She sighs, unfolds her hands and dusts a crumb from the table. Raising her eyes to meet mine, she says, 'With all your experience of police procedure, I'm sure *you* know that protocol doesn't allow me to involve a civilian in an investigation. But if you come across anything pertaining to the case, I would ask that you let us know immediately.'

'Of course,' I say. 'And if you come across the person who stashed that pesticide in my van, I'd appreciate hearing about it.'

'I can't offer that, but we can, of course, let you know as soon as we have cleared you of any wrongdoing.'

'I'll take it – thank you.'

She tilts her head in acknowledgement. 'In the meantime, you are free to go.'

But something's bothering me. 'You do realise this is almost certainly linked to the skeletons, don't you? In fact, maybe that's why someone wants to incriminate me – because I dug up their long-buried secret.'

'We are, of course, looking into any links between the two cases,' she says, 'but this is more difficult, now that Mr Patterson is dead.'

I raise an eyebrow. 'Right, but we know that the bodies in the grave are Martin's brother Charles and Charles's girlfriend, Megan . . .'

Her impassive expression gives way to shock and she leans forward. 'How did you know that?'

I consider informing her that PC Hawkins is an even more effective news transmitter than *The Green Maven*, but I hold back from blowing that particular whistle. 'Greenhaven's a small place,' I say. 'And there are people living there who still remember Charles and Megan's disappearance. Once news of the skeletons made the rounds, those people made the connection.'

She exchanges another look with her DC, but it's one that I can't read. 'Well, obviously we can't comment on an ongoing investigation.'

'Obviously,' I say.

'In the meantime, I do ask that you remain in Greenhaven until we say otherwise.'

'Of course,' I say.

'Interview terminated,' she announces, and DC Wright nods and turns off the recording equipment.

And then DS Timpson reaches across the table to shake my hand, and surprises me by holding on to it and leaning still further towards me. In a low voice – despite the lack of anyone but DC Wright and me to hear – she says, 'We don't believe you are responsible for the murder. If you were, you would have done a better job of disposing of the evidence.'

I laugh again, but this time it's with genuine humour. 'Er . . . thank you?' I say in a questioning tone.

I even receive a smile in return before DC Wright escorts me back to the entrance.

My mind is whirring as I collect Mouse from the obliging staff member at the reception desk. I thank the man, and he smiles adoringly at Mouse. 'Any time.'

And then, in the absence of our beloved van, Mouse and I walk to the station to catch the train to Witham, and then the bus back to Greenhaven. And, throughout the journey, as Mouse admires the many, varied views, along with squirrels, rabbits and diverse wildlife, I am trying to process the idea that someone would want to frame me for the murder of Martin Patterson.

43

There's no sign of my van when Mouse and I eventually reach its parking spot on Hogs Green Road outside Magpies. With a jolt, I realise the police must now have towed it away. I had been hoping to check whether there were any signs that the lock had been picked by whoever planted the pesticide. I wish I'd thought to check that with DS Timpson – although I daresay she wouldn't have told me.

It's disconcerting being on this side of the investigation, especially with my recent run-ins with police elsewhere. I must try to believe that justice will be done. At least DS Timpson inspires confidence.

I let Mouse and myself into the house, whereupon he runs to the kitchen and drinks a bowl of water before settling himself for a sleep in the living room, stretching out luxuriously in Timmy's absence. He and Nellie must be off on one of her art projects. I still haven't had a chance to talk to her about her alter ego, the Green Raven. I can't decide which revelation is more shocking: the pesticide in my van, or Nellie's poison-pen betrayal. Both are troubling.

Two coffees later, I'm about to wake Mouse and set off with him for the build site when he stirs of his own accord, barking and running into the hall with his tail wagging. This is closely followed by a ring at the doorbell. I open it to find Avery in yet another striking ensemble, this time a burgundy coat with a matching hat, shaped like a bluebell, which I think is called a cloche.

'Steph, can I come in?' she asks, stroking Mouse who has dashed out to greet her.

I hesitate. 'I'm late at the site.'

'Oh, don't worry – I've let them in, as you asked, and they all seemed to know what was expected of them.'

'Oh, that's good, thanks.'

I open the door wider to allow her to enter. 'Can we go through to the kitchen?' she asks.

I nod. Despite the restless sensation that I am overdue elsewhere, I do want to hear her side of what happened with my van key.

I lead her into the kitchen, where she takes a seat at the table while I make another pot of coffee and pour us each a mugful. Mouse settles on the floor beside Avery's chair, clearly remembering her as the bestower of dog biscuits. She strokes him as I join her at the table with our mugs.

She thanks me before sipping her drink, but it's clear she's preoccupied. I haven't forgotten our contretemps when she visited the site, but I have no intention of apologising.

Instead, she sets down her mug and says, 'I'm sorry I was a bit harsh the last time we met. I was having a bad day, but I shouldn't have taken it out on you.'

'That's all right,' I say. From the way she watches me, I wonder if she's expecting me to reciprocate. I merely smile before saying, 'My van key . . .'

She pulls a face. 'Yes, that's really why I'm here – although I did want to apologise as well. Well, I mean, that's two things to apologise for.'

'What happened with the key?'

She shrugs. 'That very correct detective sergeant – Simpson, is it?'

'Timpson,' I say.

'Well, she and her partner against crime . . . Wright?' I nod. 'The pair of them turned up on my doorstep first thing this morning, while I was still in my dressing gown. They'd been to Magpies and got no response, and they had my details as chair of the Heritage Society committee – they knew I was in charge of hiring you and setting you up in the house . . .'

'So they asked you if you had a spare key,' I finish.

'Yes. And, well, I do, of course. And I let them in and supervised, to make sure they didn't start poking around. When there was no sign of your van key in the hall, I showed them up to your bedroom, where they discovered it on your dressing table. As I say, I am sorry, but I really didn't feel I had a choice. They had a warrant to search the van, and they said they'd rather access it with the key than by force.'

I sigh and pick up my mug, inhaling the fortifying aroma. 'You did the right thing,' I say. 'But, if the detectives needed the key, it means the van hadn't been broken into.'

She surveys me. 'You don't look very pleased about that?'

Not wanting to tell her about the container of poison, I take a sip of coffee and hold the rich brew in my mouth for a moment. Another thought occurs to me: 'I'm not about to be fired, am I?'

She frowns. 'Why on earth would you be fired?'

'Well, it's pretty obvious I'm under investigation in Martin's case . . .'

She waves an airy hand. 'Don't forget they arrested John first. And that was a waste of time.'

It's my turn to frown. 'They didn't arrest him. And they haven't arrested me.'

'No, of course not – or you wouldn't be here, would you? Silly me: bad choice of words.'

I'd love to ask if she has any idea who might want to frame me, but I hesitate. Instead, I settle on, 'Have you and the rest of the committee all been questioned?'

She nods. 'And not just the committee – all of us with close ties to Martin have had to supply our whereabouts for Wednesday night,' she says. 'The police even took our fingerprints. I'm fortunate in that I was with Norma till almost midnight that night. I don't envy anyone who was on their own at home – it makes it difficult to prove.'

'It does,' I say. 'But hopefully the police will get some DNA soon from the scene, and be able to rule out the majority of Martin's enemies.'

'Normally, I'd balk at the use of that word,' she says, 'but, in his case, an exception must be made. Between the failure of the factory and his unpleasant personality, the man made himself extremely unpopular.'

I nod. 'I may not have been here long, but I have gathered that much.'

She swigs some more of her coffee before getting to her feet and leaving the mug in the sink.

'Right,' she says, 'I'll let you get on. But do bear in mind that the committee will support you, should you need it. There's no way Martin was murdered by someone without a grudge against him.'

I finish my own coffee and stand to join her. As we walk to the front door, I say, 'Thanks, Avery.'

She squeezes my arm. 'We can't let you be implicated by a lazy investigation. As I said, if you need our support, we – the committee – will be happy to intervene.'

With a nod, she strides off down the drive, leaving me to clip on Mouse's lead before locking up and heading to work.

At the build site, while Mouse runs to greet Marion, I find Norma and quietly tell her why I'm late.

She frowns and says in an equally low voice, 'So, let me get this straight . . . The police think you murdered Martin, even though you barely knew him?'

'It would appear so.'

She's been digging out ivy roots, so I grab a fork and join her.

Eloise wanders over. 'I've been thinking: how about a boat instead of the bridge?' she says. 'So it's like the kids can sail to the island.'

'That's great,' I say. 'But I want to build a play car next to the little house, and I don't think the funds will stretch to a boat as well. The bridge should allow for lots of fun games.'

Her eyes grow wide with excitement. 'Oh my god! A playhouse and a car!' She grins. 'I might need to practise in the car – I can't drive yet.'

'Eloise, would you like to take on the car as a project?' I ask her.

'How'd you mean?'

'Well, I was thinking that you can't do anything with the den-building project until we've finished the garden. In the meantime, how would you feel about researching car models from 1926 to 1930, say, and choosing one that you think would work alongside the miniature version of Woodpeckers?'

Her eyes light up. 'That would be amazing! Can I really?'

'Of course. Do some sketches to scale – we can discuss measurements together before you do that – and we'll take it from there.' I decide to wait a while before telling her that I'm also thinking she might like to be in charge of sourcing the materials for the car. I know, from my own early apprenticeship, how much a little autonomy can help to build confidence and expertise, but the extra responsibility needs to come in increments.

Norma, who is standing with us, says to Eloise, 'I can teach you to drive, if you like. I have a sweet little Fiat that would be perfect as a learner car. We can start off on some of the quiet roads around here.'

Eloise looks terrified at the prospect of the scatty Norma being responsible for her driving lessons, but she manages to say politely, 'That's so kind, but I think my mum's going to take me out.'

'Ah, fair enough,' says Norma.

Eloise smiles and asks her: 'Where are you going to do your mural?'

'Good question.' Norma turns to me. 'What were you thinking?'

'Avery's somehow managed to secure some council funding for a ramp for skateboards and push scooters. How would you feel about working with some of the local young people on decorations for that? I'm thinking, maybe a graffiti style?' But she and Eloise exchange a look.

'You can't do that,' says Eloise.

'Why not?' I ask.

Norma takes a moment to tuck a strand of hair beneath her woolly hat before saying, 'You've only just won everyone over to the centenary garden. The minute they hear the word "graffiti", they'll be after you with pitchforks.'

'Really?'

They both nod, eyeing me with sombre expressions. 'OK,' I say. 'So something that everyone will approve of, and that you can get young people involved in.'

Norma nods. 'I'd love that. I'll reach out to the local primary school, and put something on the village noticeboard to attract the older kids.'

'Perfect,' I say with a smile. 'Obviously, all materials will be covered. We can discuss your fee once I've worked out all the spending allocation.'

'I don't need a fee.'

I'm about to argue with her – I feel quite strongly that an artist should be paid for their time – but Christy comes over, bow saw in hand. He must have brought this tool from home, as it isn't one of mine. 'Hi Steph,' he says. 'How long before the build starts?'

I sigh. 'I'd love to get the digger back in, but the police won't allow it until they've finished with the grave.'

We all turn to survey the trench, with its now ratty police tape fluttering forlornly in the wind.

'Surely they're done by now?' says Christy. 'Would you like me to get on to them?'

'Do you have a contact there?' I ask.

'No, but they know me,' he says in a tone of voice that leads me to suspect he makes frequent complaints.

'That's OK,' I say. 'Thanks, though.' I'm about to add that I'll call them – but this morning's visit to the station has me wondering whether I should steer clear of the Colchester constabulary.

'Did I hear you saying they found poison in your van?' says Christy, frowning at me.

'Only pesticide,' I say.

'Is that how Martin died?' Eloise asks.

I shrug, unwilling to say too much. 'I don't think anything's been confirmed.'

Christy says, 'I'm surprised they let you go, if you were in possession of the poison.'

I frown. 'I don't think they can hold a gardener for being in possession of pesticide. It's not like they found cyanide capsules or arsenic.'

'True, true,' he says. 'Well, let me know if you need anything.'

I thank him and then, keen to change the subject, suggest we all go over the road for a coffee.

I jog home to check on Mouse before joining the others at the café. He's snoring gently on the floor cushion in the living room, Mr Rabbit and his favourite blue lead both tucked under one paw. I tiptoe out, making sure the door is firmly closed against the Tiny Terror, although there's still no sign of Nellie or her dog.

44

Nellie finally returns at seven o'clock that evening. She opens the living room door, where I'm sitting on the sofa, surrounded by scrap books filled with inspiration, my laptop open as I make adjustments to my design for the new garden, adding in the vegetable plot on the far end, in the rectangular area behind the playhouse. Even if I can't speak to Kieran about it, it will make a great addition to the community garden. I have sent emails to the village school and the local branch of Mencap, a charity for adults with additional needs, and I'm hoping they will both want to make use of it.

'Hiya!' she calls. Timmy races in, his little paws slipping on the polished floorboards. When he reaches the rug, he jumps on to Mouse, who greets him good-naturedly, nosing his friction-powered ball to invite the little dog to join him in a game.

Nellie holds up a carrier bag. 'I hope you haven't eaten yet?'

'Not yet. I got immersed. What have you got?'

'Chinese takeaway.'

'Sounds great.' I get to my feet, leaving the dogs to play. Timmy is emitting low growls, while Mouse knocks the ball for him to chase.

I wait until Nellie and I are seated at the table with our bowls of steaming noodles and deep-fried tofu with carrots, baby sweetcorn and mangetout before asking, 'Where have you been?'

She forks up a water chestnut and says, 'Visiting my relatives nearby. I didn't mean to be there so long, but I had some . . . stuff I needed to talk to them about. It got kind of heavy. Actually, I need to talk to you as well.'

Meeting her eye, I say, 'Is this about you being the Green Raven?'

She blanches and asks quietly, 'How did you find out?'

'Mouse discovered Timmy's secret treasure hoard. There were some of your Green Raven columns there.'

'Oh.'

'Oh indeed.'

She sighs and pushes a copper curl off her face. As she's still holding her fork, this results in her adding a long noodle to the curl. I leave it for now – there are more important things to sort out.

'What's going on, Nellie?' I ask at last, when she doesn't say anything. 'Why would you write such horrible things?' I keep my voice gentle, because I can see she's close to tears.

'I didn't write that stuff,' she says, gazing at her bowl. She sniffs loudly, so I fish in my pocket for a tissue which she takes and uses to wipe her eyes and nose. 'Thanks.' She manages a weak smile, and finally lifts her gaze to meet mine. 'It was Jeremy's idea,' she says.

'Jeremy, as in the husband of Stella? The man you've been meeting in private?'

She nods. 'You see, we're not having an affair.' She shudders. 'Like you said, he's way older than me. And he's married. I'd never sleep with a married man.'

'Nellie, can you get to the point?' I say, keeping my voice neutral.

She looks down at the tissue in her hand and then her back straightens and she nods and begins: 'My grandparents lived here in Greenhaven.'

I frown. 'I thought you didn't know anyone here until you arrived for your residency.'

'I don't. My dad grew up here, then they moved away when his sister went missing.'

My eyes grow wide. 'Was his sister . . . ?'

She nods. 'My granddad was John Hughes. My dad's sister was Megan, Charles Patterson's girlfriend. She allegedly ran off with him. But my dad always maintained the Pattersons had done away with her to prevent the match, and then sent their son away, to protect him. Like Avery said, my nan died within the year. Everyone said it was because of what happened with Megan.'

'So that's why you seemed upset, when you found out about the skeletons' identity,' I say softly.

She nods again. 'Yeah. And that's why I went to my cousins' last night, instead of coming home after the dress fitting. I wanted to let them know as soon as possible.'

'So, did your dad have other siblings?'

'No, but these are like . . .' She wrinkles her nose in concentration. 'Second cousins once removed? Or maybe third cousins? I think my granddad was brothers with theirs or something.'

'Ah OK. That makes sense.' There's a pause, then I say gently, 'So your dad was half right – someone did do away with his sister.'

'I know. I can't decide if it's a good or bad thing that Dad died last year, not knowing what really happened to her.'

'Either way, it's awful,' I say.

'Yep.'

I squeeze Nellie's arm as she swipes ineffectually at more tears with the now soggy tissue. I hand her another and sit quietly for a moment while she dries her face. At last, I ask, 'So . . . how is the Green Raven connected to all this?'

Nellie takes a deep breath. 'OK, so, yes: Dad died still filled with loathing for the Pattersons, and for what he believed happened to his sister. I came here to get closure, for Dad's memory and for my own peace of mind. It's hard inheriting that kind of hatred and not knowing, you know?'

'So, you aren't just here to be artist in residence? Why didn't you tell me the truth? Didn't you trust me?'

Her eyes well up again. 'It's not like that. I wanted to tell you, but I couldn't work out how. It's like, the closer we got, the more I didn't want to do anything to jeopardise that.'

A thought occurs to me: 'Does Avery know who you are?'

She shakes her head. 'I use my middle name, Dawn, as my surname for my art, so there was no way for anyone to connect me with the family who lived at Magpies before. Not that Hughes is an uncommon name!'

I stare at her. 'They lived in this house?'

She nods. 'Granddad was a manager before they fired him.' Her voice is bitter, and I don't blame her. I remember what she told me, about the man who fought for fair pay for women workers.

'Your grandfather sounds like an amazing man,' I say.

She nods. 'He never stopped campaigning. He believed everyone deserved equal pay and equal treatment. And he passed on that belief to my dad, who continued the fight. Dad didn't deserve to die at sixty.' Her voice catches, and several tears plop on to the table.

I squeeze her shoulder. My previous anger has been pushed out by sympathy and understanding.

'He really didn't,' I say. 'So is the Green Raven column about getting justice for your dad?'

She wipes her nose again, and takes a deep breath. 'I met Jeremy when I'd just moved in. I'd gone over to take some sketches of Woodpeckers from the drive, and he came home in that fancy sports car, and we got talking. It turned out he had his . . .' she hesitates, 'own reasons to bear a grudge against the Patterson family. I can't even remember which one of us came up with the idea for the column. Because he lives with Stella, he knew she was always looking for more material for the paper. The Green Raven seemed like a good first step towards getting some kind of . . . not revenge, but answers.'

'So, is that why the two of you have been meeting in secret?' She nods. 'How did you think the column would lead to getting answers?'

'We figured we could ask people to email us with their stories, and we'd promise to keep it all anonymous.'

'So villagers could be as spiteful as they wanted, without any consequences?'

She sighs. 'I know – not the most well considered of plans, was it? But we were both buzzing with the idea of taking some kind of control, you know? And we thought people might tell us stuff that would help us with our own family histories.'

'I think I get that,' I say.

'But it got a bit out of hand,' she says.

'You can say that again.'

She nods. 'The deal was that I would email my contribution to Jeremy, then he'd compile the column – he's done a bit of journalism, so he knows how to format copy for newspapers. But he started rewriting my submissions without checking with me – and then he stopped using my bits all together.'

'Is that when the column got more vicious?'

She nods. 'I tried to get him to tone it down – it was never meant to be hurtful to anyone but Martin Patterson – but I couldn't get Jeremy to listen.' She looks me in the eye. 'I honestly didn't know about the warning to you, or the bit about eagles and crows, till it came out in *The Maven*.'

Remembering how uncomprehending she'd seemed at the time, I say, 'I believe you. Are you going to tell Stella?'

'I think she knows,' she says. 'She seemed kind of half-hearted when she accused me of sleeping with her husband.'

I frown again. 'But why doesn't she just refuse to publish the column?'

'I have a theory on that . . .' says Nellie, grabbing Timmy as he hurtles past, and restraining him on her lap, eliciting grumbles from the little dog.

'Go on,' I say.

'When I first met Jeremy, he told me that his wife doesn't know about his history with Greenhaven. Although he clearly believes that, I don't think it's true. I think Stella knows that Jeremy is looking for answers, but she doesn't have the courage to confront him about it. Instead, she pretends not to know who's writing the column, in the hope that he'll get what he needs in the form of answers from residents, and they can settle down properly here.'

'I've been wondering something,' I say. 'How did Jeremy know to warn Martin?'

'Oh I don't think he did.' When I look sceptical, she adds, 'The whole village was buzzing with how the skeletons must be Charles and Megan, and how Martin must have killed them. I think he just realised Martin was bound to be targeted before too long. He swears he didn't imagine someone would murder him, though.'

'What is Jeremy's history here?' I ask.

But she shakes her head. 'That's not my story to tell.'

'Ah, well do you want the latest instalment in mine, in that case?' I start to fill her in on my morning visit to the police station, breaking off to tell Timmy he won't be getting any of my dinner. He sighs and shuffles off into the corner to stare at me while chewing on my old trainer.

Nellie is horrified by my tale. 'You mean, someone's framing you?'

'It looks like it. But there won't be any proof that the poison belongs to me – I mean, I've never seen it before.'

She nods. 'I just can't see why anyone would choose you.'

I shrug. 'Newest arrival, fewest ties in the village.'

'Put like that, I'm lucky they didn't pick me,' she says.

'Ah, but it also needed to be someone who farmed or gardened, so that would rule you out.'

She shivers. 'This place is beautiful on the outside, but there's some really sinister stuff going on, isn't there?'

I can't argue with that.

In bed that night, it occurs to me that the motives for murdering Martin Patterson continue to stack up. I don't envy DS Timpson her job, when there are so many people in the village with reasons to want Martin dead.

45

Tuesday passes with more digging by my volunteers, more tree surgery by me, and a lot of wood-stacking by all of us, some in the wildlife area, and the rest in neat piles outside the site, for Greenhaven's residents. It hasn't rained for some time, reminding me once again that Essex is in an area of low rainfall, and I must take this into account with my planting.

That evening, Nellie and I eat a homemade stew so tasty that it makes me rethink the inclusion of apricots in savoury dishes. Not that I'll be doing any cooking myself. I find myself wondering how much Mike likes to cook. I know he makes most of his meals from scratch, so maybe he'd be happy with me as sous chef. *Getting a bit ahead of yourself there*, I think. *You're rarely in the same county, let alone the same kitchen.*

I've just finished clearing away the dinner things when my phone rings with a call from Dad. I answer it as I walk upstairs to my room, leaving Mouse snoozing with Timmy beside the radiator in the living room. He's clearly of the opinion that a slumbering Timmy is far preferable to an awake one, and I can't say I blame him.

'Hi Dad,' I say as I answer the phone while entering the bedroom. I close the door and walk over to the sofa.

'So,' says my dad cheerily, 'is anyone dead yet?' When this intended joke is greeted with a long silence from me, he splutters, 'What? Not again! Oh Lou . . .'

'It's not my fault,' I say, sinking on to the sofa.

'No, I know, of course not. I just . . .' I hear Mum's voice in the background, then he says, 'I'd better put your mum on.'

'Why don't you just put me on speakerphone?' I say. But he's already passing the phone to Mum.

'Louise, what's happened? Are you all right?'

'I'm fine, Mum. It's just . . .' I close my eyes and take a deep breath. 'There's been a death.'

'Not again!' she echoes Dad.

'Can you both stop acting as though this is somehow my fault? I didn't do anything.' I refrain from mentioning that the Essex police force don't seem convinced about that.

I hear Dad's voice say, 'Who was it?'

'I don't know, Nigel,' says Mum. 'Give me a moment.'

'It was a man called Martin Patterson,' I tell her.

'Patterson . . . Isn't that the name of the family who built the village?' she says.

'It is. He's the heir who destroyed the family business.'

'Did he die of natural causes?' The hope in her voice is so obvious, I consider lying. But she'll find out sooner or later.

'It looks like he was poisoned,' I say.

'Ohhhh.'

She tells Dad, and he says, 'Well, that's new. Or the last one didn't die from it, at least.'

I say, 'Please tell Dad that I'm sure that's what Martin's killer was going for: *What has Steph Williams not encountered yet?* It's clearly all about my entertainment.'

She starts to repeat this to Dad, and then comes back on the phone and says, 'Actually, that's not funny.'

'No,' I say. 'That's the thing about murder: it's hard to find the comedic angle.' I refrain from telling her that a message sent to my phone on Wednesday night may have set me up to be the one who found him – although I am now leaning towards the idea that Martin just wanted to have another go at me about the centenary garden. It occurs to me that Mum and Dad don't even know about the skeletons.

After I've finished attempting to appease my parents and we've rung off, I video call Mike and fill him in on their reactions.

He pauses for a moment, before saying, 'You haven't told your parents about the skeletons?'

'I didn't deliberately not tell them.' I pause. 'At least, I don't think I did. But I guess I didn't deliberately set out to tell them, either.'

'It seems like it might be kind of pertinent,' he says thoughtfully, stroking Edward on his lap. Glancing over his shoulder, he says, 'Oh, Celine, come and say hi to my friend Steph.'

'Your *friend* Steph?' comes a sarcastic teenage voice from off screen. 'Is that a friend-with-benefits thing?'

'Don't be crude,' he says, but his tone is appeasing rather than reprimanding.

A young person with black eyeliner, short black hair and several ear piercings looms into view. She has a yoghurt in one hand and a spoon in the other. 'Hello, friend Steph,' she says, waving the spoon at the camera.

'Hi Celine. Good to meet you,' I say with a smile.

Looking back at her dad, she says, 'Done?'

'That'll do for now, I suppose,' he says drily. 'Thank you for granting us a moment of your precious time.'

She moves away and I hear her feet clomping up the stairs.

'So, that was Celine,' he says.

'At least now I can put a face to the name.'

'Even if it is a rather hostile face,' he says.

'I didn't get hostile,' I say. 'More . . . impatient.'

He smiles. 'You're very kind. It's one of the reasons why I like you.'

'I'm not that kind,' I say. 'Apparently, I poisoned Martin Patterson.'

'I'm sure he deserved it.'

'Well, there is that.'

He raises an eyebrow. 'It feels a bit like you might have led with whatever this is, and told me the stuff about your parents afterwards.'

'Sorry. So, yeah, the DS has decided I poisoned the man with pesticide.'

Perhaps because my tone is casual, he looks bemused rather than outraged. 'Do you use pesticide?'

'I do not.'

'So, why . . . ?'

'The police found a container of it in my van.'

'How did it get there?'

'Beats me.'

He stares at me. 'You mean someone set you up?'

'It would appear that way.'

His puzzled expression deepens and he says, 'Hold on, why don't you seem more stressed or angry about this?'

I shrug. 'I think it's because it's so ridiculous. I mean, I'm about the only person in the whole village who didn't have a grudge against the man.'

'Do you think that's why they've singled you out – because the police will be slowed down trying to find any connection between you and the victim?'

'I suppose that's possible. I certainly prefer that to the idea that I've been chosen because of the trail of dead bodies I've left behind.'

He nods. 'I suppose that's another possibility: if Patterson's killer has read that you've been involved in other murder cases, they might expect the police to be suspicious towards you from the outset.'

'Yeah, thanks. Like I said, I'm trying not to spend too long considering that angle.'

'Sorry.'

'No, it's fine – I'm the one who brought it up. I mean, it does make sense: time the murder for after the suspicious newcomer's arrival, and make sure she's the one who finds the body. That way, the police look at her first – and, because she's a gardener, using pesticide ties her more closely to the killing.'

'How easy is it to get into your van?' he asks.

'The police needed the key for the search, so the lock can't have been broken.'

'Which means they either had a key or were adept lock pickers,' he says. 'Where do you keep your key?'

'On my dressing table. But I know what you're thinking, and there's no way Nellie's involved in this. Don't forget all of the committee have keys to the house.'

And now the question I've been trying to suppress rises to the surface: could someone on the committee be the murderer?

46

I have another bad dream, which wakes me at half-five, when I'm immediately hit by the memory of the poison stashed in my van.

Ever vigilant of my state of mind, Mouse pads over and jumps up to join me on the soft bed. 'I didn't poison anyone,' I tell him, stroking his head. 'But, you know what? I'm going to bloody well find out who did.' He makes his rumble of agreement.

After a long cuddle with Mouse, I pull on my running gear and clip on his lead. And then we set out, heading straight for a country footpath, and running through a mist that starts about fifty centimetres above the ground, so that our heads are in haze and our feet are in clear air. It's a curious phenomenon.

By the time we've turned back, the mist has lifted. I find myself wishing my mind could clear as easily. Instead, it's fogged with a host of unanswered questions, worry and mistrust.

As soon as we're back home and I've set out breakfast for Mouse, I run up to the bedroom where I grab my notebook, head back to the kitchen and, settling at the table, make more notes:

1. *Still to answer: Why was Avery driving Martin to a secret meeting in a desolate place?*
2. *Out of all of Martin's enemies, who killed him? Is his death linked to Charles and Megan's skeletons?*
3. *Is Martin's murderer also the person who's framing me or is more than one person involved?*
4. *What made me their target? Is it just my background, or have I done something to upset them (such as intending to build a garden that they consider a waste of village funds)?*
5. *Did Jeremy really not know Martin was at risk of death when he wrote the ominous Green Raven piece?*
6. *Can I trust the Heritage Society committee, or are they the ones trying to frame me for Martin's murder?*

Nellie appears as I'm finishing my notes, and offers to make breakfast while I go for a quick shower.

As we tuck into our full plates of field mushrooms, veggie sausages and grilled tomatoes, I ask her, 'Do you have any idea who could have planted the poison in my van? You know the village better than I do.' I sit back and swig my coffee while she deliberates.

'I keep coming back to it being a committee member. I mean, they got your van key from your bedroom, so they must have had access to a house key.'

'Could someone have come in without needing a key when you were home – without you hearing, I mean?'

She reflects on this. 'I guess I often have my music really loud when I'm working. It helps me block out random thoughts and just tune into the process, you know?'

'I get that,' I say. 'So, you're saying someone could have come in?'

She nods slowly. 'I reckon pretty easily, if I'm honest. If Timmy knew them, he might have run to say hello, but I probably wouldn't have noticed if I was in the zone.'

'So, the committee is Avery, Christy, Marion . . .'

She nods. 'Also Jeremy.'

I look at her. 'As in Green Raven Jeremy?'

'Yeah.'

'It would be pretty easy for him to watch for me going out from over the road, wouldn't it? Does he know you play loud music when you're working?'

'He's probably heard it from outside,' she says. 'But I can't see why he'd want to frame you.'

I huff. 'Yeah, but can you think why anyone would want to? I've only just got here.'

'Fair point.'

'Is Norma on the committee?' I ask.

'She used to be, but I think they threw her out when she kept turning up late or forgetting to turn up at all.'

'That sounds like Norma,' I say with a smile. 'I really like her, though.'

Nellie smiles. 'Me, too. She's one of a kind – and a fantastic artist. I've been trying to persuade her to send some of her work off to a couple of galleries where I have contacts.'

'That's kind,' I say. Slicing into a mushroom, I consider the roll call of suspects for my framing.

'I keep wondering what time he was killed,' I say. 'It would really help with looking into where people were.'

'Between ten and midnight on Wednesday night,' she says without hesitation.

Staring at her, I say, 'And you know that . . . ?'

'Vera from the Co-op,' she says. 'She heard Hawkins telling Midge the barman in the Feathers. You know what Hawkins is like: give him one drink and he spills everything.'

'Vera seems to be always in the right place at the right time,' I say.

'Yes,' she says with a shrug. 'But she works at the only grocer's in the village, and hangs out with her best mates in the only pub. It's a pretty easy way to keep up on all the goss.'

'Especially with such a loose-lipped village constable,' I agree.

'Right? Anyway, so Hawkins lets slip about time of death on Friday night, and Vera tells anyone and everyone when they go in the Co-op yesterday.'

'That PC should lose his job,' I say.

'It has been said. But most of the people here like being kept in the loop, so no one's rushing to report him.'

'So the message I received may really have been from Martin,' I say.

'Oh, that's true! Do you think he just wanted to have another go at you about the garden?'

'If it was from him, then that seems highly likely. Do you know, I feel a bit better, knowing it might not have been the murderer who summoned me there, to find the body.'

She shivers. 'Don't!'

'Sorry . . . Did Hawkins say anything else?'

She takes a moment, cutting a tomato into neat quarters while she thinks. Timmy has noticed we have food and has now positioned himself in his entreating position at her feet.

'You've just had breakfast,' she tells him. 'Go and play.' But he whines quietly, watching her fork as it moves to her mouth.

I eat a couple of mouthfuls of my own food before swigging some coffee. At last, I say, 'Does your silence mean you're deep in contemplation or are you done?'

'I'm trying to remember,' she says. 'I'm sure there was one other thing he said . . .'

I butter a piece of toast and spread raspberry jam on top before taking a big bite. 'This jam is delicious,' I say.

'It's local, from the jam factory in Tiptree,' she says. 'They've got a tea room. It's only about fifteen minutes from here; we'll have to go for a cream tea.'

'Sounds good.'

'I've got it!' she says then, dropping her fork on to her plate with a clatter. When I look bemused, she says, 'I've remembered what the other thing was that Hawkins let slip. He said the murderer would've had to be strong, because Martin's body had been dragged from his study to halfway down the garden.'

'Yeah,' I say. 'That's pretty obvious.'

'I suppose it is,' she says. 'Makes you wonder what the police were thinking, when they arrested poor John.'

'I don't think they arrested him – just took him in for questioning. But don't dismiss him because of his age. He's been gardening since he was a teenager, so he's got to be pretty fit and strong.'

'That's true,' she says thoughtfully. 'What about you? Do you think you could drag a dead man's body?'

I raise an eyebrow. 'Do you know, that's something I've never tested, for some reason.'

'Maybe it should be included as an event in the next Olympics,' she says.

'Yeah,' I say. 'Right between throwing the discus and tossing the hammer.'

We look at each other and grimace. As I told Mum, murder is really not a suitable topic for comedy.

47

'Do you know, I always thought Greenhaven was a safe place to live?' says Norma. 'But now it turns out there's a murderer just walking around.' She shudders, and Mouse, beside her, licks her fingers. She crouches to cuddle him. Looking up at me, she continues, 'It's hard to feel safe.'

She's just arrived at the site – twenty minutes after the others – and I've stopped work to allocate her a job.

'I'm sure you're quite safe,' I say. 'It seems likely Martin was targeted for a specific reason.'

She looks unconvinced. 'There are those skeletons as well – the ones you dug up.' She points to the ditch, where the ragged police tape is still blowing in the breeze. I take a deep breath, trying to select some appropriate platitudes, but she continues, 'I'm so glad I wasn't in the village the night Martin died.'

'Oh yes, you were out somewhere with Avery, weren't you?' I say.

She appears puzzled. 'No, I was at my daughter's in Maldon. We watched a film after we'd put the kids to bed, and it got so late that I slept over.'

'So, Avery wasn't with you?'

Looking even more bemused, she asks, 'Why would Avery come with me to Vicky's? They've only met once.'

Christy comes over at that moment, still carrying the fork he's been using to dig out ivy roots. 'I think you've got your days mixed there, Norma.'

She glares at him. 'Don't gaslight me, Christy. I know what night I saw my own daughter and grandkids.'

He holds up a hand. 'I only meant that you . . .'

'. . . I know what you meant, thank you very much. You and the others keep trying to persuade me that I'm losing my mind. I know I can be a bit . . . disorganised. But I'm not senile just yet.'

'No, no. Of course,' he says.

With an angry tut, she strides off to attack another of the ubiquitous buddleias. As soon as she's out of sight, Christy whispers to me, 'Norma saw her daughter on Monday night. Whatever she'd like to believe, she does get her days confused, I'm afraid.'

'Right,' I say. He nods before going back to his task.

I'm left feeling unsettled. Why did it matter so much to Christy what I believed?

* * *

Over a break that afternoon, I take Mouse home before deliberately seating myself near to Christy's perch on a fallen birch. I'm still unsure whether to remove this tree, or turn it into a feature.

I pour coffee from my thermos and offer a spare cup to Christy, which he accepts with thanks.

'It's black and strong,' I warn him as he takes a sip and chokes. 'Sorry!'

He shakes his head, laughing. 'No, I should have remembered you always ask for an extra shot at the café.'

'Awful about Martin's death, isn't it?' I say, sipping my coffee and trying to appear nonchalant.

'It is,' he says, putting down his cup and surveying it as if it might contain organophosphates. Turning to me, he says, 'Where are you up to with the police?'

'How do you mean?'

'Well, you said they'd found the pesticide used on Patterson in your van?'

I shrug. 'They obviously don't have anything on me, other than a container of pesticide that doesn't belong to me. So, I think that's probably an end to it.'

'That's good,' he says.

Trying to regain control of the conversation, I say quietly, 'You seemed very sure that Avery was with Norma on Wednesday night. Were you with them?'

'Oh, no. But I remember hearing them make plans for Wednesday, that's all.'

'What were you up to that night?' I ask him.

'"Up to"?'

'Well, were you out somewhere?'

He thinks for a moment before saying, 'Oh, yes – I was at the Feathers with Jeremy. Do you know him?'

I nod. 'We've taken our dogs out together.'

'Ah, yes. Good chap, Jeremy.'

I let this slide. My own feelings about Jeremy are far from positive since learning he is the Green Raven. I make a mental note to check whether the two men were really at the pub when Martin died.

There's a long silence, and then Christy gets to his feet, dusting his trouser legs for plant debris, before picking up his fork and returning to battle with the ivy roots. I had originally intended to dig up all of the bramble and ivy roots with mechanical diggers – but the police have vetoed my bringing in any machines until they're done with their investigations. I wonder how long it will be before the skeletons' grave can be reclaimed and turned into something positive.

As I take a walk around the site, envisaging the finished garden, I sift through everything I know so far.

I still don't know who planted the pesticide in my van. Which means I also don't know who poisoned Martin. I wonder if they put it in his tea. I remember reading that organophosphates don't have much flavour. I don't know exactly how much he would have needed to consume for the dose to be fatal, but I do know they're potent chemicals.

I think back to seeing him in Avery's car, being driven to the factory. It was clear they were disagreeing about something. And Avery's alibi for Wednesday night appears to be false.

But Martin would have needed to trust whoever poisoned him. It seems to me that the only way his killer could have administered the pesticide is if he let them into his house, and had a drink with them.

I need to find out who, if anyone, Martin spent time with. Given his unfortunate reputation, the numbers must be limited. In my experience, though, even unpleasant people have a few like-minded cronies.

I decide that a visit to the Co-op might be in order. We're running low on a few things. And this will give me an opportunity to run into Vera, who seems to know everything that goes on in the village.

48

When we finish at the site, I lock up and head over to the Co-op, where I'm pleased to see Vera is present, stocking shelves with tins.

I grab a basket and begin to fill it with bars of Fairtrade chocolate, strong filter coffee, and a couple of bottles of red wine. I check that this last has the green v on the label, as I've discovered that not all wine is suitable for a vegetarian diet – some has been made using fish bladders or gelatine. I'm still learning as I go.

Finally, I head to the pet food aisle, where I pick up a box of dog biscuits, plus a few sachets of Timmy's food and some of Mouse's favourite flavours.

I take my basket to the till, and Vera comes over to let herself in behind the counter.

'Hiya. Find everything OK?'

'Yes, thanks. Got all the essentials.'

She grins upon seeing my basket of dog food, wine, coffee and chocolate. 'I like a woman who knows what's important in life.'

I fish a folded bag out of my pocket and begin to fill it as she scans. 'Awful about Martin Patterson, isn't it?' I say, in a casual tone.

'Terrible,' she says. She stops scanning and, leaning towards me across the counter, says, 'And I heard the police tried to pin it on you.'

'Yeah. They found the same type of poison in my van, but it wasn't mine.'

'Course it wasn't,' she says. 'Why would you kill him? You can't have known the man.'

I smile. 'Thanks for that. I'm not sure everyone's as convinced as you are.'

'Well, stands to reason it's got to be a member of that girl Megan's family. Or someone who lost their job in the factory closure.'

'Why do you think Megan's family would want Martin dead?'

'It's obvious, isn't it? Because he bumped off her and Charlie.'

'That does seem to be what people are saying.'

'Well, who else could it be that killed them? He was Charles's brother, and that statue thingy in the grave came from Eagles. Poor Nancy – I keep remembering how they blamed her for nicking it. Everyone knew she wouldn't do something like that, but would they listen? I think the Pattersons knew Martin was a bad lot, but they didn't want to admit it.'

'That would make sense. I've been wondering, did he have any friends in the village?'

'Martin?' When I nod, she thinks for a moment. 'He sometimes got a drink with Jeremy – you know, from Woodpeckers?' I nod again, and she says, 'And I think Christy sometimes joined them. He's one of your helpers at the garden, isn't he?'

'That's right. Were you in the Feathers on Wednesday night?'

She nods immediately. 'Wednesday night's karaoke, so I always go along with the girls.'

'Were any of those men there – Martin, Jeremy or Christy?'

'Yeah, Jeremy and Christy were there, getting pretty bladdered by their standards. They even got up and did a song – "The House of the Rising Sun". We were all gobsmacked. They're both normally kind of wet blankets, you know?'

'Did they stay all evening?'

She narrows her eyes. 'Why are you asking all this?'

'Look,' I say, spreading my hands. 'I've got the police breathing down my neck. I want to find out who really killed Martin, to take the heat off me.'

'Oh, makes sense,' she says, surprising me with her immediate acceptance. 'I think they both left around ten, ten thirty. I remember it was when Suze was singing her Kate Bush number. I thought it was a bit rude they didn't stay till the end.'

'Thanks for that,' I say.

'No worries.' She starts scanning again. When I get my card out to pay at the end, she leans across again and says, in a whisper, 'There's some round here that think they're above the law. I hope they get done for this. None of us liked Martin, but no one deserves to go like that.'

49

When I get back home, I find Nellie in the dining room, making a small sculpture out of clay.

'Hiya,' she says as I appear in the open doorway.

'Hi. What are you making?'

'Come and see.'

I walk over to the table, which is strewn with small tools. The head and body of a bird of prey are emerging from a slab of clay.

'Is this a model of the piece you're planning for the garden?' I ask.

'Yeah.' She looks up at me. 'What do you think? I know I said I was going to etch an eagle into the surface, but how about if the whole village is on the surface of a giant bird?'

'My goodness!' I say, peering more closely. 'You've already started on that.'

She laughs. 'I meant to get the legs done first, but I got distracted wanting to see how it would look if the texture was actually a map of Greenhaven, with all the main buildings.'

'It's amazing,' I say, pulling up a chair beside her. 'Do you think it will work alongside my big pieces?'

She frowns suspiciously. 'What are your big pieces?'

'Oh, I only mean the playhouse – which will be modelled on the facade of Woodpeckers – and a vintage-style play car.'

'This is the first I've heard about a car,' she says, setting down a small knife. Her hands are covered in clay, and she has a few splodges of it on her face.

I pull a face. 'I'm sorry – I forgot to tell you. Eloise, my unofficial apprentice, is researching cars from the same period as the village, so we can have a car frame built with seats in, and hopefully a steering wheel.

'Who's going to make that?' she asks.

'I'm not sure. I need to ask around and do some research online, maybe.'

'There is a sculptor out on the Dengie,' she says. She pronounces it 'Den-jee'.

'What's the Dengie?' I ask.

'It's this area of Essex out past Maldon, along the estuary. This guy I'm following online has done loads of pieces at museums and stuff all around Essex. He's even made robots; they don't move, but they have bits you can press and turn and stuff, so they're kind of interactive.'

'Do you think he'd be able to do anything with this fallen birch I've been wondering about making a feature of?'

She nods. 'He uses a chain saw to carve dead trees. He's done some work at Hyde Hall. I'll send you his Instagram.'

'Brilliant, thanks.' I continue, 'We need to look at placement for your sculpture. As you know, in the kids' area, we're going to have a take on a Japanese-style garden, like at Eagles, but with a sandpit instead of a pond. And of course, there will be the climbing-frame pagoda. The new bit so far is only the car.'

'How come I didn't know about this car?'

'Sorry – I guess I've been a bit distracted,' I say.

She grins. 'Sorry, sorry. You're all right. What with you being framed for the a-hole's murder and all that, I'll let you off.'

I smile back. 'You're too kind.'

'But can we have a sit down together later, maybe after dinner, and go through everything?'

'Great idea.'

We exchange smiles, then I say, 'It's very quiet. Please tell me Timmy's not got out again.'

'I wish he had,' she says. 'He's been driving me mad. In the end, I had to shut him in the bedroom. Oh – I let Mouse out for a wee by the way.'

'Thanks for that. It was my next question.'

'To be honest, I was hoping Mouse'd have a good effect on my one, but I reckon Timmy's beyond redemption.'

'What's he done this time?'

'What hasn't he done? He's destroyed a plant that was trailing from a shelf in the lounge; he's eaten one of my slippers; and he's somehow got into a cupboard in the kitchen and shredded two washing-up sponges and a duster.'

'Oh.'

'Oh indeed.'

'Well, at least he didn't get into anything toxic,' I say. We're both quiet for a moment, and I'm sure she's also thinking about Martin's poisoning. 'Right,' I say, 'I'll leave you to it for now.

I want to take Mouse for a walk. Should I do dinner when we get back?'

She says, 'I was thinking, how about we go out for that meal at the Feathers you've been promising me?'

'Oh yeah – great idea. Do we need to book?'

'Shouldn't do if we head over about six. Is that OK?'

'Yes, perfect.'

'No clearing away for you afterwards, so we can come straight home and start going through your designs.'

With a smile and a nod, I leave her and head into the living room. Nellie has shut the door, presumably in case the Tiny Terror manages to escape from the bedroom. Mouse comes running to meet me and, after a cuddle with him, I turn off the telly – where what looks like a potato in a superhero cape is running about the screen – and he accompanies me upstairs. After I've showered and donned jeans and a sweater, I take him for a walk.

We arrive at Avery's without my making a conscious decision to go there. I hesitate at her gate but, as a fan of the greyhound in human form, Mouse tugs on the lead, and I find myself on the doorstep, ringing the bell.

'Sorry to turn up uninvited,' I say, when she opens the door.

'It's only the same as I did to you earlier,' she points out. 'Anyway, who can resist this young man?' She bends to stroke Mouse under the chin. 'Do you want to come in?'

'Just for a minute or two,' I say.

We step into the house and she leads us into the living room, where there's a fire crackling in the log burner.

'This is cosy,' I say.

'Yes, I do love a real fire,' she says. 'Take a seat, won't you?'

I sit in one of the armchairs as she sets down a cushion for Mouse near the fire. She strokes him as he settles himself, and he licks her hand.

I wait until she's taken her seat. And then I say, 'I really did appreciate what you said earlier, about supporting me.'

'Of course,' she says. 'You're here as our invited guest, and you find yourself at the centre of a police investigation. It's our responsibility to aid you, if necessary.'

'Have you had any thoughts about who might have killed Martin?' I ask her. 'I'm keen to redirect DS Timpson's suspicions.'

'I'd like to say I've been thinking about little else,' she says. 'But there's been a lot going on with the Heritage committee. I'm afraid Martin's death has left us in something of a hole.'

'Wait – Martin Patterson was on the committee?'

'Not exactly, no. But the Patterson family has always held a largely non-active role – a silent partner, if you like, whereby he occasionally helped out on the fundraising side. As he was in talks with a few potential patrons for the centenary garden, we've had to pick up the slack and reach out to them, try to convince them still to donate.'

'How's that gone?' I ask, feeling a twinge of panic at the thought that all my work and planning might be for nothing.

'Don't look like that,' she says with a smile. 'We'll get there. They just need persuading that the committee can be relied upon to ensure their names are engraved on a plaque or some such, for posterity. With Martin's death, they may have lost their main contact, but most of them still want the local recognition – and the tax break.' She smiles wryly.

'Well, that's a relief.'

'Was there something you wanted?' she asks, smiling at Mouse as he stretches out luxuriously in the fire's warmth.

I decide to go for it. 'Only to ask where you really were on Wednesday night.'

Her gaze snaps back to me. 'I'm sorry?'

'I know you weren't with Norma.'

'What on earth are you talking about? Where are you suggesting I was?'

'I'm not suggesting anything except for the fact that you've given the police a false alibi.'

She looks uncertain – something I haven't seen in her face before – and then she says, 'I'm sure I was with Norma. What makes you say otherwise?'

'Only that Norma was at her daughter's.'

She waves a dismissive hand. 'Oh, Norma's always getting her days mixed up.'

'So you were with her?'

'Of course.' Avery smiles, and our talk moves on to safer ground – including the quite literal ground that I'm desperate to break with modern machinery.

'I'm sure DS Timpson must be done by now with that area,' says Avery. 'I'll give her a call tomorrow, see if I can move things along.'

'It's all right,' I say. 'I want to talk to her anyway, so I can ask her then.' Getting up, I say, 'Nellie's expecting me back, so we'd better be off.'

I can see from her narrowed eyes that she's desperate to ask me why I want to talk to the DS. But I smile, call to a very warm, dozy dog, and we take our leave.

50

I ring Colchester police station as soon as Mouse and I get back from our walk. He drinks from his water bowl while I perch on a stool at the kitchen table.

'Can I speak to DS Timpson, please?' I ask, when the phone is answered. I give my name and wait only a few seconds before Timpson herself answers.

'Ms Williams?' she says. 'How can I help?'

'I might be wasting your time . . .' I say slowly.

'Go on.'

'Well, it's just that I've found out Avery's alibi for Wednesday night might be false.'

'This is Avery Sinclair?' she says. 'She said she was with a . . .' She's clearly checking her notes, '. . . Norma Tobias. I'm not sure if that alibi has been verified.'

'I found out today that Norma was at her daughter's in Maldon overnight on Wednesday. I mean, it's possible she's mistaken, of course, but I thought you should know.'

'Right, thank you. We'll look into it.'

'You should also know that Christy – I don't know his surname . . .'

'Leonards,' she says.

'Right, well he seems to be trying to make Norma think she's got it wrong, that she's mixed up her days.'

'We'll look into it,' she says again.

'I might be imagining it, but it feels like the committee – the Heritage Society committee, that is – are trying to cover something up.'

'Ms Williams,' she says, 'you are aware that you are still very much a person of interest?'

Perhaps it's naive, but I had hoped the police silence meant I was off the hook. 'Am I?'

'You are. You were in possession of the same poison that was used to kill Mr Patterson.'

'So, you think I'm trying to throw suspicion on to someone else?' I say.

She doesn't answer, which I take as confirmation. 'If you look me up on the police database,' I say, 'you'll see that I help to solve crimes; I don't commit them.'

'We'll see,' she says. 'Now, I must get on. But rest assured, we will be following up on Ms Sinclair's alibi.'

'Before you go, is there any way the police tape can be removed yet at the build site? I really need to get on with the groundwork.'

'I'll look into it.'

'Thank you.'

She hangs up, and I'm left staring at my phone, feeling unsettled and more than a little anxious. Mouse, sensing my mood, comes over to lick my fingers and I stroke him. 'Well,' I tell him, 'if she still thinks I'm guilty, we'll have to press on with finding the real killer ourselves, won't we?'

He makes his rumble of agreement before gathering Mr Rabbit from a shelf that he's discovered Timmy can't reach, and trotting through to the living room, to settle himself on the cushion near the radiator. I close the door before heading into the dining room to see Nellie, but the room is in darkness.

Upstairs, I knock on her door. 'Just a moment,' she calls. 'I'm getting changed.'

'Did you get all the clay off?' I call.

'I never get all of it off,' she says as she opens the door, still pulling a jumper over her head.

'Like me with soil,' I say. 'I always have some up my nails.'

We smile at one another, then she says, 'Did Timmy get past you just now?'

'I don't think so.'

She turns back into the room and gets down on all fours to look under the bed. 'What have you got there? Come on – give.'

Timmy slinks out from his hiding place, a soggy lump of clay dripping brown water on the rug.

'Give,' she says. He eyes her, then backs away. 'Steph,' she says, without turning round, 'can you grab a couple of treats from downstairs? I need to bribe him to drop it.'

I jog downstairs and return a moment later with two of the chicken treats which I know are his favourites. I shut the door behind me before passing them to her. 'Thanks,' she says. 'Look, Timmy boy, what have I got here?' He approaches her, still chewing on the soggy clay. 'Give,' she says, holding out her palm. I can see him weighing up his options. At last, he drops the clay into her hand and accepts a treat. 'Good boy!'

she says, stroking him. 'But you've made a bit of a mess up here, haven't you?'

'Do you want to get it cleaned up before we go out?' I ask.

'Nah,' she says. 'It can wait. I'm starved.'

'What will you do with Timmy?'

'I was thinking we might take the dogs with us.'

I close my eyes for a moment, envisaging the havoc Timmy could wreak in a public place. As I open them, I see her reading my expression. 'Believe it or not, he's much better out,' she says. 'He likes busy places with lots of people to make a fuss of him.'

I cross my fingers as I agree to her plan.

In fact, Timmy is a delight. Clearly a favourite with the Feathers' regulars, he leaves us in peace for most of our meal, as he tours the room, getting hugs and attention from everyone. Mouse opted out of coming with us, instead going out in the garden for a quick wee before taking Mr Rabbit upstairs, where he settled with the toy in his bed.

The food at the Feathers is typical pub fare. I have a vegetable wellington which is good but, to my mind, not a patch on Nellie's cooking. She chooses a fish dish, which she says needs more seasoning.

When we get back, Timmy is finally tired enough to fall asleep in the living room, and, in the absence of a clear table anywhere in the house, we settle on the sofa, to go through my designs.

'I love how you've got the Japanese influence in the kids' area,' she says. 'And that mini version of Woodpeckers with the vintage car outside is genius.'

'Thanks,' I say with a grin. I point to the clearing and say, 'So, initially I was going to keep this as it is, a kind of secret spot, but I'm now planning to clear the surrounding trees and shrubs, all of which are self-seeded, so there are plenty of the same species in other areas. I'm going to build a gazebo there, so people can play or watch the board game, no matter the weather.'

'What about the outdoor gym?' she asks.

'I keep changing my mind,' I say. 'Do you think people want that out in the open?'

'Definitely,' she says. 'They'll want to show off how many foot-lifty thingies and pull-ups they can do.'

'OK. In that case, I'm thinking the gym should go on the far side, so it doesn't spoil the geometry. And what do you think about your sculpture going here?' I point to a spot.

'What is that?' she asks, squinting at my sketch.

'The sensory garden. Roses, climbing jasmine and witch hazel for smell, plus bamboo and other grasses for the rustling sound they make when a breeze blows through them, and also to tie it in with the Japanese area. I also want to put in several Japanese quince shrubs, *Chaenomeles japonica*, which have wonderful brightly coloured flowers in spring. There will be white paving-stone paths all around, wide enough for motorised wheelchairs, and a big white patio in the middle with white benches. I want to echo all the angular white houses in the village.'

'How about if my sculpture was black?' she says slowly, evidently picturing it in the streamlined setting.

'Oh, that would be amazing,' I say. 'It feels in keeping with the time period, as well as providing that black and white effect that will be repeated in the giant chessboard. We can put the white benches in a rectangle, with a space at the centre for your sculpture. As you can see, there will be some more seats in another gazebo, to give shelter from the weather.'

'It's going to be a wonderland,' she says.

'Fingers crossed,' I say.

51

The next morning, Mouse and I return from our run at eight o'clock to find the house silent. Nellie would normally be starting on breakfast by now, and Timmy would be performing zoomies like an advert for a battery-powered toy. At the very least, he should be scrabbling to get out of Nellie's room.

'Where are they?' I set out food and water for Mouse before creeping upstairs to check, but there's no sound from the bedroom. I wonder where they've gone so early in the day.

Back downstairs, I find Mouse has taken advantage of the small dog's absence to stretch out in blissful relaxation on the cushion beside the radiator in the living room. I grab my notebook from my bedroom and take a seat on the sofa to look through my notes on the murder. Not for the first time, I wish I had fewer suspects.

Timmy's excited yapping a few minutes later is the first sign that he and Nellie have returned. Poor Mouse lifts himself from the cushion with an audible groan before pushing Mr Rabbit underneath the cushion and shoving his own head beneath it to join his toy.

'Do you want to go upstairs?' I ask, but he remains silent and motionless. I wonder if he believes that Timmy won't be able to see him, so long as he can't see Timmy.

Fortunately for Mouse, the little dog runs into the kitchen as soon as he's inside, closely followed by Nellie. I leave the living room, shutting the door firmly behind me.

'Morning,' I say as I enter the kitchen, causing Nellie, who is rummaging in the fridge, to jump.

'Oh,' she says, standing up and holding the items in her hands to her chest, 'you gave me a shock.'

'Sorry. Is everything OK?' I ask. She shrugs and I see a tear roll down her cheek. 'Oh no! What's the matter?'

'I just went to see Jeremy,' she says. 'I hardly slept last night, cos I was worrying about the next Green Raven column – what is he so determined to achieve with the stupid column before he tells Stella? I've been worrying that he might be about to threaten someone else or something. So, I went over the road just now and gave him an ultimatum: he stops writing the column or I out him to everyone in the village as the Green Raven.'

'Wow, that was brave. How did it go?'

She shuts the fridge door and sinks on to her stool at the table. She's holding a pack of butter and a carton of milk, and I take them from her, placing them on the worktop, before sitting beside her.

She looks at me, her eyes brimming with tears. 'Stella overheard. I didn't realise she was in the next room. They had a massive row and she stormed out – got in the car and drove away.'

I grimace. 'Oh, dear.'

A tear plops on to the table as she says, 'He's furious with me, of course.'

I frown. 'Why of course? He's the one in the wrong here.'

She starts to sob. 'But he was going to tell Stella himself, and I let it out.'

'Hey, this is not on you, OK?' I squeeze her shoulder. 'It's like when someone has an affair and they blame the person who tells their partner. Jeremy has been writing a satirical column every week, without telling his wife – the newspaper editor – that it's him. She's probably feeling left out and maybe even a bit betrayed. But that's his fault for not being open from the start.'

'I guess,' she says, wiping her eyes on the sleeve of her top. I fish in my pocket and pass her a tissue. 'Thanks.' She attempts a smile.

'They'll make up,' I tell her. 'When she gets home, I'm sure they'll talk it out.'

'I hope so.'

Our attention is caught by a loud scrabbling sound in one corner of the room and we both look over to see Timmy, desperately trying to climb up the cupboard.

'Well, he knows where his food's stored,' I say with a laugh. 'I'll feed him.'

I get to my feet and open the top cupboard, above Timmy's head. 'Is it a bit high for you to reach?' I say, drawing out a sachet of his food and opening it, before squeezing it into his clean bowl. After filling his water bowl and placing it beside him, I look at Nellie. She's wilted at the table like a plant that someone forgot to water. 'Hey,' I say softly. 'Coffee and scrambled eggs OK?'

She nods and I set to work.

Although we begin breakfast in silence, by the time we've had a second round of coffee, conversation has resumed.

'Did I mention that the police still think I might have poisoned Martin Patterson?' I ask her, when we've finished discussing the Green Raven column, and how it needs to either revert to its original tone, or be terminated. Nellie is determined the latter is the only option, and I tend to agree.

She splutters on her mouthful of coffee and wipes her mouth on her sleeve. 'They what? But I thought when they let you go that it meant they knew you weren't guilty.'

'Yeah, I hoped that was the case. But I rang DS Timpson yesterday about . . . something and she said I wasn't off the hook. Her exact phrase was that I was "still very much a person of interest".'

'Shit,' says Nellie.

'I know.'

She says, 'Remind me why you think someone picked you as the fall guy, woman, whatever?'

'As you know, I have a few theories. First, I've been involved in other murder cases, so that might make me look suspicious or even guilty. Also, it's neat, isn't it? I get here, and someone dies soon afterwards – that looks pretty suspect. Plus, the murderers wouldn't want to inculpate someone else in the village – it's such a small place, everyone must have friends and allies. I'm new, so no one's going to come rushing to my defence.'

'Well, they got that wrong,' she says. 'I'll be defending you. And I know Norma will, and Avery. And what about that Eloise girl you've been mentoring? I bet whoever framed you didn't expect you to have made an impact so soon.'

'Thank you,' I say. 'I like the sound of having people on my side.' We smile at one another.

'I bet there are even more,' she says. 'I've just remembered, I was in the library the other day, and Fleur was saying how pleased people are, with your plans for the site.'

'OK,' I say. 'So, I just need to prove that the pesticide isn't mine, and then maybe I can get back to making a mind-blowing modernist garden for a stunning modernist village.'

'With an awe-inspiring modernist sculpture,' she adds with a wink.

'Absolutely.' We smile at each other, but then my smile falters. How on earth am I going to prove that a container of pesticide found in my van did not, in fact, belong to me?

Nellie insists on clearing away the breakfast things so I leave her to it. From the hall, I hear Timmy upstairs somewhere, making growling noises. I leave him to it as well.

In the living room, I find Mouse has ventured out from beneath the cushion and is gazing out of the French windows, Mr Rabbit dangling from his jaws.

'Do you want to go outside?' I ask him. When he rumbles his assent, I unlock the door and he trots out. I leave it open so he can come back inside when he wants.

Perching on the sofa, I call DS Timpson again. 'Ms Williams?' she says as she answers. 'Twice in one week, you're spoiling me.'

I decide to ignore her sarcasm and say brightly, 'Did you find any fingerprints on the pesticide pack?'

'You know I can't share details of the case with you, Ms Williams.'

'Let me phrase this differently: did you find *my* fingerprints on the container?'

There's a pause, and then she says, 'We did not.'

'Well, that's something.'

There's a pause, and then she says, 'I did follow up on that information you mentioned earlier.'

'Avery's alibi?' I check, feeling a surge of hope.

'You were quite right: it turns out Ms Tobias was at her daughter's, and Ms Sinclair was not with her.'

'Why did Avery lie?' I ask.

'I'm afraid I can't say more, but we are looking into it.'

'Did I mention the secret meeting at the disused factory?' I ask her.

There's another pause, during which I imagine her scanning through her notes on a computer screen. At last, she says, 'I don't believe you did. When was this?'

I fill her in on my evening sighting of Avery in the car with Martin.

'It can be hard to see into cars from the outside,' she says. 'Are you sure it was Mr Patterson in the car with Ms Sinclair?'

'Definitely. The car passed right by me, and there was still enough light to see who was in it.'

'Was anyone with you?' she asks.

'No.'

I hear her sigh, no doubt feeling that, once again, it's my word against Avery's.

'Thank you for this,' she says. 'I'll make sure we follow up on this as well.'

'Thank you,' I say. And I mean it.

52

'Did you catch 'em yet?' My dad rang after dinner, and I'm sitting at the kitchen table, having just finished loading the dishwasher and washing the pan. Nellie made a pie filled with lentils and butternut squash. It was so good that, although I'm full, I'm wondering whether I could squeeze in another slice.

'Catch who?' I say absent-mindedly, eyeing the remaining pie in its dish.

He sighs. 'The murderer, of course.'

'Oh! Not yet. The police still seem to think it might be me.'

He tells this to Mum in the background, and I hear her response, her voice raised in indignation.

'Your mum wants to talk to you,' he says.

'Put me on speakerphone,' I say, but he says,

'How'd you do that again? Is it this button here?' and we're cut off.

When my phone rings again a moment later, I say, 'Press the button that looks like a megaphone.'

'Ah,' says Mum. 'I think that's it. Can you hear, Nigel?'

'Loud and proud,' he says unnecessarily loudly. 'Or is that about being gay?'

Ignoring Dad's musings, Mum says, 'Please tell me you're not really under suspicion, for that pesticide.'

'I think I've succeeded in directing the lead detective's attention elsewhere,' I say. 'Fingers crossed.'

'How did you do that?' booms Dad.

'Dad, there's no need to shout,' I say. 'Your voice carries easily.'

'The local AmDrammers are always trying to get me to join them,' he says. 'Good lungs, that's what it is.'

'And are you going to?' I ask him.

'I might,' he says. 'They're doing a musical for the next show.'

'You can't sing, Nigel,' says Mum.

'Hey, I have a good voice, I'll have you know.'

Ignoring him again, she says, 'So, what about those skeletons? I saw on the news that they've been identified. Did you know them?'

I don't point out that I've only been in the village a few weeks, so there wouldn't have been time for a pair of bodies to rot down. 'No, but one of them was the older brother of Martin Patterson, the man who's just been killed.'

'And the other was a young woman?' she says.

'That's right – his girlfriend, Megan.'

'So awful for both families,' she says.

'I know.'

'You're being careful?' she says.

'Always.'

'She'll catch the baddie,' says Dad. 'Louise always gets her man.'

'Or woman,' I say, deciding to leave out non-binary, as that might start off a whole new discussion. Dad is curious about everything – a trait which can become exhausting. 'Thank you for the vote of confidence,' I say instead.

'You didn't do it, though, did you?' he says then.

'Do what?'

'Poison that man's tea with a pinch of pesticide.'

'Well, yeah, of course I did,' I say. 'But please don't talk about it over the phone, in case MI5 are bugging the lines.'

'Good point,' he says.

'You two,' says Mum. I can practically hear her head shaking in disapproval. 'People have died. This is not a matter for joking.'

'If we don't laugh we cry, 'eh, Lou?' says Dad.

'You've got it,' I say. Remembering something my brother told me, I say, 'Dad, is it true you got into trouble with the allotment committee for planting on other people's plots?'

He clears his throat and there's a pause. At last, Mum says, 'It is true, I'm sorry to say. They've banned him for three months. If he does it again, he'll be banned for life.'

'Why did you do it?' I ask.

'Well, they weren't using their plots to their full potential,' he says.

'Ah! So you were setting them an example,' I say.

'See, Louise gets it,' he says. There's a pause while he catches on. 'Oh!' he says slowly. 'You were being sarcastic, weren't you?'

'I was,' I say. 'You can't just do what you like, Dad – the world doesn't work that way.'

'Says the woman who conducts her own murder investigations, regardless of what anyone says to deter her.'

'Touché,' I say.

I steer the conversation away from Dad's and my misdemeanours, and we chat about forthcoming garden visits that Mum has booked through the older people's educational organisation, the University of the Third Age or 'U3A'.

'I was looking on the map,' says Dad, 'and you're near Beth Chatto's where you are, and a nice garden run by the Royal Horticultural Society.'

'Hyde Hall,' I agree. 'It's meant to have some lovely prairie-style planting and a good veg garden. And there's a sculpture garden at Harlow called the Gibberd Garden, which I'm dying to visit. I'm going to make sure I see all three before I leave Essex.'

After finishing the call with Mum and Dad, I have a quick video chat with Mike.

'So, where are you at?' he asks.

'Well, I've told the police about Avery's alibi being false, and about that secret meeting with Martin Patterson at the old factory.'

'I meant with the garden, but OK,' he says.

Ignoring this, I say, 'I think I'm going to take a look at the factory. There may be some clue as to why they were meeting.'

'Er . . . didn't you say Martin was meant to be rounding up funders, so it could all have been perfectly legit?'

'True. But they wouldn't need to meet in a secret rundown place if that's all they were discussing.'

'You might have a point.'

'Anyway, the garden progress is still slow, thanks to the discovery of the bodies.'

'Still no movement from the police on bringing in machines?'

'Still nothing, though I did manage to get DS Timpson to say she'd look into it.'

'Look into it? I thought she was the chief wotsit on the case?'

'Senior investigating officer,' I say automatically. 'And yes, I was a bit bemused that she didn't sound more in control.'

He sighs. 'We don't get difficulties like this at Coleton Fishacre.'

I stare at him. 'What are you talking about? What about the big murder case you had this summer?'

He grins. 'Well yeah, apart from that . . .'

'How's your work going?' I ask him. 'Still mulching?'

'Oh yes, lots of that. And the autumn crocuses . . .' He pauses then says, 'Croci? Crocii? Anyway, they're still in flower. They're looking spectacular in the main lawn next to the house.'

'I bet.'

We chat for a while longer, and then I say goodnight.

'Just don't take any risks,' he says before I press the button to end the call.

'I won't,' I say.

We both know that's a lie.

53

As Mouse and I reach the factory gates for a spot of investigating at around seven on Friday morning, I'm glad Mike can't see what we're up to. My heart is beating a little too loudly and, even while I seek an access point, part of me is hoping that the perimeter will prove impassable.

It's beginning to get light, yet the grey of the side panels against the equally grey hardstanding, all over-arched by an even greyer winter sky, offers the foreboding aspect of an Escher drawing.

But, as usual, my curiosity outstrips my nerves. I want to have a scope around for some idea as to why Avery and friends brought Martin Patterson here shortly before he died. If they've been holding meetings here, there might be some useful information lying around.

The heavy padlock is unlocked when I examine it. If I wasn't already on high alert, this sign that someone might already be on the premises would be sending extra signals to my internal warning system.

Luckily, my companion makes a fine external warning system. I push open the gate and say to Mouse, 'Is there anyone here, boy?'

When he merely wags his tail and strains at the lead in his eagerness to explore this new territory, I take a deep breath and relax.

'OK, let's go,' I say, leading him towards the factory entrance, near the far end of the stegosaurus's long body.

Mouse takes his time to cross the tarmacked area, stopping every couple of metres to sniff at a puddle or patch of moss. His tail is still wagging as I push open the factory door. I notice an old camera angled above the entrance as we step into the building.

For a moment we're in darkness until I locate a big lever, which I push down. At first, there's no response, and I think that I've got the wrong switch or the electricity supply has been cut, but then there's a flicker overhead, and rows of pendant ceiling lights come on. Blinking in their yellow glow, I look around. The place is deserted and grimy. Cobwebs hang from the high ceiling, and leaves scurry about like vermin, driven by the draughts squeezing through holes in the windows and roof.

In contrast to the squalor, a long rectangular table opposite the entrance and surrounded by chairs is clean, a pristine island in the midst of a swamp. I let Mouse off the lead so he can sniff around while I head to the table.

As I survey its blank surface, I realise how naive I was to hope there might be the minutes of a meeting just waiting for me to discover them. I glance underneath the table and spot something maroon on the floor at the furthest end. Walking around, I bend to pick it up. It's a silk handkerchief, like the one I saw poking from Martin Patterson's pocket the last time I saw him alive.

Careful to touch only one corner, I slip it into my jacket pocket. I don't have an evidence bag, so I can only hope my pocket doesn't contain enough lint to contaminate any fingerprints or DNA. I can't imagine convincing DS Timpson to search the factory, but at least this square of silk might be enough to prove that Martin was here. But will it prove that he met secretly with Avery and others? I doubt it.

As I turn from the table, Mouse barks, alerting me to a new arrival. Although his tail is wagging, I call him to me and clip on his lead. When the door opens to reveal Avery Sinclair, he starts to whine and strain to run to her. But I wind his lead around my hand to keep him close.

'Steph, what are you doing here?' says Avery, but there's no real surprise in her tone. It's been getting lighter outside while we've been in the artificially lit factory, and her silhouette in the open doorway seems eerie, as if spotlit by the grey light of another world.

'I think you knew I was here,' I say. 'Does the security camera work?'

'It does,' she says.

'And you keep an eye on the place?' I say.

She makes a scoffing sound. 'We have security for that kind of thing.'

'So . . . what? The security people alerted you to a breach?'

'The security person told me that a certain gardener had entered these premises without permission.' She steps inside and the door swings shut behind her. 'What are you doing here?' she asks again.

'Research,' I say. She cocks her head like the sight hound she resembles, and I continue, 'As you told me yourself, this factory was once the hub of the village. In fact, more than that – it was its raison d'être. Without Patterson & Sons, there would be no Greenhaven.'

'True,' she says. 'But if that's your real motive for coming here, why not just ask?'

I shrug. 'The gates were unlocked when we were passing by, so I thought I'd check there weren't any intruders, like the vandals Norma mentioned to me. Once I was sure everything was fine, I thought I might as well stay and have a look around. The building is so striking.'

'Yes, it is – from the outside.'

'I wanted to see where it all happened.'

'You have to remember that this is only the shell of what it used to be. Everything that was here – the electric saws, the work benches, the lathes – was all sold off by Martin Patterson to that asset stripper.' She says Martin's name like it's a curse.

I meet her eye. 'It seems like almost everyone in the village held a grudge against him. Who do you think killed him?'

She arches a perfect eyebrow. 'If I knew that, do you not think I would be talking to the police, rather than our hired *garden designer*? Now, shall we get out of here? I have things to do today, and I know you do.'

We walk back to the gates. When we are safely on the other side and Avery has secured the padlock, I finally let Mouse approach her. She crouches down to stroke his ears and murmur sweet things to him, and he licks her hand. When she straightens up, I'm taken aback to see her face harden. 'You do not come back here,' she tells me. 'And you stop whatever this nonsense is.'

Confused by her change in tone and mood, Mouse grumbles quietly and returns to my side. I place a calming hand on his head.

'You never did tell me why you drove Martin over here for that meeting,' I say.

'I don't know what you're talking about,' she says. 'Now, I'd appreciate it if you could focus on the job you were hired to do. Have the police agreed to remove the tape?'

'I'm waiting to hear.'

We stand in silence for a moment. When it's clear I'm going to get nothing out of her, I give her a nod of farewell and lead Mouse away.

When we get back to Magpies and I open the door, there's a note on the doormat. I lean down to pick it up before stepping inside with Mouse, shutting the door and locking it behind me.

I nearly drop the rectangle of white paper when I see the message written on it, in thick black marker:

STOP SNOOPING

54

My phone rings at eight thirty, just as I'm dressing after my shower. I recognise the dialling code as Colchester, and pick it up immediately.

'Ms Williams?'

'Speaking. Hi, DS Timpson.'

'Hi. Just to let you know, you can collect your van today from Colchester police station.'

'Can someone not deliver it back to me?' I ask. She says nothing. Eventually, I say, 'OK, thanks. Can I ask, does this mean I'm no longer a suspect in Martin Patterson's death?'

'We are following other lines of enquiry at present.'

'That sounds reassuring,' I say.

Again, she chooses not to respond. But she surprises me by saying, 'Also, you'll be pleased to know that I'm sending someone over to clear the crime scene on your garden site today, so you'll have access to the full area.'

'Oh, that's great news – thank you.'

'We'll be in touch if there's anything else, but you can collect your van keys from the desk in the station entrance,' she says.

Before she can hang up, I say, 'There's just one thing . . .'

'Yes?' Her tone is wary.

'I received a note. It was pushed through the front door this morning, while I was out.'

'Go on.'

'It's in black marker pen and it says, "Stop snooping".'

There's another long pause. At last, she says, 'And do you know what this refers to?'

'I suppose I have been asking questions around stuff like alibis for the night of Martin's death, and who might have a grudge against him.'

'Didn't I ask you to leave the investigation to us, Ms Williams?' she says stiffly.

'You did. But you also told me I was a suspect, so I wanted to clear my name.'

'Again, that is for the police to resolve.'

'I know, but—'

She interrupts: 'Ms Williams, this is not a game. We're dealing with an actual murderer here. It isn't safe for you to be going around asking questions. I am no longer asking you to keep out – I'm ordering you, for your own safety. You do understand that, if anything happens to you, I'll be the one taking the flak?'

'Did you say "murderer" singular?' I ask. 'So there's only the one?'

There's another pause. At last, she says stiffly, 'Please try not to handle the note more than necessary. If you have latex or rubber gloves, it's best to wear those. Please place it in a plastic bag and leave it at the desk when you pick up your key today.' She ends the call without another word.

* * *

Nellie stares at me when I tell her about the note over breakfast.

'Why didn't you knock on my door?' she asks.

'To be honest, I wasn't sure whether to tell you. I guess I didn't want to worry you. But really, you should know if threats are coming to the house.'

Her eyes grow wide. 'Do you think it might have been meant for me?'

I shrug. 'Have you been doing anything to stir up trouble?' I say this jokingly, but then our eyes meet and we say in unison,

'The Green Raven.'

'Even so,' I say after a moment, 'it seems a bit coincidental that the note was pushed through the door while I was at the factory. I reckon either Avery left it on her way to intercept me, or she had one of her cronies do it.'

'I don't think Avery would be writing threatening notes,' she says. 'She's too nice for that.'

'I don't know. She's been a lot less pleasant since I've been investigating.'

'Isn't that because she's paying you to build a garden?'

I laugh. 'I guess it might just be that.'

She pushes back her chair. Timmy, who's been sitting at her feet in the hope of edible offerings, looks disappointed. 'I want to see the note,' she says.

'OK. It's in my room. Do you have gloves we can use to handle it?'

'Sure. I sometimes use latex gloves when I'm working with clay.'

She leaves the kitchen, Timmy trotting after her, and returns a minute or two later, holding out a pair of gloves, with Timmy chewing on what looks like another glove.

'Is he meant to have that?' I ask her.

She glances down at him. 'Oh, it's just an old glove. I don't think it will do him any harm.'

'Unless he swallows any of it,' I point out.

'Oh!' She wrests the glove from Timmy's jaw and puts it in the kitchen bin. He grumbles and slinks into the corner, regarding her sulkily.

I look at the very small intact gloves in her equally tiny hands. 'I reckon I'll rip those if I try to get my hands into them. Also, do we have any sandwich bags?'

She opens a drawer and takes out a box of small sandwich bags, before donning the gloves.

'Can you grab two of those bags?'

She surveys me with curiosity but does as I ask. And then we shut Timmy in the kitchen, and allow Mouse to accompany us upstairs, where I get Nellie to bag up the silk handkerchief and the note.

'You've got quite the evidence stash here,' she says.

'I forgot to tell DS Timpson about the hanky, but I'm picking up the van this morning, so I'll leave it on reception for her with the note.'

'Do you need me to open up on site?'

'That would be brilliant.'

She nods and I hand her the key to the site. Then we go back downstairs to finish our breakfast.

Nellie offers to clear away, so, as soon as I've cleaned my teeth, I pull on my boots and jacket and say to Mouse, 'Shall we go and get the van?'

He makes a rumble of approval on hearing one of his favourite words. And then we set out into the cold.

55

After taking over an hour to reach Colchester police station by public transport, Mouse and I are delighted to be back in our beloved van. I have left an explanatory note for DS Timpson with the two pieces of evidence, and now we are eager to get home.

Our drive back is much more straightforward. I put on a music CD, and we sing along as we drive the short distance down the A12 to the turn-off for Greenhaven. After I've parked in our usual spot on Hogs Green Road, I walk to the back of the van to examine the lock. It doesn't look like it's been tampered with, so it would seem as though someone did, indeed, brazenly walk into Magpies, grab the key from my dressing table, plant the evidence in the van, and then return the key to my room.

At least there's no sign of any poisonous substances in the van now.

'Right,' I tell Mouse. 'I'm going to work. Do you want to come?' He makes his rumble of agreement, so I grab my holdall from the hall and we jog the short distance to the site.

Nellie has been as good as her word, and has let my volunteers on to the site. But they're clustered just inside the entrance when Mouse and I arrive, deep in conversation.

'Morning,' I say, and they all turn to greet me in return. 'What's going on?' I ask.

'Oh, the police are taking down the tape and filling in the trench,' says Christy. 'I offered to help, but they said it was best if we kept out of their way.' He sounds offended.

'Ah, great stuff,' I say. 'We can get the machines in!'

'No more digging out bramble roots?' Leo asks hopefully.

'No more manual root excavation,' I confirm.

Everybody cheers.

We are passed a few minutes later by two uniformed officers, carrying holdalls.

'Is that it?' I ask them.

'All done,' says the female officer.

We cheer again, and she and her colleague smile and wave goodbye.

'So, do you still even need us?' Leo asks me as soon as the officers have left.

'Leo!' says his mother.

'What? I'm only asking.'

'It's a fair question,' I say, smiling at him. 'You've all done amazing work. It would be great if I could get some of you back when it's time for planting, but I probably don't need all of you from this point on.'

Leo cheers once more and his mother says, 'Leo!' again, making us all laugh.

'I'd like to treat you all to coffee and cake, if you can find enough work to occupy you for about an hour,' I say. They all smile and grab tools before heading off to find something to tackle.

My phone rings around ten minutes into my own task. I'm at the filled-in trench, trampling down the soil so that it will be less likely to subside over time if we lay paving slabs on top of it. Mouse is snoozing with Mr Rabbit beneath a glorious yew tree which will look stunning as a feature in the new garden.

I stop, panting for breath, take off my glove and draw out my phone. Seeing the Colchester dialling code, I answer at once.

'Ms Williams?' says Timpson's voice.

'That's right. Morning.' I manage not to say, *Twice in one day – you are spoiling me.*

'Are you all right?' she asks. 'You sound out of breath.'

I laugh. 'I was stamping down the area your officers dug up.'

'Did they not fill it in? I instructed them to.'

'They did, thanks. I just wanted to make sure it was all properly firmed down, ready for the build. How can I help?'

'Can you explain this handkerchief to me? Your note said it belonged to Martin Patterson?'

'That's right. I saw it in his jacket pocket when I went to his house to warn him about the Green Raven's threat.'

'And you found it at the factory?'

'Yes. You know I said I'd seen him in Avery's car, about to head in through the factory gates?'

'I remember.'

'Well, the handkerchief is proof I didn't imagine it – he was there.'

'I just don't see what this is proof of, exactly.'

'Only that he was in the derelict factory not long before he died. It seems a strange place to hold a meeting, don't you think?'

'I did ask Ms Sinclair about this after you first mentioned it,' she says. 'She explained that the meeting was about development possibilities for the factory. So, it seems perfectly reasonable that the meeting would be held at the site under discussion.'

'Oh, right.'

'As for the note you received . . .'

'Yes?'

'There are only your fingerprints on it, I'm afraid.'

'Oh.'

'Just . . . be careful, please,' she says. 'I don't want to be investigating a fourth murder in Greenhaven. And do let us know if you receive any further notes or warnings of any kind.'

'Of course,' I say.

We ring off, and I'm left feeling suspicious and more than a little uneasy. I don't believe that the meeting was about the factory. And I'm not happy that the police were unable to trace the writer of the note, though I guess it was a long shot, given that they'd need to have taken fingerprints from everyone in the village. But I shove my phone back in my pocket and return to my stamping. It's possible that I stamp slightly harder than is really necessary.

Once I've got some of the frustration out of my system, I announce that it's coffee time.

The volunteers and I have a nice chat over our morning coffee, and end up staying on for lunch. Mouse sleeps beside the table, only stirring when it's time to leave. We all walk back to the site entrance together, whereupon I thank and dismiss them.

Marion, Norma and Christy have all agreed to come back to help me when needed, and I've also arranged for Eloise to come to the site on non-college days, to watch the build progress.

I'm determined to spend the rest of the day contacting the various local firms who have offered their services for the build. This is a whole different scenario from my usual projects, where I employ one landscaping firm to do all of the structural work. Instead, the committee have signed up one company to donate flagstones and bricks; another to lay them; a third to build the children's play area and a fourth to build the gazebo structures. There are even three separate nurseries providing the plants – so I can only hope that, between them, they stock everything I need. It's going to prove quite a feat to coordinate everyone and everything. I have emailed the sculptor Nellie mentioned, about the children's car and the fallen birch tree, and I make a mental note to chase him.

I grab my large holdall filled with tools and lock up the site, then Mouse and I walk back to Magpies. The poor boy seems worn out. He received a lot of attention in the café after he woke up from his nap, and now he trails along beside me, seeming to have barely more muscle than Mr Rabbit, dangling limply from his jaws.

'Home to bed,' I tell him softly, and he makes a little rumble of approval.

* * *

'You managed to contact every firm on the list?' says Nellie later, over dinner.

'Yeah. It took me three hours but, apart from two where I just left messages, the others were all surprisingly keen.' I fork up some of the stuffed cabbage. 'This is really tasty, by the way. I love the chestnuts.'

'Yeah, they weren't in the original recipe, but they definitely add something, don't they?'

We lapse into silence for a moment, sipping from our wine glasses and enjoying the hearty meal.

Nellie breaks the silence. 'Have you heard any more about Martin's case?'

'Only that the police don't get why I thought the hanky might be important. Oh – and that they don't know who wrote the note. I feel like all I've got at the moment is questions.'

'How'd you mean?'

'Well, did someone kill Martin because of Charles and Megan? Or was it because of something else altogether? I mean, everyone – even you – seems to have a reason to resent Martin.'

As I sip some more of the wine – a fruity Fairtrade Merlot from the local Co-op – I reach a decision. 'Nellie,' I say.

'Yeah?'

'Do you know when the committee are meeting again?'

'No, but the date and time are normally included in the village listings in the *Maven*. Hold on.'

She gets up and fetches the paper from the worktop, opening it in the middle. 'Yeah, here we go. It looks like they're meeting at six tomorrow night, in the village hall.'

'Thank you.'

'Why did you want to know?' she asks as she retakes her seat at the table.

'I think it's time I got more involved in village life,' I say.

She surveys me with a puzzled expression, but I don't elaborate.

56

'Don't let her leave!'

I am at the Heritage Society committee meeting, where I have discovered that its members do not like being asked questions about their alibis for the night of a murder.

I guess I might have seen this coming, but I've been frustrated by the committee's apparent subterfuge, so I've decided it's time to bring things to a head.

I did not plan to risk my own head in the process.

'Sit back down, Steph,' says Avery from the head of the table.

'No, that's all right. I think I'll be heading home.'

Christy bangs his fist on the table, making me jump.

'Really, Christy,' says Marion, and I notice it's the same tone she uses on Leo.

'Oh do shut up, Marion,' he says, not taking his eyes off me. Addressing me, he says, 'You'll sit down and listen to what we have to say.' I hesitate, but he adds, 'You can't just come in here and accuse us all of murdering Martin, and then get up and leave. I mean, Marion and I are the same people who've been volunteering our time to help you clear the site. Surely you owe us the courtesy of listening to us, at least.'

He might have a point, so I sit back down. 'I wasn't accusing you,' I say. 'I was only asking.' I can hear how feeble that sounds. I think I might be on his side in this one. 'Sorry,' I say. 'Please, go on.'

Marion shoots a look at him. 'Are we really going to tell her?'

Avery says, 'I think it's time, don't you? It's the only way to stop this nonsense.'

She looks around the table. Christy nods, Jeremy shrugs, and Marion looks appalled. 'I don't think it's a good idea,' she says.

'Sorry, Marion, but you're outvoted,' says Avery. Turning to me, she says, 'We were blackmailing Martin. That's why you saw me driving him to the factory. We were extorting funds from him for some . . . events we knew about from his past.'

I don't know if she's under the impression that this somehow clears them of being suspects in his murder. I ask, 'What kind of events?'

'Burning down the bungalow – do you know about that?' she asks me.

'Yes, Kieran told me. His grandparents died, didn't they?'

'That's right.'

'So you had actual proof?'

'Not direct proof of the arson, but proof that the then village bobby was paid off,' says Avery.

Christy chimes in: 'We found it when we were filing old police records for the village archives. Eddie gave us all his dad's old police notebooks, and it turned out Hawkins Senior kept meticulous notes. Believe it or not, he even kept a separate notebook for his less . . . legitimate police work. It wasn't hard to tie the days and the payments to the fire. He'd even included the initials S.P. – Simon Patterson, Martin and Charlie's father – so it was clear where the payment came from.'

'So Martin's parents knew he'd killed Kieran's grandparents?' I say in horror.

Christy shakes his head. 'From old Hawkins' notes, it seems more as though Mr Patterson didn't believe his son had done anything wrong – but knew he hung out with the arsonists, so would be under suspicion,' says Christy. 'A quiet backhander ensured Martin wasn't even interviewed.'

I rub my face, trying to take it all in. There's a long pause.

At last, Marion speaks up, breaking the silence. She seems to have decided it's too late to prevent me from knowing the facts, so she might as well join in. 'As far as the . . . blackmail is concerned, you have to understand how much Martin owed to the village. We felt it was only fair that he shared any wealth with Greenhaven, to improve the quality of life for people living here.'

'After all,' says Christy, 'the village was built by Martin's grandfather to provide a decent lifestyle for his workers – electricity, indoor plumbing, large gardens, allotments . . . It was all part of the package. But all of it only made sense as long as the factory was profitable. Martin put paid to that.' He sounds bitter.

'The man was a monster,' says Jeremy, who's been quiet until now.

'And you're telling me all this to prove you didn't kill him?' I say.

'Steph has a point,' says Christy. 'We're not coming out of this looking squeaky clean.'

'No, but blackmail is a long way off murder,' says Avery.

I laugh – I can't help myself. They all turn towards me, nonplussed. I put up my hands. 'OK, so you're not murderers. Have you told DS Timpson about the blackmail?'

'Not yet,' says Marion. 'We're hoping it might not come up.'

'If Martin's been making big payouts to you, it will show up on his accounts,' I say.

'It might not,' says Christy. 'He's been paying us from personal bonds which are a separate entity to his other finances, and we set up an account just for this.'

'A special blackmail account?' I say. 'This gets better and better.'

'Look,' says Avery. 'We understand that, to an outsider such as yourself, our behaviour may appear . . . unorthodox.'

I nearly say, *Try illegal*, but I hold my tongue.

She continues, 'But, to anyone who grew up here, it will appear quite justified.'

Jeremy nods. 'Like when you get those class actions, to claim compensation from a negligent employer or a dodgy manufacturer.'

I consider this. 'OK. So, the meeting at the factory?'

'It was an ultimatum,' says Avery. 'Martin had said he was going to go to the police.'

I frown. 'Why? Presumably he didn't want the truth to come out, or he wouldn't have been going along with your blackmail.'

Christy clears his throat. 'He said he'd had enough – and that the evidence we had on him was slim, at best.'

'He was right,' says Jeremy, and they all nod.

'So, we had to make it clear that going to the police was not an option,' says Avery.

'And how did you do that?' I ask, not sure I really want to hear the answer.

'Oh, you know,' she says breezily, 'we mentioned an accident that might befall him if he tried to blab to the police.'

I suppress a shiver. 'An . . . accident?'

'Oh, we weren't really going to do it, were we?' says Marion brightly.

There's a chorused mumble of 'No, no,' which, to my ears, doesn't sound entirely convincing.

'So, why are you telling me all this?' I ask them.

'Because we didn't kill him,' says Avery. 'And we need you to stop acting as if we did.'

'What am I doing, exactly?'

'Snooping,' says Christy.

I narrow my eyes in his direction as I recognise the wording. 'So, the threatening note came from you, then?'

'We had to warn you off,' he says, as if delivering a menacing note is a perfectly reasonable action. 'We've been reading up on you, and you're good at solving crimes. We didn't want you to work out what we've been doing, and tell DS Timpson.'

I sigh and rub a hand across my face. 'It's just . . . You haven't really told me why I should believe that you didn't kill him.'

'Because we didn't,' says Marion.

'Well, where were you all that night?' I ask. 'I already know that Avery's alibi was false.'

'You can't trust Norma's memory,' says Christy.

'Will you stop gaslighting Norma?' Marion says sharply. 'Just because she's a free spirit and you're a . . . stick-in-the-mud . . .'

'Well, thank you for that, Marion,' he says stiffly.

She continues, 'Look, I know she turned you down. But that was more than twenty years ago . . .'

He turns bright red, and splutters. There's an awkward silence, before he says, 'Look here, it has nothing to do with that . . .'

Before they can begin a full-scale row, I say loudly, 'Unless you all want to tell me what you were doing on the night that Martin died, I think we're done here.'

'I was on my own,' says Avery.

'As was I,' says Christy.

'And me,' says Jeremy. 'Stella was in London.'

'And Leo was at his girlfriend's,' says Marion, 'So I was on my own at home.'

Avery spreads her hands. 'So, you see, none of us has a witness who can testify that we didn't leave our homes.'

'Hold on,' I say, turning to Christy and Jeremy. 'I thought you two were in the pub, performing karaoke.'

'Only at the start of the night,' says Christy. 'At least I think so. As for karaoke . . .' He looks worried. Glancing at Jeremy, he says, 'Tell me we didn't.'

Jeremy looks unsure. 'I don't think so. I don't remember much about that night, to be honest.'

Christy says, 'I had a splitting headache the next day. Oh – and there was that trophy . . .'

'Oh yeah,' says Jeremy. 'What did it say on it again?'

'World's best dad,' says Christy. He catches my eye. 'I don't have any kids, so I'm not sure where that came from.'

Avery claps her hands. 'If we can get back to the matter in hand.' Turning to me, she says, 'So, as you can see – unless Christy and Jeremy stayed at the Feathers later than they remember – nobody here can prove they weren't murdering Martin on that Wednesday night. Hence, the fabricated alibis. Of course, if you hadn't interrogated Norma, we might not have needed to tell you all this.'

'Oh yeah,' I say, raising an eyebrow. 'Of course, it's all my fault. So, can I leave now? Or are you going to threaten me with an accident?'

'Of course not,' says Marion. But I see a look pass between the other three, like a flea beetle leaping from plant to plant. And, as I get to my feet and stride out of the room, I try not to show that my legs are shaking.

57

I fill Nellie in about the meeting over a late dinner of caramelised onion quiche with minty new potatoes and broccoli. The food is nearly good enough to distract me from my sense of disquiet. Nearly, but not quite.

'So, they threatened you?' she says, squaring her shoulders as if about to go into battle on my behalf. 'You've got to tell the DS.'

I spear a mini potato and shrug. 'It's my word against theirs, and there are four of them. It's not like I was recording it.'

'Shame. Wish I'd come with you.'

'There is a reason I didn't tell you what I was going there for – there's no need for both of us to put ourselves in potential danger.'

'Look, I'm your wing woman, whether you like it or not. You need to keep me in the loop. I mean, what if you'd never come back, and I didn't know what had happened?'

'You knew where I was going, at least.'

She narrows her eyes. 'Better communication from now on, promise.'

'I promise,' I say meekly. In truth, it makes me feel safer, just knowing that Nellie is watching out for me.

'Anyway,' I say, 'I've been looking at one of the clues – you know how my birth mum and I do the cryptic crossword and exchange notes on it?'

'Way to change the subject.'

'Actually, this is weirdly on theme.'

'Go on.'

'"Brave night to find this nesting."'

She squints as she tries to solve it.

'It's easier if you see it written down,' I say. Grabbing my notebook, which is on the table, I write out the clue and pass it to her.

'Oh!' she says, wide eyed. 'That's funny!'

'I know,' I say. '"Raven" hidden right in there. Anyway, it's got me thinking . . . What if Jeremy's more involved than we realise? I mean, what if he isn't just a blackmailer with the rest of the committee, but he's the murderer as well?'

She stares at me. 'No, he wouldn't. There's no way.' But, as I watch her, I see her conviction waver. 'I don't think so. I mean, unless . . . I guess he did really hate Martin.'

'Why is that?' I ask. 'You haven't told me.'

But she shakes her head, sipping her wine. Setting the glass back down, she says, 'You'll have to ask him.'

I scrape my plate clean, stopping short of licking it. As I sit back, I say, 'Do you know what? I think I might.'

She doesn't look too thrilled about this, but she also doesn't try to dissuade me, for which I'm grateful. She merely says, 'Just be careful, OK?'

I nod.

After dinner, Nellie heads into the dining room to do some more work on her maquette – the miniature model for her sculpture. I clear the kitchen and check the time. It's nine o'clock – hopefully not too late to visit Jeremy.

I head into the living room to fetch Mouse, and find him knocking the self-powering ball for Timmy to chase. He reminds me of a patient parent desperately trying to tire out an apparently inexhaustible child before bedtime.

'Hey, Mouse,' I say, as he comes to say hello. 'Do you want to see Greta and Marlene?' He makes his rumble of agreement and fetches his lead from a shelf that's too high for Timmy to reach. I'm quite impressed with how he has found ways to outwit the little hoarder.

'Sorry, Timmy. Be back soon,' I tell him, feeling a bit guilty when I see the little dog standing forlornly in the middle of the room.

I call out to let Nellie know that we're leaving and that Timmy might need attention, and then I pull on my shoes, clip on Mouse's lead and we head outside and cross the quiet road to Woodpeckers. The vintage car is missing from the driveway but, as Jeremy was at the meeting, I suspect it just means that Stella has taken it out.

I ring the brass bell push and we wait. But, although we hear the dogs barking from inside, nobody comes to the door. 'It looks like the girls are home alone,' I tell Mouse. But he ignores me. His ears are pricked and, at first, I think it's just because he can hear his friends. But when he drags me round to the back garden, I know he's picked up on something beyond my sensory abilities.

A security light comes on as we cross the garden and head for the French windows to the living room. I step close to the glass doors. Mouse is making a strange, almost uncanny noise, somewhere between a whine and a question, and I feel my heart rate rise in response.

The light is on inside the house, so we can see that Jeremy is lying on the floor. As I try the door handle, I can only hope we aren't too late.

58

'Jeremy!' I shout, as the door thankfully opens and I burst into the room and rush over to the prostrate figure, closely followed by Mouse.

Greta and Marlene are standing beside their human, clearly distressed.

Nudging the dogs gently aside, I kneel on the floor beside Jeremy. He's frighteningly pale, and there's a pool of blood on the wooden floor beside his head. Taking a deep breath to steel myself for the worst, I take his wrist between two fingers and a thumb – letting out the breath in relief as I feel the faint but definite beat of his pulse against my fingers. Gently palpating his scalp, I locate the injury, feeling alarmed that this doesn't cause him to groan. I run to the kitchen and bring back a towel, which I wad up and press against the wound, trying to slow the bleed.

Taking hold of his hand, I place it over the towel. 'Here, hold this,' I say, as I fumble for my phone. Although he doesn't respond, he manages to hold the towel in place, albeit with less force than I would like.

Fumbling for my phone, I call 999 while addressing him: 'Jeremy, can you hear me?' His eyelids flutter. 'Hi. Can you tell me what happened?'

'Kieran . . .' he says, his voice as faint as his pulse.

My call is answered. I ask Jeremy, 'What did Kieran do?' before speaking into my phone: 'I need an ambulance and police, please.'

'No, no police,' says Jeremy, his voice surprising me by its intensity. He opens his eyes and grabs my arm. 'No police,' he says.

'OK . . .' I say, and his hand falls back to his side, as if exhausted by its exertions. His eyes close again. On the other end of the phone, a voice is saying, 'Caller, are you there?'

'I'm here,' I say. 'Just an ambulance, thanks. The patient has hit his head hard. There's a lot of blood and he's very pale and barely responsive.'

I give the call handler the address for Woodpeckers, and she informs me that an ambulance is on its way.

I hang up and survey the three dogs, who are sitting side by side, watching us with concern. 'It's going to be all right,' I tell them, desperately hoping it's true.

'Kieran,' says Jeremy suddenly, with another surprising burst of energy. 'You have to stop him.'

Alarm flares in me like the flick of a lighter. 'Stop him from what?'

He takes a deep breath and says just one word: 'Suicide.'

59

I'm back on the phone to the emergency services when, to my relief, Jeremy's ambulance draws up outside, much sooner than promised.

'Where is Kieran?' I ask Jeremy while I'm again being put through to the ambulance service.

'Eagles,' he says. 'Roof.'

I run to open the door to the emergency medical team while giving the call handler the details about the suicide attempt.

Hard though it is to leave Jeremy in such a weak state, I have no choice. I greet the two medical staff on the doorstep with, 'He's through here,' and lead them to him. 'He's hit his head and he's in a bad way. I can't stay. Where will you take him?'

'If he needs admitting, it'll be Colchester,' one of them says, and I nod and thank them.

Ignoring their bewilderment, I tell Jeremy to hang in there, then I call goodbye to him and the girls as Mouse and I squeeze past the medics and head off at a run towards Eagles. At least I am leaving Jeremy in good hands.

As I run, I ring Nellie.

'Steph hi. What's going on? Aren't you just over the road?'

'Jeremy's hit his head. I think he had a fight with Kieran. The ambulance is with him. Please can you tell Stella?'

'Oh my god! Is he OK?'

'I don't know. His head seems quite bad. She'll need to make sure someone looks after the dogs.'

'I'll call her now. Why are you panting?'

'Running to Eagles. Will explain later. Tell her they're taking him to Colchester Hospital.'

'Will do.'

I finish the call, and Mouse and I increase our pace to a sprint.

And then, as we near the imposing white edifice that used to be home to the Patterson family, I slow right down. Mouse looks up at me questioningly.

There's a streetlight outside Eagles and it clearly lights the paving stones beneath.

And, within that pool of light, lies the body of Kieran Galloway.

60

My heart beating hard from exertion and fear, I race to Kieran's side. Beside me, Mouse lets out a whine and, for a moment, I fear the worst.

But then the figure on the ground whimpers.

'Kieran, thank heavens!' I say, crouching beside him and taking off my jacket to drape over him for warmth.

I can see tears streaming down his face, and I touch his cheek. 'Hey. It's all right. Where are you hurt?'

'No, it's not all right . . .' He turns his face away from me and his crying turns to loud sobs.

I have to raise my voice for him to hear me. 'Hey, come on, talk to me,' I say. 'I've called an ambulance, but I need you to tell me where you're hurt.'

At last, he stops sobbing, but he looks up at me in evident anguish. 'No ambulance. I don't want to be saved.'

'Come on,' I say softly. 'You'll feel better about everything in a day or two.' It's a stupid platitude, but I can't think what else to say.

'No, he says, shaking his head. I . . . I killed him but it hasn't made anything better.'

'You mean . . . Martin?'

'He murdered my grandparents.'

'That fire . . .' I say gently. 'Did he intend to kill them, do you know?'

'They weren't meant to be home that day. But that doesn't mean he should just get away with it.' His voice is full of bitterness.

I stop myself from pointing out that there are other ways for a grown man to handle such matters; now is hardly the time. Instead, I'm about to ask why he has chosen now, after all these years, to exact his revenge upon the man he hated – but, at that moment, the ambulance pulls up, turning off its siren but leaving its blue lights flashing. I turn back to reassure Kieran, but his whole body is jerking, as if an electric charge is running through him.

As the medical team run over to tend to him, Mouse and I move to one side, my beloved dog whimpering at the distressing situation.

We wait, looking on helplessly. And, after a few minutes of listening to the clinicians calling out urgent instructions to one another, there is sudden silence.

Before the lead clinician has even stood up to approach me with my jacket, I know that Kieran is dead.

* * *

When Mouse and I return to the warmth of Magpies, we find Nellie and Timmy curled up together on the living room sofa. Nellie mutes the telly.

'You've been gone ages. Is Jeremy OK?'

'I don't know. Like I said, he had a bad knock on the head . . .'

She frowns up at me. 'You look like you're in shock.' She pushes Timmy off her lap and gets up to help me into an armchair.

'Thanks,' I say. 'It's just . . . Kieran.'

She crouches in front of me. 'What about Kieran?'

I begin to cry. 'He's dead.' Mouse, who has followed me to the chair, puts his paws up on the armrest, and I stroke him.

'Dead?' says Nellie weakly. 'What . . . ? How . . . ?' She runs a hand through her curls. 'I don't understand.'

'He jumped off the roof at Eagles.' Meeting her eye, I say, 'Kieran killed Martin.'

She rocks back on her heels. 'It was Kieran?' Reflecting for a moment, she says quietly, 'He never did get over his grandparents' death.'

'No, and he blamed Martin for the fire,' I say.

She shudders. 'It's so sad. Let's hope Jeremy is all right. What happened to him?'

'I'm not sure. I think he and Kieran had a fight. It was Mouse who led me round the back at Woodpeckers, to find him.'

She reaches across to pet Mouse. 'You are a marvel,' she tells him. 'Fancy knowing Jeremy was in trouble like that.' Mouse licks her hand.

'It might have been more to do with him hearing Marlene and Greta,' I say. 'They were pretty frantic.'

'Either way.'

'Yep. He is a wonderdog.'

We're quiet for a moment. 'Oh, did you get hold of Stella?' I ask.'

'Yep. She sounded shocked. She was going to head straight to the hospital. Apparently there's a friend nearby with keys who will look after the dogs.'

'That's great; thanks.'

'Right: hot chocolate and bed for you, young lady.'

I manage a smile, despite my harrowing night. 'Yes, please.'

* * *

As I get into bed after my hot, sugary drink, I realise that DS Timpson still doesn't know about Kieran's confession. It takes me three attempts to type her a message which doesn't just say: *Kieran murdered Martin. Kieran now dead.* I eventually settle on:

> Kieran Galloway admitted to murdering Martin Patterson in revenge for the arson Martin committed in his youth, which killed K's grandparents. Kieran told me this after jumping off Eagles' roof. He had a seizure and died after ambulance crew arrived. Jeremy Pargeter and Kieran also had a fight just before this, during which Jeremy sustained a bad head injury. A different ambulance crew have taken him to Colchester Hospital.

I figure it's a lot, but that Timpson is not a family member, and can take it.

Weirdly, when I lie my head back on the soft pillow, instead of my brain whirring from the drama of the evening's events, I find myself going over the previously unsolved crossword clue.

Unoccupied, I start organising group holiday.

Another word for 'unoccupied' is 'vacant'. So . . . And I get it! VACATION – meaning 'holiday' – equals 'vacant' plus the 'I' and then the 'O', from the *start* of 'organising'. I message Verity: Vacation!

She sends a thumbs up emoji, and I fall into a deep sleep.

61

DS Timpson interviews me for around ninety minutes the following morning but, with my post-adrenaline exhaustion, it feels like hours. As well as answering all her questions about my encounters with Jeremy and Kieran the night before, I tell her about the committee's confession to me that they had been blackmailing Martin Patterson. She doesn't seem too thrilled about me introducing a whole new thread to her investigation, just when it looked like it was neatly tied up by Kieran's confession. She is evidently also upset about his death – and, as she's a decent human being, this isn't just because she's lost the murderer in her case.

By the time I leave the station, I would love to curl up with Mouse and sleep for a whole day.

But I've heard that Jeremy has thankfully survived the night and is stable, and I want to visit him while we're in Colchester. So I take Mouse for a walk along the River Colne before driving over to the hospital and parking the van.

'Are you OK here, boy? I won't be too long.'

He gives me a rumble of agreement and curls up on his seat with Mr Rabbit. I drape a blanket over him for warmth and leave him to sleep, double checking the doors are locked before I go.

In the hospital, I get directions to Jeremy's ward. Stella has notified the reception desk that I'll be coming. I find him in a room of his own, lying in bed, with Stella sitting on the chair beside him, holding his hand.

'Hiya,' I say. 'How are you doing?'

He gives me a weak smile. 'Oh, it's all good.' This seems a strange response, given the death of his friend. But I'm happy to talk of other things.

'How did you wangle this?' I ask, gesturing to the private room.

'Oh, I think they were worried I might go on the rampage and attack other patients,' he says wryly. 'I was in a fight last night, after all.'

'What was that about?' I ask.

'Kieran came to say goodbye. He told me what he was planning, and I tried to stop him leaving. He shoved me and made a run for it, and I fell back and whacked my head on the hearth. I honestly don't believe he had a clue he'd left me injured.'

'That makes sense,' I say.

Stella stands up. 'I'll leave you two to talk while I go and get some air.' As she passes me, she takes my hand and squeezes it, whispering, 'Thank you'. She plants a kiss on my cheek.

After she's left, I settle on the chair she's vacated and turn to Jeremy. 'How are you really doing?' I ask, taking in his bandaged head and bloodshot eyes.

'I want to visit Kieran, but they won't even let me get out of bed.' His voice is croaky and weak.

I swallow hard. Does this mean it's my job to tell him that Kieran has died? I realise that, if Stella's been at the hospital with Jeremy, she might not have heard.

'You've been so kind,' he says, and I'm happy to delay the awful task.

'Hey, you'd do the same for me.'

He closes his eyes. When he opens them, he says, 'Actually, I wouldn't. You see, I owe you a huge apology.'

I frown. 'What for?'

'The container of pesticide in your van.'

My eyes grow wide. 'You mean you planted it?' When he nods, I realise I feel more confused than angry. 'But why?' I ask him.

At that moment, a nurse enters and strides over to the bed. 'Don't tire him out,' she instructs me as she takes his temperature and notes it on his chart.

As soon as she's left, Jeremy takes a deep breath and says, 'Kieran told me what he'd done. He'd basically been over to give Martin one last chance to confess to the arson. He had the poison on him – and, when Martin claimed he didn't have anything to do with the fire, Kieran pretended to accept it. They shared a drink or two but, as soon as Martin turned his back on his glass . . . well, you know about the poison.'

'So, where does framing me fit in?' I ask.

'Kieran had been keeping an eye on the scene. He told me he'd seen you turn up at Eagles in the morning, meaning you were the one who found Martin.' He shrugs. 'I love Kieran – we've been mates since school, you know?'

I stare at him. 'You grew up here? I thought you were an incomer.'

'No, I used to live here. Kieran and I weren't in the same year, but the village is small. You must have noticed how everyone knows everyone . . .' He takes a deep breath. 'And Kieran had his teenage years stolen from him, thanks to Martin.' The bitterness in his voice reminds me of Kieran's tone last night. He continues: 'Typically, Martin got let off. I mean, two people died, for fuck's sake. The village policeman was Hawkins Senior back then – the current Hawkins' dad – and he had that kind of deference for the ruling classes that lends itself to bribery and cronyism.'

He's breathing hard, so I say, 'I should leave you.' I'm wondering if it would be very cowardly to find Stella and let her give Jeremy the bad news.

But he shakes his head, wincing as he does so. 'Please stay a while longer. I haven't told you why I framed you.'

'Was it really just because I'm the one who stumbled on Martin's body?' I ask.

He pulls a face. 'That, and the fact that you were one of the few people who might be expected to carry a pesticide for your job. Oh, and . . .' He trails off and I notice his pale cheeks start to flush.

I raise an eyebrow. 'Let me guess: and no one in Greenhaven would care much what happened to me?'

He closes his eyes again. When he opens them, he says, 'Pretty shitty, when you say it out loud. And not even true, from what I've gathered from Nellie. I just thought no one had had time to get to know you properly.'

'Have you talked to the police yet?' I ask him.

'Yeah, a detective constable came by first thing, after Stella called to tell them I'd planted the evidence.'

'How's it looking for you?'

'The police officer didn't say, but I can't really worry about that right now, while we're waiting to hear about Kieran.'

I realise I am going to have to tell him, though I can't imagine why the police haven't done so. First I say, 'Can I ask: why now? I mean, what brought all of this to a head for him?'

'It was a combination of things,' he says. 'Kieran and I had heard a rumour since secondary school, that there were bodies buried on the site of the destroyed bungalow, and that Martin was responsible. But we never fully believed it. But when I heard from Marion and Christy that you were planning on using the whole site for the garden, and not just one section, as had originally been discussed, I realised we were likely to find out once and for all if the rumour was true. When I put the hints in the Green Raven column, it was really just to see if I could get a rise out of Martin.'

He gestures to his water cup and I help him to sit up just enough to take a couple of sips. After he's sunk back on to the pillows, he continues, 'But then Kieran started to talk to me about the Raven, as if it was some all-knowing being. Despite my best efforts to persuade him otherwise, he became almost obsessive about it. I tried to tell him it was me, but he thought I was just saying it, to put him off.'

'But the bodies I dug up weren't those of Kieran's grandparents,' I point out.

'No, but Kieran's reasoning was that, if Martin could kill once and keep it a secret, it stood to reason he could have done it again. By the time you unearthed poor Charlie and Megan's skeletons, he was very clear about what he had to do.'

He sighs. 'I only found this last part out after the event. If he'd told me beforehand, I might have been able to talk him out of it. But after he'd . . . killed Martin, all I could do was try and draw attention away from him. I knew Kieran wouldn't cope in prison.' He looks at me with eyes that are almost pleading. 'They can't charge him with this.'

I squeeze his hand. 'I'm really sorry, Jeremy, but I have bad news about Kieran.'

As soon as I tell him about his friend's death, he becomes so distressed that I have to press the alarm button on the bed, and staff come running.

I wait for Stella outside the room. 'What happened?' she asks, picking up her pace as she catches sight of all the activity around Jeremy's bed. 'What did you do?'

'I'm afraid I had to tell him that Kieran died last night.'

'Oh!' she says. 'I asked the police officer not to tell him that yet.'

'I'm sorry – I didn't realise.'

But she just nods and strides into the room.

I wait just long enough to be sure that Jeremy is settled again and stable, and then I head out to the van and my beloved dog, for our short drive home.

62

'Did you find out why Kieran attacked Jeremy?' asks Nellie over dinner that night. She's made a dish featuring tagliatelle with tomatoes, chillis and mushrooms. It's delicious as always, but I haven't yet asked if the dish has a name – I've been too busy filling her in on my visits to the police station and hospital. Timmy is in his usual position at her feet, while Mouse has taken the opportunity to retreat to the living room for some peace.

I tell her what I know: 'It seems Kieran went to see Jeremy, to tell him he was going to kill himself, and Jeremy tried to stop him from leaving. Kieran fought him off, and Jeremy fell and hit his head.'

'What a mess,' she says. 'I know Kieran was a murderer but, given what my family went through, never knowing what happened to Megan, I can't imagine having to live with knowing Martin killed your grandparents and got off scot-free.' She pauses, clearly reflecting, then adds, 'Poisoning, mind – that's pretty cold blooded, isn't it?'

We look at one another. 'It's so complicated,' I say. 'Martin seems to have thought he was above the law, so I kind of get it.'

She sighs. 'Well, at least Jeremy wasn't in on it – apart from framing you, obviously. I was starting to worry, with all that stuff in the Green Raven column. Do you think Stella will forgive him?'

'She was there in the hospital with him, so maybe.'

'I wish I had that kind of love.'

'What? Someone who'd forgive you for covering up a murder and framing an innocent bystander?'

She pulls a face. 'Yeah . . . Maybe not *quite* that kind of love.' She sips from her wine glass and looks down at Timmy. 'Nothing for you. You won't like chillis.' He surveys her with an expression that suggests she must be mistaken.

Mouse appears. I've noticed he's been checking up on me since yesterday's events – as if he's worried that, if he turns his back, I might end up on the floor with a head injury. I stroke his soft head and say to Nellie, 'You know, you do already have that kind of love. Timmy would forgive you anything.'

'Would you, Timmy?' she asks. The little dog barks once at the sound of his name, and we both laugh.

We toast to the astonishing loyalty of our dogs. And then we refill our glasses, and our conversation moves on.

63

Ten days later, Jeremy is released from hospital and taken straight into police custody.

The Green Maven is put on hold for three weeks. When an issue finally comes out, the front page is devoted to the story of Martin's death at the hands of a resident – albeit without naming Kieran. Of course, everybody in the village already knows the identity of the unnamed party.

After a reminder from Stella, I have finally finished collating all of the villagers' responses to my questionnaire, and supplied her with a mock-up of the design for the centenary garden, complete with a key to the different areas and features. She has awarded this a double page spread, and it looks pretty good, even if I say so myself.

To my surprise, there is also a Green Raven column.

'Did you know about this?' I ask Nellie as I walk through to the kitchen with the paper, which I found on the doormat when Mouse and I got back from our run.

'About what?' she says. She's busy frying mushrooms and tomatoes, and barely glances my way.

'There's a new issue of *The Green Maven*, and the Raven has a column.'

She instantly switches off the hob and turns to face me. 'Read it.'

I read aloud:

> **'Farewell from Your Feathered Friend**
>
> This little bird is ready to fly away. First, though, my heartfelt apologies for the suffering I have caused. Please believe that I have only ever taken wing in search of truth and justice.
>
> May the wonderful rookery of Greenhaven settle back into a tuneful chorus.
>
> You will be forever in my avian heart.'

Nellie sits down on her stool and sinks her face into her hands.

'Are you all right?' I ask her.

She shakes her head. 'That stupid sod.'

'I know.'

She looks up at me, and I can see tears on her cheeks. 'The column was only meant to be a bit of fun, plus a chance to raise some questions.'

'I know,' I say again.

She sighs and wipes her cheeks – a gesture I'm coming to recognise as a sign that she's ready to change topic. 'I've been meaning to ask if there's any movement on the whole blackmail thing?' she asks. 'I keep seeing Avery and the other two about the place. They don't look like people who're about to go to jail.'

'Yeah . . . I have heard from DS Timpson about that, actually, though I'm not meant to tell anyone.'

'Go on – I won't say.'

'It's just that she's been having trouble finding proof that there was any blackmail going on.'

She frowns. 'So that's it, then? They just get away with it?'

'I don't know. Timpson did say she's got forensic accountants on the case, so I guess it's going to be a long-term thing.'

She sighs and wipes her eyes before getting to her feet. 'Fancy some brekkie?'

'Yes, please,' I say with a smile at her swift recovery.

'Right. You feed the dogs and get showered, and I'll get this finished. If you're not down, I'll put it in the oven to keep warm.'

'Brilliant, thanks.' While I set out food and water for Mouse and Timmy, I wonder if I should tell her about a national headline that I spotted outside the Co-op this morning, confirming that Martin Patterson has been found to be the murderer of both his brother Charles and Charles's girlfriend, Megan Hughes.

But, while I can't protect her long-term, I decide to let her enjoy her breakfast before I tell her that Martin was definitely behind the death of the young woman who should have gone on to become her aunt.

As I have a quick wash, I mull over everything that Nellie has had to deal with. Reflecting on how amazingly resilient my housemate is, I realise that she is going to be OK.

64

'Where do you want the bamboo?'

Norma points to three large pots of the black-stemmed bamboo, *Phyllostachys nigra.* John was delighted when I told him that I was putting in a miniature Japanese-style area, inspired by the garden at Eagles.

I have somehow managed to coordinate everything, project managing delivery of every service and material. It's taken months – from bringing in machinery at the start of November to now, early March. And it's been exhausting. But it's also proved worth it.

What's more, in all this time, we have unearthed no additional skeletons. Considering how much I held my breath at every digging session, this has been a great relief.

The main build is finished, and we're finally bringing the life and colour to the centenary garden with the planting. A local carpenter has built wonderful raised beds for the Galloway Vegetable Garden, and I have it on good authority that both Mencap and the village school are already sowing quantities of seed in pots, ready to plant out once the seedlings are sturdy enough.

Smiling at Norma, I say, 'The bamboo's for the island in the children's sandpit. You remember that barrier we dug in, around its perimeter?'

'That was a nightmare,' she says.

'Well, this plant is very invasive. I chose it for its vigorous growth, but that barrier will prevent the roots from escaping into the sandpit.'

'Oh, I forgot that's what it was for.' She shakes her head. 'You think of everything.'

'Not quite. I'd never have thought of those,' I say, gesturing to the giant murals that she has painted, assisted by a number of young villagers. The paintings are on both sides of the new skateboard ramp. One includes the faces of almost everyone in the village, taken from a giant group photograph that Norma orchestrated. Only Martin and Kieran are missing from the painting. There are even two faces from a bygone era: Charles and Megan, taken from an old photograph.

The other side depicts a dragon, breathing fire. It's a stunning piece of work. Both have featured in the *Essex Chronicle* newspaper. The journalist who interviewed Norma for the piece has promised to be back to do another feature when the garden is finished.

As I glance around the streamlined, minimalist white-and-black garden, several pieces stand out. These include the miniature version of Woodpeckers, complete with a racing-green vintage MG 'parked' outside, as project-managed by my protégée Eloise alongside the very talented Essex artist whose details Nellie supplied. He has also carved an intricate dragon from the fallen birch, to tie in with the Japanese theme and Norma's mural. Eloise has begun creating her den-building area, in a small section of woodland that we've retained specially for this purpose.

Other striking features include the giant chessboard set into the ground with its neighbouring black-and-white games table; three white pergolas built from brick and rendered to match the houses; and the metal fencing, painted green, which runs around the whole perimeter and mimics the railings on the balcony of Woodpeckers. There are also two pairs of stunning gates, one facing the shops, and the other directly opposite the first pair, with a paved white path to link them. These gates have been made by a local blacksmith, and they include within their detail a rose, a daffodil, a thistle and a shamrock – a nod to the fact that the original workers were drawn from throughout the British Isles.

But the pièce de resistance out of all these works of art for me has to be Nellie's astonishing sculpted bird at the centre of the sensory garden. This jet-black bird towers over the gardens on a plinth, its wings spread wide as if offering fierce protection. Anyone who chooses to inspect the sculpture more closely will be able to see – or feel – the intricate webbing of etched detail that covers the bird's body.

When asked at the unveiling what type of bird it embodied, Nellie had replied that it was a rook. She explained that she wanted to represent everyone who lived in the village, as if we were all members of a rookery.

65

When nine-year-old Alice comes to visit at the start of the Easter holidays, she gives her seal of approval to the children's play area. I have trouble getting her out of the playhouse when it's time to go home for tea. Mouse, who isn't allowed in the children's play area, has sat good-naturedly throughout, watching her play, his tail wagging.

I didn't have enough space to incorporate an area into the garden for exercising dogs – but the Heritage Society committee managed to acquire some grassland from the council, which only needed secure fencing to become the perfect dog park on the outskirts of the village. Alice and I made sure Mouse had some playtime there before we came over to the garden.

'I wish we had a house and a car in our park,' says Alice as we walk back to Magpies with her holding Mouse's lead.

'You have a wooden boat in your playground,' I point out.

'Yes, but a car's better,' she says. 'And a house is much better.'

'I forgot to tell you that I loved your story,' I tell her. 'Your dad sent it over to me. I've never heard of a penguin with magic powers before.'

'Oh, I've written lots of better stories since that one,' she says dismissively.

'I'm sure you have,' I say with a smile.

My next – and final – visitor is Mike, who has thoughtfully waited for everything to settle down on the crime front, and for the garden to be complete, before descending. He and Nellie hit it off immediately, as I knew they would – and he even copes superbly with Timmy's manic attentions.

He's only able to stay for two nights, as Coleton Fishacre demands a lot of attention to the grounds in late spring, but his visit reinforces our awareness that we don't want to be apart for so long again.

66

Before leaving Essex at the end of April, I make excursions to nearby Beth Chatto's garden, where my parents went on a day trip a little while ago. Here, in an area known for its low rainfall, Mrs Chatto made a dry garden out of a car park and turned it into an ecological lesson by never watering it. Filled with Mediterranean plants that thrive in drought, the area is a testament to the 'right plant, right place' maxim of which she was the driving proponent.

I also visit the much less structured but no less lovely grounds of The Gibberd Garden in Harlow. Designed by architect Sir Frederick Gibberd (pronounced with a hard 'G'), it is a stunning, semi-wild site, featuring a collection of sculptures strategically placed for maximum impact. Nellie comes with me on this outing, and I leave with far more knowledge relating to the different forms of sculpting than I had upon arrival.

I finish with the Royal Horticultural Society's renowned garden at Hyde Hall, where there's an immaculately planned vegetable garden, arranged in a circle around an octagonal glasshouse. There are also large gardens filled with perennials that will be beautiful as spring moves into summer, plus woods and stunning views.

My final trip, the week before Mouse and I leave Essex, is with Nellie to the tea room at Tiptree jam factory, as she promised. After a cream tea (or coffee in our case), I buy lots of the tiny sample-size jars of jams from the shop, knowing my niece and nephews will enjoy the doll-size treats in various flavours.

On my penultimate day, Greenhaven holds a tree-planting ceremony, at which we plant three trees: one for Kieran's grandparents, another for Charles Patterson and Megan Hughes, who should have lived to become Nellie's aunt, and a third for Nancy O'Donoghue, the housekeeper who was falsely accused of stealing the statue. Her daughter Olivia comes over from the States with her own children for the ceremony, and she and Norma enjoy a long-awaited reunion.

The trees we plant are silver birches. As well as being a favourite of mine, their slim white silhouette fits perfectly into the black-and-white framework of the centenary garden.

67

Mouse seems fairly happy to leave Greenhaven. There's no denying that he has found living with Timmy a strain. I, on the other hand, have loved living with Nellie – the brief spell of upset over the Green Raven column notwithstanding.

'Don't be a stranger,' she says, giving me a big hug in the hall after I've loaded the van. She's holding Timmy in her arms, so he can say his goodbyes without overwhelming us – or making a bid for freedom when we open the front door.

'Send me food parcels,' I say.

She laughs. 'I'll make you a meal when I come to visit you in your next place,' she says.

'It's a deal.' I grin as she releases me from the hug.

I've never had a sister but, as Mouse and I climb into the van and I wave to Nellie through the window, I feel as though she's the closest I've come.

'Right, boy,' I say to Mouse, strapped into the passenger seat beside me with Mr Rabbit. 'Peterborough to see Alice and the boys.'

He barks happily and watches through the window as I start the engine and take us through the village for a final look. I pull in for a moment alongside the railings at the centenary garden.

It's another sunny but cold day – but I can see plenty of figures inside, including children clambering over the playhouse and playing in the car, and adults seated at the games table.

'It looks like the garden's proving a success,' I say to Mouse.

He barks once and I start the van again, saying goodbye to the white buildings and flat roofs of Greenhaven. Despite the awful events of November, the little village has got its hooks into me like the barbs of a wild rose, and I know I will remember it more for its charm and sense of community than for its tragic history.

I head to the A12 and turn on the CD player. Mouse sings along to the music at the start of the audiobook. The story turns out to be about a woman who finds a body buried in her garden. I switch on my sleuthing brain and settle in for the drive.

Acknowledgements

My thanks are due to a number of wonderful people, as detailed below.

The Silver End Heritage Society for much help, support, advice and information! Special thanks to Alan and Victoria Waine for letting me view their beautiful home (and for yummy cheese scones!), to Jackie Nesbitt for showing me lots of reference pictures of the village and answering various questions, and to Natalie Banks for her excellent talk, helpful feedback, and the invaluable copy of *Mister Pink* (details in bibliography, below).

Jenny Todd at The Literary Office for being a simply wonderful agent.

The dedicated and inspiring team at Embla Books: Jane Snelgrove, Bea Grabowska, Emma Wilson, Vishani Perera, Tia Ungar, Chelsea Graham, Martina Arzu, and anyone I've missed.

Laura Gerrard for her ever-vigilant and thoughtful copy editing. Sandra Ferguson for her keen-eyed proofreading.

Shazia Nicholls, for bringing Steph and my other characters to life in her brilliant audiobook narration.

My wonderful consultants for their continued generosity in sharing their expertise and correcting my mistakes. All errors are, as ever, my own:

Christina Erskine of The Urban Hedgerow (www.urban-hedgerow.co.uk) and Detective Inspector Scott Kingsnorth.

Richard Ogle for the stunning cover.

Thanks also to Dawn Ratzlaff Drzaic from the wonderful Cozy Mystery Lovers/Meg's Cozy Corner Facebook group, for entering my competition to name a character, thus naming Nellie Dawn, the sculptor!

My mum, Maureen Sandler, for providing Steph and Verity with excellent cryptic crossword clues.

Michael Barter, sculptor extraordinaire (www.bartworks.co.uk), for inspiring my Dengie-based sculptor who builds structures for Steph.

Reference/bibliography

Mister Pink: The Architectural Legacy of W. F. Crittall Robin Carpenter (2007, Essex County Council).

A Note from the Author

Greenhaven is based on the real – and stunning – Essex garden village of Silver End, which was built in the 1920s and '30s by Francis Crittall with his son Walter 'Pink' Crittall for their workers at the Crittall window factory. As in this book, workers were, indeed, drawn from far and wide, lured by the promise of gardens, allotments, electricity and indoor bathrooms. As with the furniture factory in this book, Crittall ensured that 'small parts' jobs were devised for workers who had been injured in the First World War.

In *Murder in Season*, I have renamed the roads as well as the village itself, because it's never a good idea to imply that a community might contain murderers and hidden bodies!

I have also taken some liberties with the layout of the village, and the naming and descriptions of the houses, but I have tried to be historically and geographically accurate wherever it worked alongside my plot. For instance, Manors in Silver End – the model for Eagles in the book – does not have a flat roof. Apologies to the wonderful – and hugely supportive – Silver End Heritage Society committee for this and other liberties.

About the Author

Rosie Sandler lives in Essex, UK, where she writes novels and poems. She loves wearing home-made colourful outfits, which often leads to joyful encounters with strangers. Rosie is gradually redesigning her own garden, which now features prairie-style borders, a willow 'house', piles of rotting wood to encourage wildlife, and a pond which is home to newts, pond snails, beetles, and damselfly larvae. She dreams that she and her husband will one day live beside a lake. Or at least a big puddle. Rosie is co-author of the Agatha Oddly trilogy of children's detective novels.

About Embla Books

Embla Books is a digital-first publisher of standout commercial adult fiction. Passionate about storytelling, the team at Embla believe our lives are built on stories – and publish books that will make you 'laugh, love, look over your shoulder and lose sleep'. Launched by Bonnier Books UK in 2021, the imprint is named after the first woman from the creation myth in Norse mythology. Embla was carved by the gods from a tree trunk found on the seashore; an image of the kind of creative work and crafting that writers do, and a symbol of how stories shape our lives.

Find out about some of our other books and stay in touch:

X, Facebook, Instagram: @emblabooks
Newsletter: https://bit.ly/emblanewsletter